Drifting
in the
Push

Drifting in the Push

Daniel Garrison

Tongue & Groove Publishing

ISBN: 0-9976363-0-0
ISBN 13: 978-0-9976363-0-7
LCCN: 2016908427

Tongue & Groove Publishing
Salem, Oregon

www.driftinginthepush.com

Cover photo by Daniel Garrison
Cover design by Mallory Logan, www.go-roshambo.com
Editing by Lindsey Nelson, www.exactedits.com

This is an autobiographical novel. It is a merging of factual accounts from the author's life with fictitious events and people. Some character, business, and place names have been changed.

To my fantastic and talented mother.

Let us follow our destiny, ebb and flow. Whatever may happen, we master fortune by accepting it.

—Virgil

CONTENTS

Chapter One

Kick Off

I couldn't compose a deep thought to save my life, not that I understood my life could ever be taken from me. My hair was ruffled, one shoe was untied, and my green-and-orange plaid pants were a bit too loose around my bony waist.

"I want that!" some kid yelled as she grabbed the ball right out of my hands. I watched in horror as the bandit darted across the room and vanished behind the coatrack.

"Hey, that was *mine*. I was playing with it!" I shouted.

I didn't see the teacher, and nobody else seemed to care. Tears rolled down my cheeks. I hiked up my trousers and shuffled over to a red plastic chair, thumping down on it.

"I'm Bryan."

I sucked a trickle of snot back into my nose and looked at the kid sitting on the floor next to me. I liked his

Spider-Man T-shirt.

"She took my ball."

"You don't need that. I got these. They're lots better."

My whimpering slowly eased while Bryan dug several well-used Matchbox cars from his pockets.

"Wow, those are neat," I said.

"Want to play race cars?"

"Okay." And so we did until nap time.

In the afternoon, we continued our game while some gangly-looking kid stood nearby, eyeing us. Finally, he asked, "How come you got them?"

"They're his." I pointed at Bryan.

The kid continued to watch us push the cars between piles of wooden blocks.

After a while, Bryan said, "You can play with them too, if you want."

"I don't feel good," the kid said as he plunked down on the floor next to me.

"My name's Dan," I said.

"I'm Shane."

"You want to play with us?" Bryan asked.

"My tummy feels real bad," he groaned.

It was a remark we were unequipped to deal with. Our focus quickly returned to the cars while Shane sat cross-legged, slowly rocking back and forth.

After a few minutes, Shane lifted himself onto rubbery legs and sobbed. "It hurts. I want to go home."

Pools formed in the corners of his eyes as he gazed down at me. Then his mouth grew unbelievably wide, and out came a rush of chunky, sand-colored vomit. I sat there stunned, splattered from the top of my turtleneck sweater to the bottom of my Snoopy sneakers.

I had just met my two best friends.

Chapter Two

Pioneer

A year or two earlier and I would have been bawling my head off, but then a couple of years ago, I wouldn't have dared to be where I was now.

Ouch, it stung. I gingerly plucked the last few pebbles from the scrape on my knee and wiped at the blood with my sleeve. I guess it wasn't too bad, but it was bad enough to show off to the fellas Monday morning when I told them about my adventure! Dusting off my behind, I straddled my bike once more and continued in the footsteps of Columbus, Captain Cook, and all those other guys the teacher was always blabbering about.

Veering between pine trees and sliding across tilted granite slabs, I silently counted the times my legs turned the cranks...ninety-nine, one hundred. The ground was getting much steeper, and I was really puffing, but that was yet another hundred pedals into the unknown. Panting, I stopped and checked out the view. I could see my house tucked in a small neighborhood with a half dozen other homes. There were a few other buildings scattered around the mountain-ringed valley, yet there were no signs of life. I was really out there!

My folks would freak out for sure if they knew where I was. I wasn't really supposed to leave our neighborhood. Nevertheless, over the past few months, I had secretly begun exploring the mountainside behind our house. Little by little, I was venturing farther up the hill. Today, if my lungs and legs would let me, I was going to reach the large rocky cliffs near the top.

My knee was really throbbing, and I started to waver.

Maybe I should go back?

Maybe Mom and Dad were looking for me?

Boy, I could really be in for it. My indecision was interrupted when a fist-sized rock fell from the boulders above and tumbled down the hill twenty yards to my right. It bounced off a tree trunk and came to a stop. I searched the area but found nothing peculiar. It was probably just a loose rock, nothing to spaz about. No sooner had I decided to push on than I heard a sort of soft crunching sound. It was barely audible and very sporadic, yet after a few moments of concentrated listening, I was certain it was real. There was something more here than just a loose rock. It took less than a second for me to change my mind about continuing on my quest. Just as I began turning my bike around, I caught a fleeting glimpse of a very large brown form leaping from the top of one boulder to another. Then it was gone.

Slipping on pine needles, I frantically spun around, stomped on the pedals, and headed down the hill. I steered around groups of trees and past several rocky patches, making it to a large clearing. I took a chance and skidded sideways to a stop.

The landscape was silent. Gulping down air and wiping the sweat from my eyes with my bloodstained sleeve, I continued to scan the hillside. After a couple of minutes, I began to calm down. Heck, I probably just imagined it. I mean, it could have been any—my thoughts froze as I locked eyes with a massive cat, which was effortlessly loping down a patch of loose shingle a mere fifty yards above.

"Holy cow, holy cow, holy cow."

I twisted around and furiously pumped the pedals with my shaking legs. I launched my trusty bike down the uneven slope at rocket speed, never daring to look back. In seconds, I was covering ground that had taken me all morning to climb. The homes in the valley rapidly grew larger, the mountains taller. I was nearly back to the road that led to my front door…nearly there!

Thud.

The front tire struck something unforgiving. All at once, I was traveling even faster, unfortunately without my bike. My time sailing through the air was so unexpected and brief that I didn't even have time to utter a cry. I slammed into the ground and tumbled to a stop. Nothing was working—not my arms, not my legs, and not my brain.

Gradually, neurons began to fire.

Lots of me hurt. Wheezing, I crawled to my bike. It looked like it was still in one piece. Slowly, painfully, I got up and onto the seat. I began sobbing. My parents were going to kill me. And there was a mountain lion chasing me. I had nearly forgotten—there's a mountain lion chasing me!

"Mom! Dad!"

Crying as hard as I ever had, shrieking for help, and nearly blind with tears, I finished my retreat down the hill in a painful panic. I dropped my bike in the front yard and dashed into the house like a maniac.

"Yep, and then he chased me all the way down the hill."

"Wow," the fascinated group of boys said in near unison.

"He was totally going to eat me," I said. "I know for sure he was."

"Holy crap!" Shane yelled. "You got that broken wrist fighting him?"

"Yep. He cornered me, but I wasn't going to give up." I had them totally spellbound. "But I already told you guys about all that."

"Tell it again," a few of them hollered.

"Okay. But first, who wants to sign my cast?"

Chapter Three

Trouble

For a ten-year-old, it was utopia. I would have traded my entire collection of Star Wars action figures to be there. I wasn't aware of my parents' slowly disintegrating marriage. I didn't fully realize my dad couldn't find work and had slipped into an unrelenting depression. I had no knowledge that our family was on the brink of financial disaster. I didn't care my sister had taken it upon herself to rebel against the world. My entire family was a half step away from implosion, yet I was unwittingly overjoyed.

We had left our little town in the Rocky Mountains, shifting west to a fifty-acre orchard in the Willamette Valley. Our section of land was the center of my universe. And what a cool universe it was—streams to build dams on, trees to build forts in, gravel tracks to ride my bike on, a barn full of animals to play with, and dirt to roll around in. It was fantastic.

During the weekdays, I attended a two-room schoolhouse. The only other building in the vicinity of the squat brick institution was a single-room church across the peaceful country road. Thirty students received the attention of two teachers, both of them named Mrs. Powers since they were sisters-in-law. My house was just a couple of miles away and often times, when the skies were clear, I rode the family horse to class. Mornings when it was raining, I caught the school bus, which had already picked up the rest of the kids, some of whom lived twenty miles away from the isolated school.

It was a typical drizzly Oregon winter morning, so I zipped on my rain jacket, grabbed my lunch, and headed down our long, winding driveway. Walking along, kicking stones into standing puddles of muddy water, I noticed my cat, Trouble, following closely at my heels.

"Trouble, you can't go to school with me," I said. "Go home. Go back."

He didn't listen. He never did. He was a cat. A black-and-white striped one. So we traveled, more or less together, to the end of the driveway and waited at the road's edge under a dripping, leafless oak tree.

"Trouble, come back here." I set down my Pac-Man lunch box. "Come on, get over here." He had crossed the road and was sniffing around in the damp ferns.

"Trouble, come."

He didn't. He never did anything I said.

"Okay, stay over there. See if I care. Here comes the bus anyway."

Here comes the bus!

"Trouble, get over here now!"

The big yellow vehicle was headed down the hill at a seemingly high speed.

"Trouble, Trouble, come on!"

Surprisingly, he finally responded to my squeaky yells just as the bus hit the brakes. Millions upon millions of unnoticed, unremembered seconds pass in life—this wasn't one of them.

Paths intersected.

While the bus slowed to a stop, I sprinted to the rear, my stomach revolting as I spied a tangled, bloody mess stuck behind the rear axle. Without thought, I pried Trouble loose just before the bus lurched forward and the occupants continued their journey, somehow unaware of me or the tragedy that had just ensued.

I stood motionless in the road, tears falling silently down my cheeks, looking down at my twitching cat. His guts spilled outside of his mangled hide. His eyes were open, and he stared at me in shock and pain. I cradled him in my arms and pumped my stubby legs to the house, hoping Mom and Dad could fix him but knowing they could not.

A few weeks passed, and as happens more readily in childhood than in adulthood, I had moved on from the sadness quickly. Trouble's terrible demise was now far in the background of my everyday thoughts.

It was yet another gray winter day, this one a Saturday, and I was entertaining myself with a couple of buddies in the steep pasture that bordered the north side of the barn.

"It's my turn!" Jason yelled. He yelled everything he said.

"Yeah, but I pushed it back up the hill," Scott protested.

"That's the deal, stupid. You roll. You push. Then it's another guy's turn."

"Yeah, that's the deal, stupid," I agreed.

"Here," Scott curtly replied, pushing it toward

Jason.

He'd tried to scam another turn and lost. Every so often, a guy has got to try to get a free turn; we all understood that. Heck, we all wanted as many turns as we could get in the tire. It wasn't really a tire at all. It was two six-foot-tall inner tubes lashed together with some coarse rope. Scott and his older brother had dreamt up the simple contraption, and Scott brought it over that day. It was his invention in a way. I guess that's why he kept thinking he was entitled to a free ride now and then.

Standing at the top of the hill, Scott and I steadied the tire while Jason wrestled his way into the center.

"Boy, this is tight."

"Shut up, and just get your fat butt in there," I barked.

"Hang on, okay, wait, yep, just wait a second." Jamming himself into the tightest of all possible fetal positions, his nose hard against his knees, feet squashed and twisted under his bum, and arms pinned beneath his ankles, at last he was ready for takeoff.

"Ready," Jason announced in a muffled voice.

Scott and I were all smiles. We each grabbed a side. "One, two, three!" With a mighty push, the tire ripped down the steep slope, Jason tucked inside, spinning faster and faster as it gained momentum.

"Go Jason!" I snickered.

"He's really cruising!"

"It's my turn next!"

"No way, it's—"

Boom!

The blast echoed across the small valley. Halfway down the hill, at a speed of perhaps twenty miles per hour, one of the highly inflated inner tubes found something sharp and exploded into rubber tatters. The left half of

Jason was still packed into the remaining tube, while his right arm and leg alternately flew to the sky and smacked into the ground, the wounded beast rolling drunkenly down the hill.

Scott and I burst out laughing. Within a few seconds, the tire and its occupant reached the valley floor, Jason spilling out into a heap on the wet grass. Tangled rope, shreds of rubber, and the remaining inner tube flopped over and buried his crumpled body.

Cupping his hands to his mouth and trying to suppress his laughter, Scott yelled, "Hey, Jason, you okay?"

The sad, deflated mess slowly shifted as he pushed out from underneath it and stood up on wobbly legs, only to fall back down on his rear end. "That was excellent!" we heard him shout up the hill.

"Ah, he's okay," I said.

"Yeah, well, the big loser just wrecked the tire. Turds and gravy! You got another tube 'round here maybe we can fix it with?"

"I dunno."

"I'm going down to check out the tire," he said, "and numbnuts."

"I'll have a look around; maybe I can find something."

I poked around the barn without success, and it wasn't long before I was sitting on a bucket, scratching my head. Hmm, I knew there were some tubes somewhere, but where? Then it hit me—the pump house.

I couldn't find the light switch. In fact, I couldn't remember if the pump house had a light because I so infrequently entered it; therefore, I simply left the door open on the cramped, musty-smelling hut and began searching the dark corners for the inner tubes. I found them wedged beneath a couple of old cherry crates. I tried to yank one of the larger tubes loose, but the whole tangled pile resisted. I'd have to do it the hard way. I lifted the crates off and backed out the door into the light, my eyes refocusing on a future reoccurring nightmare. In the top crate, in my arms, inches from face, was a badly decomposed, maggot-ridden corpse.

It was the unburied and long-forgotten body of Trouble.

Chapter Four

The Battle of Bull Run

"W e'll see you next Sunday," Dad said, "behave yourself."

I was staying at Matt's for the week. His parents owned an eighteen hundred–acre farm down the road from our orchard. I was both excited and nervous. Matt was a good friend, and I was sure we'd have lots of fun, but I was already missing my parents. Yet it wasn't long before my anxiety faded, as I found myself gripping onto the back of Matt's Honda dirt bike, speeding along one of the farm's many gravel roads. We spent the day riding around, searching for anything stupid enough to be in range of Matt's .22-caliber rifle. The next morning at breakfast, however, I quickly realized the beginning of my holiday was also the end of it.

While I endeavored to eat around the milk in my cereal bowl (it smelled sort of funny and tasted a bit like grass), I listened to Matt Sr.

"You and Dan move that hay in the barn like I told ya, and get the cats while you're at it. Tomorrow we'll drive up top and check the creek. If it's on the wane, you two can take 'em up. Might just work out well. I'll be up there dealing with the loggers anyhow, so I can make sure you boys done your job right."

He downed the last of his coffee, thanked his wife for the meal, and left for the day. I had no idea what the heck he had been talking about, other than it sounded like work.

I was right. We spent the day pushing immense bales of hay from one side of the barn to the other. Every so often, we'd encounter a hidden litter of kittens. Sometimes there was just one or two, and sometimes there were four or five of them. Some appeared quite old, and some still had their eyes closed. But if they could be caught, we nabbed them, Matt stuffing them into grain sacks.

"What are you gonna do with them?"

"I told you, just wait and see." Matt grinned mischievously.

"You gonna give them all away or what?"

"Just wait and see."

Several hours later, we pulled the last bale into place and went in for supper. I could barely concentrate on the meal because I was itching so badly from the hay. Matt didn't seem bothered by it. We sat patiently, watching his dad finish his post-dinner coffee. At last he spoke.

"You boys get that hay sorted?"

"Yes, sir."

"Got the vermin rounded up?"

"Yes, sir," Matt repeated.

"Then best go deal with it."

We followed him to the barn.

"Go get 'em, Matty. And the can."

Matt disappeared, returning with two squirming sacks and a blue metal container. Without hesitation, Matt Sr. dropped the bags into a blackened steel barrel and followed it with a big dose of pungent smelling liquid from the container. Reaching into his shirt pocket, he produced his pipe and a box of matches. With an empty expression, he struck a match and tossed it into the barrel. Instantly a cloud of flames erupted and high-pitched screams of terror and pain ensued. He methodically struck another match, lit his pipe, and drifted back to the house, Matt in tow.

I wanted to join them, but I couldn't. I stood transfixed, staring at the flames and listening to the worst sounds I had ever heard.

The next day, we piled into a battered old truck and traversed several badly rutted tracks, which snaked deep into the hills. Every time I thought we must be nearing the conclusion of the mysterious journey, we continued on, into another valley and over yet another hill. Ultimately, the trail ended in a grove of untended cherry trees. Matt's dad shut off the truck. "We walk from here, boys."

After a short hike, we reached the bank of a small river.

"Good. It's even lower than I reckoned. Shouldn't have a problem gettin' 'em across, eh, Matty?"

"Nope. Probably even shallower up at the crossing."

"Good enough."

I was no closer to ascertaining the whys and whats of their scheme, but I didn't want to divulge my ignorance by asking stupid questions, so I held my tongue during the return trip. Bumping along through an orchard of apple trees, Matt Sr. hammered the brakes of the old pickup and, with a few quick motions, snatched the rifle from the rack behind our heads, pointed it out his window, and fired.

"Damn if I didn't get him!" he shouted, darting from the truck.

"Get out! Get out!" I could barely hear Matt over the ringing in my ears.

"Come on, boys, he ain't down!"

We sprinted to catch up, charging into a wall of brambles. Another shot rang out. Within seconds, we were at the scene. The deer lay bleeding, tangled in a barbed wire fence.

"Nice shootin', Dad!"

"Naw. Should have had him on that first shot. Least he didn't get past the fence, would of never got him then," he said, shouldering his rifle. "Grab a leg, boys. We'll deal with him back at the house."

I tasted bile. I was going to blow chunks. I just knew it.

"Come on, Dan, get in here," Matt's dad commanded in a stern yet amused voice.

"Go on." Matt nudged.

I obeyed. There really wasn't any choice. I climbed the stepladder, struggling to avert my gaze from the bloody mess that hung mere inches from my face.

"I'll spread the ribs. When I do, you reach in with this knife and cut loose the innards. Careful you don't knick the stomach," Matt Sr. instructed.

"Gross, don't cut open the stomach," Matt echoed.

I nervously stuck my arm in, fumbling around the warm, squishy goo with the blade. Big Matt reached in and guided my hand. *Splash!* A big pile of guts dropped into the large pan set below the deer. Blood splattered me from the waist down.

"Good job."

I looked at him with glassy eyes and an inflated mouth.

"Go do it over in the corner, son."

The next morning, we were out of bed before the sun was up. At least today I knew what I'd be doing. Matt had clued me in the night before. At the moment, half of the steers the farm possessed were milling about in a large field directly behind the barn. Every spring, the herd needed to be coaxed up the gentle slopes to the upper pastures where they would spend the duration of the summer months. Matt and I were going to do the coaxing this year. I asked him if that was the reason his dad had checked the level of the river yesterday.

"If it's too high, you really got to force 'em to cross. I don't think we could have done it with just the two of us. But it's nice and low now, so we shouldn't have a problem." He was totally rapt. This was the first year he would do the job unassisted by his uncle. "Come on, let's get going!"

On our way out of the house, Matt's mom handed us each a backpack and told us to be careful. A few minutes later, big Matt was giving us last-minute instructions while he helped us get the herd moving up the hill.

Over the next several hours, the apprehension I felt over my sudden responsibility lessened as the sun broke across a cloudless sky, and the steers virtually led themselves through the winding paddocks. Matt and I trailed the smelly pack at a leisurely pace, never needing to do much more other than walk and talk. By late afternoon, Matt reported that we had reached the halfway point of our journey. He left me to block the path of any steers that might decide to reverse their course and made his way to the front of the herd where he unlocked a large wooden gate. As soon as they were through, Matt swung the gate shut.

"This is the high pen. It's about an acre and all fenced off, so we don't have to worry about them going anywhere tonight."

"What about us?"

"Over there," he said, pointing to a small but well-maintained shack situated at the edge of a grove of trees.

That night we built a larger fire than we probably should have and gulped down the delicious venison sandwiches his mom had sent with us. The steers seemed content enough, and Matt said there weren't any wild animals to worry about. "Except maybe a few coyotes, but they wouldn't go for anything that's much bigger than a rabbit. Even if they did mess with us, I'm a good shot with my twenty-two." It was such a perfect night that we decided to sleep under the stars by the fire. It was all a fantastic dream to me.

The following afternoon, nearing our final destination, Matt was chattering away about the two girls that made up the other half of our sixth-grade class when he abruptly went silent, grabbed my arm, and urgently whispered, "Run."

He sprinted for cover among the trees, and I automatically darted after him. I thought maybe he was just messing with me, trying to make me look stupid or something, until I saw him glance back, focusing on something directly behind me, with wide, terror-filled eyes.

"Holy crap! Run, run!"

It was no joke. Matt ducked and bobbed into a dense thicket, dodging tree after tree. Blindly, I followed, until his arms reached out and grabbed me. Safe in our hiding spot, we peeked through the branches. Thirty feet away stood one very big and very angry bull. He had an impressive set of dangerous-looking horns, and a big metal ring hung from his nose. Like a caged lion, he paced back and forth in the pasture, his head shaking from side to side.

"That was a close one," Matt wheezed.

"Holy moly, Matt, what the heck is that?"

"I can't believe it. It can't be."

"Can't be what?"

"It's Duncan!"

"What?"

"I can't believe it's really him. It's Duncan, the meanest damn bull you'll ever see. The bastard gored Dad."

"Gored?"

"Dad got him in the corral once; I think he was trying to catch him because one of the neighbors wanted to buy him or something. Anyway, he had him cornered, almost got him into the chute, when he charged and stuck Dad in the leg with one of his horns."

"Geez."

"He busted out pretty much right after that, and he's been on the loose since."

"He's just been loose?"

"Yeah, 'bout two years I guess. Dad's been trying to put a bullet in him ever since. But nobody's seen him for a long while; we figured someone else killed him, or he just died or something."

"He doesn't look dead to me," I said, watching the irate creature stomp away toward the herd.

"Maybe we can change that."

"Hey, a coyote's one thing, but I don't think your gun would hurt him much. Besides, he's too far away."

"It's time for a plan."

As Matt predicted, Duncan was too busy mingling

with the steers to observe us. At least, not yet anyway. Wiggling on my belly through the tall grass, I had no way of knowing if Matt was following me as promised. He better not be chickening out! No, I knew he wouldn't. The truth was, if anyone was going to run down the hill screaming, it was me.

We were sixty feet downhill from the back of the herd, slowly making our way from the tree line to the center of the field. I had no idea where Duncan was; all I could see were the stalks of grass that surrounded me. I just hoped the brute was still standing where we last saw him. The farther from the trees I crawled, the more I regretted agreeing to Matt's plan. I was quickly realizing this was not just stupid but possibly suicidal. I was about to reverse course when I felt a hand on my foot.

"Stay put until you hear me whistle," Matt whispered.

I heard him crawl off. Before I could fully work myself into an all-consuming panic, I heard a shrill whistle and jumped to my feet.

"Hey, idiot, over here." I waved a long stick with a shirt tied to the end of it. "Over here, stupid!"

The bull emerged from the herd and promptly broke into a run straight toward me. Screaming, I turned and fled toward the trees. Don't trip, don't trip, don't trip…the tenth time I heard the dire warning in my head, I was back in the safety of the forest.

I had actually beaten Duncan by miles, just like Matt said I would, but that hardly decreased my fear. He had slowed to a trot when he neared the edge of the pasture. Keeping low and in the bushes, I quickly moved downhill, leaving Matt and the bull above. When I figured I had gone far enough, I crouched behind a log just as a rifle shot split the air. I pushed out of the forest and caught sight of Matt standing in a shooter's pose, his rifle pointed straight at the bull, which was scarcely ten feet away, swaying on wobbly legs. For a long time, nothing seemed to move—the steers, Matt, the bull, even the breeze seemed to be frozen in time. Then Duncan gave a grunt and crashed over on his side.

"Yeeeeehaw!" Matt yelled, swinging his rifle triumphantly above his head. "Dan. Dan. I got him! Goddamn if I didn't!"

"I still can't believe it," I said.

We were walking side by side, Matt twirling Duncan's nose ring around his index finger, king of the world.

"What a plan. What a shot!" My adrenaline high seemed to be never ending.

"It worked perfectly." He threw his arm around my shoulder. "After he chased you, and I knew you were away from where I was gonna shoot, I waited till he turned toward me, popped up and—blammo!"

"You must have been freaking out with just that little gun."

"I was so close, I couldn't miss. Smack! Right between the eyes. I've seen Dad shoot lots of cows and a twenty-two is all he ever uses. Says if you hit 'em in the forehead, they'll drop like a stone every time."

"He's not going to believe it."

"That's why we got this," he said, still twirling the ring.

After we locked the gate of the upper pasture, the herd safely delivered, we hiked for another hour, making our way across a ridge of dense fir trees.

"Do you hear that? We're almost there. Come on, I'll race ya."

We took off toward the faint noise of machinery, rushing through the forest until we emerged into a vast clearing where everything had been leveled.

Matt told me earlier that his dad was selling off some of the timber at the edge of their property. We skirted around huge stacks of logs and brush. Just past a group of gruff-looking men wearing hard hats and holding chainsaws, Matt spotted his dad.

"Dad. Hey, Dad. I got him!"

Matt Sr. was facing a heavily bearded man who held a roll of large papers. "Hold your tongue, boy. I'm busy."

Matt could barely contain himself. Eventually his dad concluded his business and turned to us. "I take it you have something to say? Before you tell me, did you get the herd up okay?"

"Yeah, yeah, they're all safe and sound. But guess what?"

"Well?"

"I got him!"

"Matty, I'm pretty busy here, I—" He stopped midsentence when Matt produced the nose ring.

"I got him," he whispered through smiling lips.

"I'll be a son of a bitch."

After we recounted our tale twice, Matt's dad led us through the woods to another clearing.

"I was gonna send you boys back down the way you came, but I think you deserve a reward for your good deed." Stepping around a pile of branches, he pointed to a large helicopter. "How 'bout a lift off the hill?"

"That was so cool."

"Which part?" Matt grinned. He was certainly the happy host.

"All of it. But I meant riding in the logging helicopter. That was so cool."

"Yeah, that sure was awesome. It stinks you have to go."

"Yeah, but I'll see you tomorrow at school."

"Yep, see you tomorrow, bull chaser."

"It's time to go, Dan," my mom said. She thanked Matt's mother one last time and led me to the car.

"So how was it?" my dad questioned as I slid into the backseat.

"It was okay."

"Did you do anything fun?" Mom asked.

"Not really. Just sort of hung out and stuff."

Chapter Five

Ashes

The school year was nearly at an end, but I wasn't thrilled about it, for my parents had sold the orchard, and in a few short weeks, we'd be packing up and heading back to Colorado. I was beginning to understand depression. I didn't feel like doing anything except lying in bed. From the stillness of the house, that's what it seemed like everyone else was doing on this quiet Sunday morning, so why should I get up and do my chores? Gradually, I decided to get them over with. Maybe afterward I'd return to bed.

I sluggishly got dressed and scuttled out across the driveway, lost in thought, barely attempting to lift my feet as I went. The stupid chickens, the stupid horse, always needing to be fed, but not for much longer, I sourly realized. I was really in a funk. There was no doubt about that. Before I reached the barn door, it dawned on me— something was not quite right. No, it was more like *everything* was not quite right. It was well past dawn, but the sky was very dim, gloomy even. Under the faint light, the world seemed to be encased in some sort of giant eggshell.

Roofs, cars, fences, trees, all of it was painted a dull gray, like I woke up that morning color blind. Gazing down at my boots, I was dumbstruck to find myself standing in a thick dusting of what looked a lot like frost. It couldn't be. It was almost summer. What in the world?

I jogged back to the house, stirring up whatever it was that blanketed the ground. "Mom, Dad, come quick!" A few moments later, I was joined on the porch by my parents.

"What in God's name?" Mom said, taking in the sight.

"It must have finally blown its top," Dad said.

"The mountain?" she asked. "Oh my God, they were right. Mount St. Helens erupted!"

"How fitting," Dad said. He turned and went back into the house.

Chapter Six

Busted

Things sure hadn't been going my way lately. I switched off my battered flashlight and munched on a stolen ham sandwich in the dark. Better save the batteries. It was the seventh night in a row I had slept here. I was almost at the breaking point, ready to let my emotions crush me. Instead, I let my mind wander while I settled down in the dirt and closed my eyes.

Three years ago, I was ripped from my friends in Oregon, and now it was happening again. I wasn't going to let it. All my friends were here. My girlfriend was here. This was my town. It was my world, the only one I had. Deep down, I knew I didn't possess the weapons to win this battle, but fighting it I was, nonetheless.

My mind began to wander, and suddenly I was reliving the day I got the crap beat out of me in seventh grade. I turned a corner and ran straight into a group of guys wearing the dreaded hoodlum costume—a black concert T-shirt, jeans, and a leather jacket. I had just given them something more interesting to focus on than their cigarettes. It was all over in seconds. I received a few bruised ribs and a matching set of black eyes, but the worst was the broken nose. I had to wear *the mask* in order to finish the wrestling season. The contrivance hooked onto the headgear and covered the entire face. It was close to impossible to see or breathe out of the eye and mouth slits. I hated it almost as much as I hated wrestling itself. I had wrestled since I was six years old and despised every moment of it. All the anxiety of a one-on-one sport, all the training, all the starving for months on end to reach a lower weight class—why did I keep signing up for it?

"And why are you living like an animal in such a dangerous place?" my dad asked. He was standing over me, reaching for my left wrist.

I woke abruptly, hitting my head against the flimsy wall. Thin bands of light filtered through the cracks of the structure. It was time to go.

I stuffed the flashlight and rubbish into my backpack and left the shelter through a badly warped plywood door. Reaching the edge of the vacant park, I felt a strange urge to turn back and say good-bye to my current residence. Hundreds of little kids would probably be thrilled riding the miniature train through that poorly built tunnel this summer, but I doubt they'd appreciate it as much as I did. "I'll see you tonight," I said to the peculiar little building. Yet for some undefined reason, I doubted it.

After walking a few miles along the real train tracks, which roughly divided Longmont in half, I reached my school. The cooks were always the first to arrive, and I had discovered they invariably left a rear door unlocked. I slipped down the bricked corridors, making my way to the boy's locker room. After a heavenly shower, I changed into a pair of semiclean jeans and a T-shirt my friend Andy had generously loaned me. I still had some time to kill before the students and faculty arrived, so I hunkered down on a worn bench, head in hands, and tried to think my way out of my predicament for the umpteenth time.

I was in a jam, no doubt about it. It just seemed so unfair. Everything was going great up until last year. That's when my parents got divorced. The divorce was bad enough, but then Dad decided to move back to the familiar surroundings of Evergreen (where we had lived when I was in elementary school). My sister had dropped out of school and vanished. So it had just been me and Mom holding down the fort in Longmont. But a couple of months ago, Mom had married a guy named Phil and shifted to California. Since then, both Mom and Dad had fervently been insisting I move in with one of them—a fifteen-year-old boy cannot, and should not, be left on his own to do as he pleased. Yet that's exactly what I had been doing.

For a while, I spent every night at Andy's. I called my dad regularly, begging him to let me finish the school year where I was and led him to believe that everything was great—Andy's mom was cool with me staying with them; I was eating well, keeping up my grades, and so forth. The truth was, Andy's mom didn't even know I was staying under her roof. Andy slipped me in through his bedroom window after dark. I was struggling to get enough to eat, and my grades were plummeting. One night, Andy's mom was waiting for me, arms crossed, as I exited the bathroom. The jig was up. I managed to stay with a few other friends, but their parents were just as uncomfortable with the situation. That's when I found the train tunnel. I was making my last stand.

I could hear people filing into the building. It was time to get to class. After a brief stop at my locker to collect my books, I made my way to first period.

"What's up?" my buddy Jerry asked.

I slid into the desk next to his. "Nothing, man, still

waking up."

"Hey, I was thinking last night that you could probably stay in the loft of my old man's workshop. He never goes up there, and there's plenty of room."

Before I could smile, a loud bell rang, and the teacher started in on the lesson. Normally I would have made a weak attempt to pay attention to the boring lecture, but I was lost in thought, doodling on my notebook, too excited about Jerry's proposal to concentrate. Perhaps that's why I was the only one in the room who didn't notice them walk in.

"Dan, will you come up here please."

Hearing my name instantly snapped me out of my daydreaming. I looked up, and every eye in the room was focused on me. At the front of the room stood the teacher, bookended by two cops.

"Oh shit, dude," Jerry whispered.

I nervously stood up and made my way forward.

"Uh, it seems that these, uh, two officers want to speak with you, Dan." I wasn't the only one caught off guard; even Mr. Morton was tongue-tied. It wasn't every day the police walked into the junior high school and removed one of its students.

The cops gently steered me out of the building without uttering a word. I don't know what was worse, the overwhelming fear or the humiliation. To my surprise, I was directed away from their police cruiser and toward a familiar-looking sedan. The taller cop opened up the passenger door and stuck his head in. "Here he is, Mr. Garrison. He didn't give us any trouble."

"Thanks, officer. I appreciate it," my dad said.

I was completely dazed, hardly noticing as the other officer guided me into the car and shut the door.

"The party's over kid. You're going home with me."

Chapter Seven

Fate

Asteady stream of sunshine warmly collects along endless golden beaches and turquoise-colored surf, while bikini-clad women laze under the cool protection of majestic palm trees. Such was my illusion of California, and I was intent on making the most of it.

A week earlier, I had graduated from Longmont Junior High School. At least, that's what I had been told. Frankly, I didn't see how it was possible, since I never actually finished the school year. I guess my dad had sorted it out somehow. What I did know was that it was decision time, and this wasn't your garden-variety decision either—this one was a biggie. I could continue living high up in the Rocky Mountains with Dad and his new wife, Annie, or I could move to sea level with my mom and Phil. It would determine where I would go to high school, who my friends would be, *everything*. So I decided. I decided not to decide, at least not yet. I agreed to spend the summer in the Bay Area with Mom and Phil, at the end of which I promised everyone I would have an answer.

Immediately, California took a shine to me. With

little effort, I found employment for the summer in a relaxed, fun, and, most importantly, tropical environment, which confirmed my belief that this place really was the paradise portrayed in the movies.

"Have you ever been a manager?" asked the hyper twenty-year-old blonde.

"Uh, no."

"Like, that's cool. I'm totally going to recommend you anyway." And just like that, I was working as one of several new assistant managers of beverages at the recently opened Marine World/Africa U.S.A. theme park.

Cool.

My job consisted of walking around the massive entertainment park, casually dressed in the company uniform—a short-sleeved Hawaiian shirt, crisp khaki shorts, and gleaming-white socks stretched to the breaking point just below the knee—checking in with the employees of the fifteen scattered beverage booths and carts. I had to make sure supplies weren't running too low (sugar-drenched, artificially flavored drinks sold in little plastic fruit-shaped containers). It was also up to me to make sure everyone got his or her lunch breaks in a timely fashion. It was a vital and important job to be sure. Moreover, it had a very unique perk. Every evening, just after closing, the place magically transformed into an animal playground.

I stood there with a small chimpanzee on my shoulders. "You sure she doesn't bite?"

"Oh no, Ollie loves everything and everyone. She's very gentle," the trainer replied.

I felt her picking through my hair, looking for hopefully nonexistent bugs.

"Are you getting tired of her sitting up there? She can get a bit heavy. Come on down, Ollie. That's a good girl."

"She's really cool. Thanks for letting me play with her."

"Yeah, she's a real sweetie. I guess I'd better be getting back. It's past her dinner time."

"Okay. I'll see you later."

"See ya."

Hands down, it was the best time of the day. Walking through the vacant park, checking the inventory of each kiosk, I found it difficult to stay on task when the handlers passed by, exercising their different animals. I contemplated sauntering over to the killer whale tank. Maybe they would let me help feed them again? Just then, I remembered I had promised Jimmy I'd be at his house for supper in an hour. I hustled to finish counting fruit drinks and caught the bus.

Jimmy wore the same uniform I did. We met shortly after I was hired and quickly struck up a friendship. Although his parents lived in Northern California, he spent the majority of the year at a boarding school in Philadelphia. He was home for the summer.

"What are you two up to tonight?" Jimmy's mom asked as she cleared away the dishes.

"Oh, we thought we'd go into the city and do some browsing at Guido's House of Sex," Jimmy replied.

"Is that so?"

"They're having a big sale on all their toys. If we don't hurry, we'll miss out."

"Okay, Jimmy, that's enough," she scoffed.

"Keep an eye out for me, fellas, a good sale is a rarity these days." His dad chuckled.

"Is it cool if we borrow the car? We'll probably just

go over to Dan's and hang out."

"Put some gas in it this time, will you?"

In keeping with our normal nocturnal routine, we jumped in the large imitation-wood-paneled station wagon, Jimmy's small frame dwarfed by the massive ship-like steering wheel, and headed down the road with absolutely no destination in mind.

"Where to, slick?"

"I don't know. Hmm, why don't we go into the city?" I asked.

"Hang on then. The Shwagon is on the move." He hammered the pedal to the floor and tugged at the wheel. The tires let out a slight squeal as we flew around the corner, the huge engine roaring to life, propelling us up the freeway onramp. We erratically entered three lanes of traffic, and he squeezed the enormous car into a slot behind a semitruck. "San Francisco, here we come!"

Jimmy was obnoxiously flipping through radio stations when a sports car zipped past us in the fast lane, the girl of my dreams behind the wheel.

"Dude, follow that car!"

"Breaker one-nine, we have the target in sight."

He yanked the shifter into overdrive and abruptly swung into the adjacent lane. Within moments, the mighty wagon was closely tailing the sleek red car.

"Man, you've got to see this chick. Long blond hair, the works, dude, the works!"

Jimmy made several attempts to maneuver us alongside our speeding mark but was thwarted by a constant stream of neighboring vehicles.

"Shit, I can see her up there, but I can't get closer."

"She's switching lanes. I think she's going to get off and head for the bridge. Don't lose her."

"Roger that."

We drifted across the three lanes, cutting off a few cars in the process, just in time to catch the exit and follow the elusive woman whose beauty was godlike. The bridge was tightly packed with vehicles, but after several tense minutes, Jimmy managed to bring us alongside the flashy coupe. We goggled over at her, but she was concentrating on the road ahead, her wicked, long hair shading her face.

"Honk the horn! Honk the horn!"

Jimmy laid into it and wildly waved his left arm out the window. "Hey, baby, what's shakin'?"

She couldn't ignore us now. Slowly, she turned her beautiful head our way.

"Son of a bitch, she's got a beard!" I was horrified.

"She's a dude!"

"And he's flipping us off."

We took the first exit beyond the bridge and circled back toward home.

"He did have very nice hair," Jimmy said.

"Very nice, very silky."

Before long, we discovered a way to spend our time away from the tourist park more constructively. We pursued the noble art of surfing. Well, Jimmy did. He continued to hone his abilities while I floundered alongside, eager to learn and overjoyed to be acting out the California surfer-dude persona. Initially, we joined the throngs of wave riders on the constrained beaches south of the bay, but after taking a moment to examine a map, we discovered the less-frequented shores of Stinson Beach. It was perfect. A beautiful forty-five-minute drive north of the city, the forested cliffs gave way to a wide, sandy beach, which curved into the hazy northern horizon.

"Hey, check out the seals," Jimmy called out. "Looks like they're waiting for the waves too."

To our right, three shiny black heads popped out of the calm water. They were the only sign of life along the expansive coast. Once again, Stinson Beach was our own personal playground. Twisting around on my floating island, (Jimmy insisted I first learn to surf on the giant platform of a board before I could graduate to a smaller cool surfboard like his.) I glanced over my shoulder. Jimmy was lying there, forearms propping up his head, staring out at the great expanse of the Pacific Ocean. We had been drifting on the placid water for an eternity.

"Where are the waves?"

"It's just one of those days I guess," he said. "Flat, man, flat."

The warm afternoon sun and the gentle roll of the swells were making me dozy. I closed my eyes and felt certain a nap was imminent. The waves would wake me if they ever decided to arrive. My thoughts were slipping into the fuzziness that precedes sleep when a loud splash jerked me back to my surroundings.

"Hey, man, I was just about asleep." I paddled with my left arm, forcing a 180-degree turn out of the behemoth board. "You're not giving up are…"

Jimmy's board was abandoned. He was nowhere in sight.

I was instantly on my hands and knees, scanning the water, but just as panic was setting in, he exploded to the surface ten feet in front of me. His features were so contorted by fright that I didn't recognize him. He appeared to be silently screaming. He frantically drove his arms into the water, propelling himself forward in a splashing, disorganized frenzy. His eyes threatening to launch from their sockets, his mouth stuck open and full of saltwater, he recovered his board. Urgently, his arms resumed digging water, furiously paddling for shore.

I was stunned, unsure what was happening or what to do, but the large blue fin that appeared a few feet from my face answered everything in a heartbeat. Terror wiped my mind clean. Luckily, I didn't need to think—my arms knew what to do. Through the splashing water, I glimpsed the impossibly distant beach and Jimmy, who appeared to be nearing it. I willed my arms to swing even faster. It was like moving through oil. After what felt like days of paddling, I lifted my head and discovered the beach was close. Jimmy was there, jumping up and down, yelling something indistinct and pointing at something beyond me. Just then, my board was hit with the force of a torpedo, knocking it onto its side and savagely dumping me into the ocean. My arms never stopped turning. I didn't know if I was swimming up, down, left, or right. I didn't know anything but undiluted fear. I battled the water until my lungs ached. My vision grew black. And then something grabbed me, and I was lifted from my prison.

"I got you. I got you. It's okay!" Jimmy was dragging me through the shallow water. "We're on the beach. We're safe. Here, sit down. Can you breathe?"

My reply was a stomach load of salt water vomited onto the sand.

"Take it easy…take it easy." He was kneeling next to me.

I wiped my mouth and fell onto my back, giving Jimmy a slight nod in the process. He lay down next to me, and for several minutes, the only sound was our heavy breathing and coughing.

After a while, I managed to sit up. I was trembling. "What? What the? Jimmy, what the hell happened?"

He stood up on unsure legs and retrieved his

surfboard from the water's edge; mine was nowhere in sight. He dropped it in front of me and sat back down. It had a small crack running down the middle of it and part of the right side looked like someone had taken a belt sander to it.

"Oh my God."

"One second, I was just lying there, listening to you snore, and the next thing I know, my board flips, and I'm in the water. And then…Jesus…and then…" He began sucking in deep, short breaths.

I put my arm around his shoulder.

After a few minutes, he continued. "I saw it. Underwater, I mean. I saw it."

"Shit."

"It was only for a second, but it was right there. I mean, I could have touched it. God, I can't believe it. That was one big fucking shark." We just stared at each other. "I don't remember much after that, not until I made it to the beach anyway. I'm pretty sure I didn't say anything to you. I should have. I should have told you to swim your ass off or something."

"It's okay, man, you didn't need to. I saw the fin."

"Yeah, it was trailing you."

"*What?*"

"As soon as I was out of the water, I looked for you. You were giving it everything you had and right behind you was this huge fin. Jesus. I started screaming at you. I don't even remember what I was saying. And then it disappeared, and I thought you were going to make it. You were pretty close to shore and then—"

"And then it hit me!"

"Yeah, and then it hit you. My God, as long as I live, I'll never forget it. It just shot right out of the water and drilled your board. The next thing I knew, it was gone, and so were you. I ran into the water just as you surfaced."

"I thought I was underwater the whole time."

"No, you were thrashing around, so I swam out and grabbed you."

I hugged his shoulder even tighter, and we both started crying.

As the god of summer felt the first subtle nudges of its weaker yet irrefutable cousin, autumn, the world around me began to shrink, and my attention seemed to be increasingly focused internally. Jimmy had returned to Philadelphia a few days earlier, and I realized the school year would have to begin soon for me as well. It was just a matter of deciding where that would be.

"I got a call from your mom this afternoon. She said she'll be back on Tuesday," my stepfather relayed.

"How's she doing?"

"Good. Getting lots of material; sounds like she's really enjoying herself," Phil said.

"I knew she would."

Mom was a brilliant artist. She had been in Arizona the past week, touring the Navajo Reservation. She was learning more about the culture and taking heaps of photos for future sculptures and paintings she would create.

"I guess our pizza days are numbered."

The next day I gave my two-week notice at the park. I was running out of time. If I was going to go back to Colorado, I should have reserved a plane ticket days ago. I just could not decide. I was driving myself crazy. One moment, I'd firmly make the decision; the next, I would reverse it. During the bus trip home that day, I managed to make at least one decision I felt confident I would stick to—I *must* decide that very day and live with it.

I walked up the short driveway, unlocked the front door, and took a seat in the living room. Like every day since Mom had been away, I had the place to myself until Phil got home from work a couple of hours later.

Maybe I should let fate decide? That wasn't such a stupid idea actually. Why not just flip a coin?

The phone rang.

"Hello?"

"Dan, are you all right?" Phil asked with a tone of urgency I was unaccustomed to hearing in his voice.

"Yeah, sure, fine. I just got home from work."

"Did you come in the front door?"

I thought that was an odd question. "Yeah, well sure. Why, what's going on?"

"I'll tell you about it when I get home. I'll be there within the hour. Stay put."

"Okay."

I hung up the phone and sat back down on the couch. I had no idea what that was about. Phil was the president of a brick company. He had a lot of work responsibilities; the call probably had something to do with that. Maybe some bigwig was flying in unexpectedly or something? Guess I'd find out when he got home. I pulled a quarter from my pocket and rubbed it between my thumb and finger.

"Heads Colorado, tails California." I flipped it. It bounced off the carpet once and came to rest. I stared at George Washington. To my surprise, I didn't flip it again. I just clicked on the TV. The decision was finally made, and it was absolute. I felt a sort of odd calmness sweep over me.

Forty-five minutes later, I was halfway through an episode of Night Court when I heard a car pull up in front of the house. Phil entered a moment later.

"Hey, Dan, is everything okay?" he inquired, glancing around the entryway.

"Yeah, Phil, just like I told you on the phone, everything is fine. What's going on?"

"Let's go for a ride. I'll tell you on the way."

As we accelerated out of our pocket of suburbia, Phil recounted an alarming story. "I've been having some problems with one of the employees at work for quite some time. He's lazy, has a constant problem with showing up on time, and basically he's just a bad egg. I've had several talks with him about it, even warned him he better straighten up and fly right or I'd be forced to let him go. It never seemed to do any good. So last week I called him into my office and canned him. He apparently didn't take it so well." We zipped underneath the freeway and headed into the center of town. "Last night, he built a pipe bomb in his apartment. The police found evidence that he was planning on wiring it to the front door of our house."

"Are you serious?" The thought of unlocking the front door earlier that day ran through my mind.

"I wouldn't blow smoke up your ass about something like this." He pulled the car into a parking lot and rolled to a stop. "Look."

We were sitting in front of a two-story building that was wrapped in yellow police tape. Part of it was missing. At one end, the second story wall had been replaced by a gaping hole the size of a swimming pool. The roof sagged over the charred, jumbled remains of furniture, cabinets, and dozens of other unidentifiable items.

"My God. What happened?"

"He screwed the cap on too tight."

Chapter Eight

Rocky

"So you've never rock climbed before, huh?" It was an incredibly steep slope. My ankles and calves were beginning to ache, and at an altitude of over nine thousand feet, my lungs were desperately searching for what they craved. My vision was restricted to the back of his ever-shifting legs. The rugged ground passed beneath my feet at an increasingly slower rate.

"No," I gasped, "never." And I didn't really care to. I was just trying to fit in.

I had stayed true to my coin toss and returned to Evergreen. So far, high school wasn't going that great. Most of my friends from my youth were giving me the cold shoulder, so I was doing whatever it took to heal the new-guy brand I had burned into my forehead yet again. When Bryan had invited me to go climbing with him and Mark, I could hardly have refused, but now I was thinking perhaps I should have. I kept puffing and climbing, all the while convincing myself this was better than eating lunch every day alone in the corner of the cafeteria. An eternity later, the ground began to level out, and I looked up, shaking off my tunnel vision.

"Whew, now that's a climb, eh, brother? Hey, chuck those ropes over here. I'll tie them off. Better get into a harness."

As my chest desperately snagged a few oxygen molecules out of the thin air, I faintly heard Mark's words and did as he instructed without uttering a reply. I pulled the tangled black webbing out of my pack and examined it. It looked like nothing more than a mess of flat ropes to me. A few minutes later, I was no closer to figuring it out; Mark saw the confused expression on my face and walked over.

"Here, let me help you. Step into this first, then this one."

It felt like I was wearing some type of Sumo lingerie over my shorts. If I hadn't been so winded, it might've made me horny.

"Right, we should be all set. Follow me, and I'll get you hooked up to the rope."

We dropped down onto a small ledge and edged our way to the top of the cliff. I very carefully leaned forward and peeked over.

"Wow."

"Higher up than you thought, huh?" He stood next to me looking down without a trace of fear.

"Uh-huh." I could see Bryan's tiny figure waving up at us.

"Okay, dude, come here. This end we connect to you."

"What's the other end connected to?"

"It's right there behind you."

The thin rope was tied to the trunk of a much-too-small aspen tree in a mess of knots.

"You just tie it to a tree, that's it?" I was hoping he would laugh and explain it was also magically attached to something else as well, preferably something like an aircraft carrier.

"Don't worry, man, I checked it out; that tree is sturdy. So we put the rope around like this and then..."

He continued muttering, but I couldn't make out the words. It was like he was talking himself through a process he wasn't very familiar with. That didn't seem like good news.

"All set. Just push off with your feet, and this is how you brake the rope." He demonstrated much too quickly. "Now back up to the face."

"Wait, wait. What do you mean, brake the rope? And what's a face?" I asked while I unknowingly walked backward.

"So you can stop between push-offs."

"I don't know about this; hang on. I don't understand..."

I lost my train of thought. I was now standing a couple of inches from the massive drop off. I felt woozy.

"Don't overthink it, dude. You'll just chicken out. What you want to do is just do it!"

And the bastard pushed me in the chest, and I went sailing into space.

Unfortunately for Mark's nose, jaw, and left eye, I lived through the ordeal with everything intact, including my fists.

Chapter Nine

Freedom

I stood outside of the department of motor vehicles giddy with victory, lost in a chaotic rush of future dreams. The things I could do now, the places I could go, and the girls—

A car horn honked right in front of me, snapping me back to reality. It was Dad. He motioned for me to get into the car.

"I passed!" I reported through a wide smile.

"Congratulations. On your first try no less."

It was my birthday, my sixteenth to be precise, and the best present I had ever received had been given to me by a plump, blue-haired woman moments earlier. It was, of course, my driver's license. It was time to clean out my wallet. The moment had come to toss out all the scraps of paper with locker combinations and class schedules scribbled on them, chuck the school photos that had crap like "Love ya lots, Tonya" and "URA sweetheart, ☺ Michelle" written in a flowery female hand on the back, ditch the library card I had never once used, and finally throw out what remained of the brittle condom Davie Hunter and I had swiped from his big brother's dresser.

Yes, it was about time! It was time to slide that stiff, glossy ticket to freedom into my previously pointless wallet.

The drive home lasted forever, but at long last, Dad swung into our driveway and pulled up alongside a deep-red 1967 Ford Mustang. It was a cool car. It was the type of car that never has been and never will be uncool. It was a dream car, and I was ecstatic Dad was considering buying it for me. It had been at our house for the past two days. The owner was a friend of Dad's and allowed him to bring it home so he could thoroughly check it out. Today would be the first time I would drive it alone, that is, if I could talk Dad into it.

"I'm headed back to work for the day," he said, without getting out of his car.

"Okay. Hey, you know Mike? Well his dad is an awesome mechanic, and he said he'd look over the Mustang. Would it be all right if I drove it over there, seeing how I got my license and all?" It was the truth; besides, I couldn't come up with a better lie.

"Is his dad at home this time of day?"

"Yeah, he works nights." (I had no idea.)

"Okay. But be careful."

No sooner was he out of sight than I was behind the steering wheel of the badass machine. I was a bit nervous but too young and cocky to let it come to the surface. It wasn't the best of weather, a cold, gloomy February afternoon. There were even a few patches of snow on the ground, but to me it felt like the height of a wonderful summer's day, and I cranked both windows down and the music up.

I decided to take the longest possible route to Mike's house. I tooled around the winding back roads for a while, gunning the powerful car here and there, until I came upon Fish Creek Hill. I knew the hill well and reduced my speed accordingly. I was traveling at perhaps thirty miles per hour. I reached the summit and suddenly viewed the smooth, shiny surface on the other side. The backside of the hill faced north, and the sun hadn't thawed the icy road. It didn't bother me. I just gently applied the brakes like I had been taught. But nothing happened. In fact, far from obeying me, the car continued to pick up speed at an alarming rate.

Oh man, okay, try slamming on the brakes.

I followed my adrenaline-charged advice, but the car still didn't respond. With both feet furiously working the brake pedal, I looked ahead and, to my horror, realized I was quickly approaching a three-way intersection, and the road I was barreling down didn't continue through on the other side. I knew what was on the other side.

"Shit, shit, shit, shit." I helplessly watched the intersection whiz by. A fraction of a second later the car left *terra firma* and whistled off a twenty-foot cliff.

I vividly remember steering all the way down, as well as working the brakes. If the car had turned in midair, I probably would have used my turn signal too. But the only thing demonstrating control was gravity.

An awful crunching sound with a background chorus of thuds signaled the end of my joyride.

Panicking and seeing through a foggy filter of fear, I scrambled from the vertically perched car and plunged into a waist-deep river of ice. I had not only managed to drive off a cliff but also parked the car smack in the middle of Fish Creek. Quite an accomplishment really, considering the state granted me my license a mere hour and a half earlier.

Chapter Ten

Beer and Bikes

I t took a while for Bryan, Shane, and the rest of the
gang to welcome me back to Evergreen, but it did
happen. By the time I graduated high school, it felt like
I had never lived anywhere else, never had any other
friends. It felt like home. Yet change is an integral part of
growing up, and it was here again.

Many of the seniors in my modest-sized class had
chosen to attend college at Colorado State University, and I
went along with the crowd. Shane and I shared a dorm
room that first year of emancipation. We were a couple of
unruly eighteen-year-old boys who had virtually no adult
supervision and easy access to cheap beer. It was awesome.

It was the dawning age of the mountain bike. It seemed
everyone had one, with the exception of Shane. He had the
Schwinn. It was an absolute wreck of a bike; why it
stubbornly refused to completely fall apart, I could never
figure out. I can't imagine that it had been in much better
shape twenty years earlier when his dad was riding it

around, for it was his dad who had given it to him. Maybe he was mad at his son, and this was his way of getting revenge. I don't know. I do know, however, the ancient ten-speed became the very bane of Shane's college existence.

The curse began one day when Bryan, Shane, and I were routinely biking to class. Bryan and I were riding next to each other on our fairly decent mountain bikes. Shane brought up the rear on the old man's bike. We were cycling down the middle of a side street, which led to the heart of the campus. It was a one-way, one-lane road with parking spaces running ninety degrees to it. Bryan and I were chattering away about this and that, pedaling rather slowly, when out of nowhere, Shane zoomed between us, head tucked down, legs furiously pumping the pedals. He was on a mission to push the Schwinn to the limit, just for the hell of it, which was the same old reason for most of what he did. He raced ahead, straining to coax even more from the rickety bike—butt pointing skyward, chest rubbing against the handlebars, nose inches from the whirling front tire. A Volkswagen Beetle suddenly backed out from between two parked cars.

He never saw it coming.

The force of the impact was immediate and brutal. The collision buckled the Schwinn's front wheel and crushed the car's door. Momentum threw Shane up and over the roof of the Beetle until his body found the unforgiving pavement to slam into. The stunned driver and passenger sat frozen in their newly dented car. Bryan and I started laughing so hard we fell off our bikes.

Shane was sitting at his desk, rocking back and forth in his chair, chewing on a pen, and avoiding his calculus book. It was Friday night, and I was just about out the door of our cramped, filthy dorm room.

"I wouldn't go if I were you," he said.

"It's a bit late for that. Besides, what's the big deal?"

"It just sounds like it would suck. I mean, why would anyone want to go on a blind date?"

"I'm sure it will be fine. Anyway, at least I'm doing something tonight instead of sitting on my ass, pretending to study."

"Oh I got big plans, loser; don't worry about that."

"Okay, big shot, I'll catch you later."

The bastard was right—my date was a nightmare. I think she said four words the entire evening, and I was out sixty bucks on a dinner that tasted like it had been created in the dorm cafeteria.

Returning to the repulsive hole I called home, I was hit with a totally unexpected sight.

"What the hell are you doing?" I chuckled.

He didn't respond, not verbally anyway. He just lifted his head off the beer-soaked pillow and directed a crooked grin in my direction. I cracked up. Damn, I was only gone for a few hours.

Shane was lying on his bed fully dressed and covered with empty beer cans. There were cans between his legs, above his head, and on his belly. With both hands, he cradled a full beer, which was sitting precariously on his chest.

He mumbled something incoherent.

"What'd ya say?"

He managed to slur, "I'm gonna drink myself to death."

"It can't be done, buddy. Not with beer," I informed him, thinking him silly for not realizing that.

"I'm...I'm gonna try," he stammered, "and won't you be sorry...really...really fucked-up-like sorry."

I moved over to the edge of the bed and sat down beside him, watching him struggle with his latest victim. He just didn't have any remaining motor skills to get it to his lips. With tensed neck muscles and tearing eyes, he let out a few grunts, but the can of beer and his mouth were as far apart as ever.

"Here, big guy, let me help." I lifted the can from his sticky grasp and held it to his lips.

His eyes shined with gratitude.

"You'd do it for me, man. You'd do it for me."

When the can was empty, the majority of the beer still running down his shirt, I placed it on his forehead.

"I looovve you, man. Goddamn, you're—" And with that, he promptly passed out.

It took around three seconds before I was crouched over him with my razor and a magic marker.

Chapter Eleven

Rite of Passage

It was the spring of 1989. Even though Shane and I had killed the final beer, taken the last exam, and packed up our belongings less than two weeks before, the carefree college life seemed years distant as I lay on my belly, sandwiched between jagged metal plates that were coated with a gooey black substance. The rays from a shop light partially illuminated the steel cavern I slid through, searching for more rust spots to knock loose with my sludge-covered rotary hammer. It seemed to me they should have offered me some type of ear protection and a respirator, or perhaps I should have requested these things, but I thought it best not to make waves, for on the docks of Seattle, I had the impression they liked things as smooth as glass. I just thanked God scraping the interior hulls of ancient tugboats was a temporary job. A week ago, I should have been standing on the deck of a ship in Alaska. However, the ship I had been assigned to was currently unreachable, so the company decided to get their money out of me in this fashion during the interim.

After the Exxon Valdez oil tanker was drunkenly steered into a reef in Alaska's Prince William Sound, Exxon reluctantly broke out the checkbook and proceeded to stage one hell of a confused cleanup operation. For maritime companies, like the one I was hired by, the race was on to send every boat they owned north. There was plenty of room in Exxon's cash trough for thousands of boats to sail comfortably. It didn't matter if they had been mothballed for twenty years and sported more rust holes than a 1971 AMC Gremlin—if it held seawater at bay, it was a potential money-maker. Thankfully, the ship I was waiting to board was in much better shape. Phil had seen to that.

A year ago, my stepfather landed a new job. He was now the boss of a brick company outside of Seattle. So when my mom had mentioned he could get me a job for the summer, I naturally assumed I'd be doing something construction related, but instead he got me a job through one of his friends who was high up in a shipping and salvage company.

I felt a tug on my boot and twisted around in order to see behind me. A heavily bearded face hung in the opening; with his grease-stained thumb, he signaled for me to crawl out. I nodded and fought my way to the main deck where a smartly dressed man wearing a hard hat was waiting for me. He glanced at his clipboard, looked at me in a questioning manner, and barked, "Go to the office and pick up your ticket. You better hurry; your plane leaves in four hours."

"Where am I going exactly?" I queried.

"Somewhere in Alaska."

Hmm, that really clarifies things. "Yeah, but where exactly? And do you know what I'll be doing? I mean, what my job will be?"

"I wouldn't have the slightest." Annoyed with my foolish questioning, he tromped off.

I climbed up to the dock and looked at the sorry,

old tug. I was fairly ignorant about boats, yet knew enough to know this one was a piece of junk. It was amazing it was still on top of the water. A few months later, it would amaze me yet again.

Twelve hours later, I found myself outside of a structure that strongly resembled a mobile home. It was the airport in Homer, Alaska. After collecting my duffel bag, I searched for the pilot I had been instructed to meet. Forty minutes ticked by, and I began to wonder if I shouldn't begin to redirect my attention toward locating a room for the night. Just then, a tall, middle-aged man rounded the corner, walked up to me, and inquired, "Hey, champ, your name Dan?"

"Yes."

"Cool beans. Come with me."

We traipsed across the silent runway to a yellow-and-white Jet Ranger helicopter. I stood back while he opened one of the rear doors, rummaged around a bit, and produced a fluorescent-orange vest.

"Name's Jim. We don't have a long flight, but most of it is over water, so sling this on. I'm going to get this bird cooking."

I fumbled with the vest while Jim sat in the helicopter and did pilot things. I threw my duffel bag in back, put on a headset when he indicated, and with the blades spinning furiously above our heads, we left the ground and headed out of Kachemak Bay. It was nearing eleven o'clock, and the last rays of the setting sun were still playing off the huge glacier-covered mountains, which thrust right out of the sea. I was awestruck. I had never seen scenery so bold and wild.

Fifteen minutes into the scenic flight, a ship came into view ahead. My nervousness was overridden by my curiosity, and I eyeballed as much as I could during our quick drop in altitude. It looked like a very large tugboat. The front third was three stories tall. Most of the roof appeared to be a helicopter deck. Behind this was a very long stern, littered with a large amount of gear, one or two small boats, and several shipping containers.

We touched down softly, and the motor began winding down. Jim gestured for me to get out. I jumped onto what I quickly found to be a constantly shifting floor. The ship was rolling in the evening swells. I was trying to adjust my balance to the odd sensation when a man of average build and height, sporting shoulder-length gray hair and wearing blue coveralls, emerged from a nearby hatch and introduced himself.

"How you doing? I'm Richard. You'll be bunking with me. I'll show you where the head is. Grab your gear."

That he did, as well as direct me to our quarters. Luckily, he was on watch, so for the moment, I had the place to myself. I latched the steel door shut and took a look around. It was the size of a large broom closet. Two narrow floor-to-ceiling lockers covered one wall, bunk beds the other, and a tiny desk was wedged in between. There was hardly enough room to turn around. And the whole thing, all of it, was moving from left to right, up and down, up and down, relentlessly.

"Oh man, what the hell have I gotten myself into?" I mumbled.

I shoved my bag into the vacant locker, stripped down, and climbed into the top bunk. I was exhausted, yet it seemed like hours before sleep arrived in this foreign, constantly moving place.

"Get up."

"Um, what?"

"New watch. Your watch. Time to roll out." Richard's silhouette filled the doorway.

"What time is it?" I rasped.

"Five," he stated, closing the door.

I rubbed my face and tried to remember where I was. A sudden clattering noise erupting from the bowels of the ship forced me into reality, and I quickly jumped from bed and searched for some clothes. What the hell is that noise? While I finished dressing, it occurred to me what I was hearing was most likely the anchor being hauled up. It was a good guess anyway. I nervously rushed to the head, feeling the vibrations of the ship's engines churning to life.

After a quick wash and shave, I found myself slowly wandering the corridors aimlessly. So now what? I noticed a sign on the wall pointing the way to the galley, so I took the hint. As I entered the small, triangular room, a dozen hardened sailors simultaneously paused eating and silently stared at me. I had absolutely no idea what I was doing, but I knew I'd better do something and quickly. I glanced beyond the rows of tables and observed an open kitchen, behind which was a cook hard at work. I guess it's breakfast time. The men went back to their meals and conversations as I walked over to the kitchen.

"Howdy," I coolly said to the cook. "What's on the menu?"

"You late. You very late. Not again I think!" he said loud enough to elicit snickers from some of the closest men.

My mind was completely blank. Late for what, breakfast? I had no idea, so I simply stood there.

"You come back here."

I obeyed and shuffled around the counter. In less than two minutes, he had me scrubbing pots.

He was, as I learned over the course of the morning, Primo, a large Filipino with an even larger temper. He had been employed as a ship's cook for twenty-six years, and I'm fairly certain he wasn't impressed by the likes of me.

One by one, the sailors finished eating, depositing their dishes in a tub next to me. One sailor grumbled about some minor aspect of the meal, which Primo threw himself into a rage to defend. I kept my mouth closed, not only because it was the prudent thing to do, but I also had a feeling if I opened it, the only thing that would come out was vomit. The violence of the waves was getting worse. I finished washing the dishes with my right leg two feet behind me, bracing myself against the counter.

"You eat now. I'll make you something. What you want?" Primo demanded.

"Whatever is easy. Uh, eggs are fine."

God, how am I going to hold down food? It felt like my upper intestines were knotted around my stomach. I sat down in the now-desolate galley, and Primo swiftly produced a plate of runny eggs and toast. I watched my meal slide to the other end of the table and back. The little rail around the top edge was certainly proving handy. I caught my plate and held it in place. I was losing the battle against the heaves. I forced myself to take several deep breaths and reluctantly picked up a fork full of yellow goo. Before I could insert it into my mouth, I was thrust sideways, nearly getting knocked from my seat. Primo was shouting obscenities as a couple of pots clattered off the counter and onto the floor. Unbeknownst to me, the ship had just left the safe waters of its last anchorage and was now crashing through the massive waves of the Gulf of Alaska. I got up and tried to navigate out of the galley.

"Where you going?" Primo shouted.

"I need some air," I managed to squeak.

"Come back soon. We start fixing lunch now."

I careened through the corridors desperately seeking the outdoors. All of a sudden, I was forced to my knees with a vicious thrust. I gripped the bulkhead and fought against the force, pulling myself back to my feet. No sooner was I up than a feeling of free-falling rushed over me. It was like standing in a rapidly descending elevator. Then gravity once again reversed, and my knees began to buckle. This time I knew what was coming and resisted. I waited until the floating sensation returned and quickly darted out the nearest hatch I could find.

I was on a sort of balcony that overlooked the rear two-thirds of the ship. I threw myself onto a large coil of rope and puked. It took several minutes for me to regain some sort of control over my gut, but finally my breathing returned to normal, and I felt a bit better. I glanced around for something to clean up my mess with but was immediately distracted by the scene unfolding all around me. A fair portion of the ship was under water, or so it seemed. The stern was constantly awash, and gear floated everywhere. Enormous waves methodically pounded both sides of the ship, and it honestly looked like we were sinking into the sea.

Oh man, I thought, if this is just a run-of-the-mill day, I am fucked.

I had just suffered through the worst weather during my entire time on board, thank you, Jesus. The harsh initiation did have one positive side effect. It seemed to have cured me of further seasickness.

I settled into somewhat of a routine that first week. I quietly did what I was told to do, which included washing the dishes, prep cooking, unloading cargo, doing the laundry, running messages to the bridge, and assisting any crew member with anything at any time.

One of the many things I learned early on was how frequently crew members seemed to rotate. When distance and weather permitted, the helicopter seemed to be constantly ferrying men to and from the nearest town. There was one exception to this rotation—me. I didn't come to relieve anyone. I just appeared, and to compound the mystery for the crew, I didn't come aboard to be a captain, a mate, an engineer, a diver, or a cook.

So why was I there? I'm sure there were many theories among the crew, but considering I was the youngest aboard by fifteen years, it probably wasn't too difficult to conclude that I was a spoiled college kid whose Daddy got him the job.

I wasn't going to do myself any favors by admitting that, so I performed evasive maneuvers. I offered no information and stonewalled any and all inquiries as to how I ended up on board. At the same time, I worked as hard as I possibly could. Through this combined effort, I managed to stay below the crew's radar. Well, most of the crew. There was, unfortunately, Joe.

He was the chief engineer, although I never saw him do any engineering. It seemed to me his main occupation was just sitting in the galley all day drinking coffee, which is why I regrettably couldn't escape him or his stench. Joe never bathed—not that I tried to determine that fact, it was just apparent. He probably weighed somewhere in the neighborhood of 250 pounds and stood around five-and-a-half-feet tall (when he did, very occasionally, stand). He wore the same clothes the entire time we were acquainted. I never figured out if he had several pairs of identically stained pants and torn, grubby T-shirts or if he wore the same outfit every day. Along with abstaining from bathing, he also refused to cut his hair and beard, producing an additional sordid effect in his overall appearance. Yet Joe's most repugnant trait wasn't his lack of hygiene—it was his frightening displays of homosexual tendencies.

Four days after my arrival, I received a quick lesson on the consequences of getting within arm's reach of Joe. A supply boat had tied up alongside, and I was busily offloading its contents, carrying them to a storage room on the far side of the galley, which unavoidably forced me to pass quite close to where he sat. I was transferring the final box—a carton of thirty dozen eggs—squeezing past him, when I felt his sausage fingers latch onto both cheeks of my ass. The box hit the floor with a crunch, and Joe's round face lit up in laughter, giving daylight to a mouth containing only a few sad, yellow teeth. Then he blew me a kiss and invited me on a date. At that point, Primo rushed over, loudly vocalizing a mixture of Filipino and English obscenities at me.

It looked like the ship would have to make do without eggs for a while. I never again approached Joe closer than ten feet, but that only made his advances louder.

Time slipped into apathy. I was nearing the end of my first month. I had settled into my low spot on the totem pole and went about my business of cooking, cleaning, and unloading cargo. The fishing and coastal scenery were fantastic, and all in all, life wasn't too bad—that is except for an annoying itch I had developed. Normally, I wouldn't have concerned myself with such a minor condition, yet this itch was alarmingly centered on my most private of parts. It wasn't long until I felt a distinct change; the sensation mutated from an itch to a feeling of very small and semipainful pinches.

One morning, I timed it so no one else was using the communal shower when I reached the head. I promptly began inspecting myself. At first, I found nothing startling, no rash, no missing hair, no weird lumps, and then I spied the movement of something very small. I was absolutely horrified; I nearly screamed out in shock. I captured one of the invaders and brought it close to my eyes. It looked like...like...like a tiny crab! I knew nothing about crabs, but in that instant, I learned all. I furiously began scrubbing until I was down a couple layers of skin. I dressed and went to work. I kept calm, resisted scratching myself, and quickly left the galley when my shift ended twelve hours later.

How was I going to rid myself of these bastards?

I wasn't sure.

How the hell did I get them in the first place?

I didn't know.

One thing was certain—I sure wasn't about to tell anyone. Then another thought hit me. What if some of them jump ship and try to conquer Richard's bunk? Jesus, he'd tell everyone, and they'd keel haul me! Every question I asked myself seemed to have no answer. The only thing I knew for sure was the sooner I got rid of them the better.

I walked down the corridor to my quarters, passing by the medical room. The door was wide open as always. I'd never entered the room, and to my knowledge, no one ever did. It resembled a hospital room, fully equipped with a medical bed and all the instruments and medication necessary for a small disaster. Surely there was something in there that could help me out. When I reached my room, I had talked myself into making a stealth incursion, rifling through the cabinets until I came upon a cure. I knew if I was caught, I would have doomed myself, but there really didn't seem to be much of a choice.

Around 2:00 a.m., when Richard was on the bridge, I slipped out of our cabin and tiptoed in the direction of what I hoped would be my salvation. I turned the corner and smacked right into the chest of the first mate. Before he could question me, I excused myself for running into him and said I was in a hurry to get to the head. I rounded the next corner and nearly dove into the med room. My hammering heart deafened me to the gentle noises I made as I tried to jimmy open the first cabinet. It wouldn't give. I tried the one next to it. It was locked as well. Reaching to check a third, I heard someone cough down the hall. Panicking, I spun around and dashed out, running all the way back to my bunk. My foolhardy scheme just went out the porthole.

Three or four days passed, and although I made every attempt to win my private war, I was still locked in a stalemate with the little pricks. I showered in the morning and at night and rubbed down a half bar of soap at each instance. It helped, but I was quickly reaching the point where I could scarcely afford to lose any more skin cells in that particular area. My nerves were shredded almost as badly as my crotch. Enduring Joe's colorful homoerotic suggestions and Primo's tantrums, slaving away seven days a week in virtual silence, all the while battling a case of undeserved crabs was taking its toll.

I had to get rid of them.

Then the idea of attrition sprang to mind. What if I wipe out their habitat? The instant the thought hit me, I began rummaging around my locker for my razor. I couldn't believe it hadn't occurred to me earlier. With my razor and a pair of scissors in hand, I grabbed my towel and raced to the head. It was the beginning of my shift, which meant the beginning of a shift for eight others as well. When I entered the head, three men were showering and one was grimly squatting over a toilet. Instantly the plan collapsed. I couldn't very well be shaved down below; that'd be a tough one to explain to the two guys next to me in the shower. Dammit! I waited my turn for a shower and trudged through the rest of the day.

After work, I sought out solitude deep in the ship's belly. I wandered in and out of the engine room and the adjoining compartments. No one was around. There usually wasn't anyone in this part of the ship. I didn't know what I was searching for, just searching I guess, hoping for sure. I slowly moped into the workshop. Pails of chemicals were strewn about; worktops were covered with wrenches and engine parts, jars of screws and bolts—and a can of Raid! It was tucked in the corner, mixed in with a bunch of spray-paint cans. I dashed over and grabbed it. It was full! Hastily, I spun it around and read all of the fine print on the back. Several times throughout the warnings it stated, "Do not come in contact with skin." On the front, it listed what it killed: mites, moths, ants, flies, and on and on. I noticed the omission of lice, however. It wasn't even a decision. I pulled down my trousers and shorts and doused myself thoroughly. The deafening *thump thump* of the six diesel engines more than masked the screams that ripped from the very depths of my gut. Perhaps dousing my tortured, raw crotch with a half can of insecticide was a bit impulsive.

The next morning, examining the battlefield, I could tell I had made the right decision. Victory was at hand. I gritted my teeth and blitzed the area again. That evening, my conquest was total. From that day forward, I washed my bedding every other day (since I was the one who did all the laundry, it drew no suspicion) and showered with frequency. I also secretly stashed the can of Raid in my quarters. I never figured out how I got the little bastards, but I had an inkling Richard was the source. I sprayed his bunk with Raid once a week thereafter.

It was the brief episodes of leisure that helped break up the monotony of endless twelve-hour workdays. In my off time, I would often find a secluded spot and read.

One evening, I was doing just that, lounging on the narrow portside deck when a small landing craft carrying two men drifted alongside my little sanctuary and heaved over a rope. It caught me off guard, but I knew they hadn't sent the rope over so I could just stand there dumbly holding it. It was one of those many situations I was thrust into, not knowing how to perform the expected duty, and since I was fully aware of my ignorance, I instantly became nervous, flustered, and failed.

The current was forcing the two boats apart, and even though I was inexperienced in the art of knot tying, I knew I better try something before the end of the line was yanked from my hand. I fumbled around with the coarse rope, looping it, crisscrossing it, sort of doubling it back here and there, doing my best to create some sort of knot-like shape. At some point during this pathetic attempt, I tied one of my fingers up in the mess. The men obviously thought I had it under control for they both jumped aboard and thanked me. I stood there with my free hand covering my trapped one, trying to act causal and ironically told them, "No sweat." While they climbed the ladder behind me, the force of the ocean pushed the boats apart once again; the weight of the pulling landing craft cinched the makeshift knot tight, instantaneously crushing my caught finger.

I let out a howl as the men disappeared on the deck above and ripped my finger free. I'm not sure why my panicked reflex didn't completely tear it off, although it might have been less painful in the long run if it had been torn off. It was absolutely mangled. I think I broke it in at least two or three places. I was never completely sure how bad it had been crushed because I kept it wrapped up with duct tape and told everyone a crate of canned goods fell on it.

Patiently, I ticked off the days on my calendar. Besides my constantly aching finger, life was steadily getting better. Most of the original crew had been replaced over the previous two months, which meant even though I was still the ship grunt, I was now far from being the greenhorn. Actually, I think I had a few of the new guys fooled into thinking I was a bit salty. Primo had also rotated out. He was replaced by some big-time cook from New York who thought it might be a fun adventure to work on the oil spill in Alaska. He spent his first two days in the head heaving his guts out and the majority of the next five on his back in his quarters. On day eight, his luck changed when he found a vacant seat on the transport helicopter. A small, mousy guy named Travis was the next cook to hold the galley reins. He turned out to be a calm, decent guy. Things were definitely looking up.

The cook's position wasn't satisfied simply by chucking two-dozen pork chops on the grill; he actually had to be quite skilled at scheduling and ordering. Twenty men can eat up a hell of a lot of food in a hurry, and it was up to the cook to make sure there was always enough fresh meat and vegetables on hand to meet this constant demand. With the recent comings and goings of cooks, no one had bothered to compile and submit the current resupply request; consequently, after Travis settled in, he found himself severely lacking in all types of foodstuff. It was becoming a slightly hazardous situation, for the quickest way to rock a boat is to deny the crew one of their chief enjoyments—good meals. Unfortunately, help was not forthcoming; the next supply ship would not arrive for at least nine days. Travis found himself in a bit of a pickle. Begging appeared to be his only alternative.

The ship I called home was the flagship for a small ragtag armada consisting of twelve Alaskan fishing boats. An inept Exxon executive randomly directed the little fleet in and out of hidden bays along Alaska's rugged southern shores. When we stumbled across a coastline bathed in oil, the entire fleet dropped anchor, and workers shuttled to the beaches in skiffs and landing craft. Armed with shovels and trash bags, they halfheartedly scooped up a tiny fraction of the mess.

As for Travis's predicament, he found twelve separate opportunities to scrounge for the food we desperately needed. After Jed, the radio operator, broadcast our plea throughout the fleet, Travis received word three boats reported having a surplus of food and were willing to share a bit of it. Jed and I were ordered to take a skiff and retrieve it. The conditions that morning were twelve- to fifteen-foot swells driven by a steady, rain-laced wind, so I can't say I was eager to be the lesser half of the expedition. Yet, Travis's first impression as cook was at stake, and as he roughly shoved me in the direction of the skiff, I figured he wanted that impression to be a good one at nearly any cost.

Cloaked in bulky, bright-orange survival suits, Jed and I timed our jump into the dinghy with the swells. A moment later, a crew member threw over the painter rope, and we were off. A wave passed beneath us, and we fell like a stone. Suddenly, the only thing I could see was a circular wall of water. The next second, the dinghy abruptly changed from a horizontal position to a vertical one as we raced out of the watery depression. The scenery instantly changed. I caught a glimpse of our bobbing fleet and the distant mountains before we sailed nose first into another canyon of water. I was situated in front, clutching anything that could be clutched; Jed was behind, doing his best to steer and manipulate the throttle. He was yelling things I couldn't make out. The boat was full of water, and I was scared shitless.

Cresting yet another mammoth hill of water, I glanced back at Jed and detected a hint of fear in his eyes. Luckily, the boat we were aiming for was also the closest, and by Jed's efforts alone, we soon floated up alongside it. For a second, I was staring into the face of a Hispanic-looking fellow, and the next, the wave that had been holding our two boats even moved out from under us, simultaneously lifting the larger boat and dropping ours. The fishing vessel seemed to jump right out of the ocean, and suddenly, I was staring at ten feet of rusty hull. We quickly regained elevation, only to have the whole process repeat. Coming up for the fourth or fifth time, a crewman yelled at me as our faces passed one another, "Jump, man. Jump!" We plummeted yet again.

"You've got to jump over when we get lined up," Jed shouted.

I shot him a look like he was mad, but he didn't catch it; he was too busy concentrating on keeping our little raft upright. We popped back up. I observed the dark-skinned guy still braced against the railing.

I jumped.

I didn't quite make it. The lower half of my body dangled over the railing as the wave broke. The dinghy was gone. I felt several hands grab at me, but it wasn't enough. I slid down, my hands unable to find purchase on the slick rails. The hull rushed past me and I was instantly underwater. My survival suit brought me quickly to the surface where I found myself wedged between the boat and our skiff.

"Grab my hand," Jed screamed.

I hugged the side of the skiff for all I was worth. A moment later, he heaved me in like a halibut.

"Are you okay? Are you hurt?"

"I'm okay," I chattered.

"Hold on to something. We need to get back."

I shook my head. "I can make it."

"Are you sure?"

"One more try."

This time I was pulled onto the fishing boat by the entire crew. They damn near threw me across the deck and over the opposite railing.

"Welcome aboard," the Hispanic guy said, helping me to my feet. Without further conversation, he and another sailor grabbed my arms and led me into the inner safety of their boat. I glimpsed Jed heading back to our ship, alone.

Jed made a safe return and waited out the bad weather on our ship. I spent the afternoon on the fishing boat, wrapped in a blanket, drinking strong coffee with the captain. The string of stories he spun made my recent adventure seem mundane. Once the conditions calmed, Jed returned to collect me and the supplies. On the ride back, I vowed never to get into a skiff again. Since a smaller craft was the only way to leave the confines of the ship, I figured the decision was a rather restricting one, but it beat the hell out of driving around the violent ocean in a tiny rubber raft.

The days continued to drag on, and I continued to work around the galley. One morning, Alan, the current helicopter pilot, was finishing up his breakfast and called me over from where I was mopping the floor.

"You want to go for a ride today?" he asked.

"Can I?"

"I have to drop off some equipment. The front seat is empty if you want to fill it."

"Awesome!"

"Meet you at the chopper in ten minutes. Oh, hey, Travis, I'm going to borrow your boy for a bit." Without turning around, Travis just raised a hand in a gesture of permission.

I guess I had forgotten—there was another way off the ship.

The fleet was anchored in a sprawling, mountain-ringed bay. Coming from Colorado, I was used to being surrounded by mountains, but Alaska's rugged peaks and glaciers put the Rockies to shame. Alan and I situated ourselves in the cockpit and lifted off in the direction of those stunning, and probably unnamed, mountains. As the machine whirled forward, over sandy beaches and low-growing willows, Alan informed me over the headset that our destination was beyond the next mountain range. All around us, the view was staggering. We passed over huge ice-enveloped peaks and smaller, jagged ranges. Alan angled the helicopter down, matching the slope of the mountain. He increased speed and quickly dropped our elevation until we were whipping along, a foot or two above the top of the dense forest. I was looking through the glass floor, watching the trees blur by, when suddenly the ground fell away as we passed over a giant cliff, which abruptly marked the end of the forest and the beginning of the sea. I was unprepared for the sudden altitude change and my stomach flipped. Before the sensation had a chance to fade, the helicopter tilted back, and we shot up like a rocket. I was plastered to my seat.

"Yeah, baby!" came through the headphones.

He was really enjoying it, and so was I. I was just glad I hadn't eaten breakfast yet. We continued climbing, and then Alan coaxed the machine into a tight turn. The nose dipped, and we sailed back toward Earth. Nearing the ground, he brought us level and resumed course.

"How'd you like that?"

"Unbelievable." I laughed.

We made it to the designated beach, unloaded the gear, and headed back by a different route. This time we flew parallel to the coastline.

"Look." Alan pointed below us. In the distance were two grizzly bears.

"You want me to land so you can get some pictures?"

Of course I did.

We set down in a gravelly area between the sandy beach and forest. I eagerly jumped out, camera in hand. I could only just discern the bears in the distance, so I jogged down the shore for a few minutes until I was close enough to get some good shots with my telephoto lens. While I merrily clicked away, I thought I detected a change in the noise emanating from the helicopter. It sounded like it was winding up in preparation for flight. I turned around. It took several seconds for me to process the scene I beheld.

A hundred yards in front of me a very large female bear and her three cubs were trotting directly at me. Beyond, I could see the helicopter lifting off. Startled and confused, I remained motionless, watching in horror as the clan of bears grew nearer. Belatedly, I brought my legs back into use, turned, and ran as hard as I could. A few seconds later, the whining engine of the helicopter deafened me as it zipped over, the rotor wash causing me to stumble and fall to the ground. As I rolled to my side, I saw it make a low-banking turn and head back toward me. By the time I was back on my feet, Alan had landed his machine in front of me. I ran for all I was worth. He had the passenger door open, and I dove in and slammed it shut. Moments later we were airborne.

As soon as I put on the headset, I heard, "Holy bejesus, Dan, you okay? You're bleeding."

I followed his gaze and found my left arm was a bit scraped up.

"No, it's okay. I'm okay. Just a bit shaken up." I took a couple of deep breaths. "Where the hell did those other bears come from?"

"I don't know for sure. I was working on the logbook and glanced up and saw them running in your direction. The chopper must have scared them out of their hiding place in the woods. I could see you still had your back turned, so I decided I'd better run a little interference for you. You sure you're okay?"

"Yeah. Thank God you scared them away."

"As soon as I flew over the top of 'em, they darted back into the trees. But I saw the other two were still standing out there on the beach. You were the meat in a bear sandwich for a minute there." He chuckled.

"Geez, that was freaky."

"Listen, I vote we keep this little adventure to ourselves."

"Agreed."

After my outing with Alan, I added helicopter joyrides to the list of things I refused to do. Now I really was trapped on board. I continued with my duties, resigned to the fact my world consisted of three decks of steel. However, just as before, I was mistaken in my thinking. For one short week later, I found myself off the ship yet again.

Even though the beach cleaners were far too few in number, eventually their efforts did add up, and the point was reached when every boat in the fleet had a full cargo hold of oil-filled plastic bags. When this situation developed, the fleet lifted anchor and made its way to the nearest dump site. On this occasion, the site was in a small bay on the virtually uninhabited southern shores of Kodiak Island. It took the better part of two days to reach the bay, where a large barge was waiting. I stood on the bow with a rope in my hands as we led the fleet single file through the narrow inlet. As the hull bumped the side of the barge, I tossed my line over to a ragged-looking man who sluggishly tied it off. The ship's engines rumbled down.

"You guys got any food?" the man pleaded.

"Um, yeah, sure," I responded. He was standing a few feet away and below me, as our ship was considerably taller than his barge. A feeling of pity struck me as I looked down at him. His clothes were filthy, his skin had a yellowish hue to it, and his face was gaunt. His overall appearance was one of desperation, and the first words out of his mouth were an appeal for food, my God.

"Can you come over?" he implored.

I glanced around. The rest of the crew was busy directing the other boats.

"Sure." I jumped over the rail and dropped down on the deck of the barge.

"I'm Peter," he said, taking my hand and shaking it hard.

"Dan."

"Where the hell am I, Dan?" he said in all seriousness.

"Somewhere on the south end of Kodiak Island, I think."

"Come with me." He clutched my arm and led me to a catwalk. We slowly made our way along the rusty-metal bridge. Below was the barge's expansive belly, half filled with stinking bags of oil and trash.

"Besides the two guys trapped here with me, I haven't seen another human since I got here," he said as we neared the far side of the barge.

"When was that?"

"Over six weeks ago," he said. "Check this out."

I followed his lead and hopped over the rail onto a tiny tugboat.

"This is fucking home, man."

I honestly thought he might start crying, and I wouldn't blame him if he did. The little boat was a wreck. It was literally rusting right into the water. Wood planks were strewn all over the deck, covering the holes. The crews' quarters and kitchen were scrunched into one tiny room. The place was disgusting. There was so much junk crammed into the tight space it was impossible to take it all in, which was probably for the best.

"This is our only heat source," he lamented, showing me a decrepit potbelly stove in the corner. "We tried to start the engines, thought they'd give off some heat, but Lamont couldn't get it to turn over, and he's a pretty good mechanic too. How the hell did they even get this piece of crap here? Huh? Riddle me that?" He was on the verge of losing it. "I should have never left Jersey, man. You got to get me off here."

"Uh, look, you're talking to the least-important guy on the boat. I don't think I can help you out."

"Shit, shit, shit!" Tears formed in his eyes, and he began pacing. "We ran out of fresh food the third week I was here. I...I mean...God." He was sobbing now.

"Hey, listen"—I grabbed his shoulder—"I'll go back and see what I can do. I can at least get you some fresh veggies and meat."

"Oh, thanks, man, thanks. Sorry, I didn't mean to fall apart like that."

"I'll be right back." Turning to go, a question struck me. "Do you smoke?"

"Yeah, we all do, but we ran—"

"I'll try and steal you some."

"Thanks."

Fortunately, the galley was deserted when I returned. I quickly threw together two large boxes of food, grabbed a couple cartons of generic smokes, and hustled back. As I approached the rotten tug, I stopped and took a good hard look at it. It seemed so familiar. Then it hit me. It was, without a doubt, the same disintegrating tugboat I had worked on in Seattle. I had come full circle. And I truly had. Two weeks later, I boarded a transport helicopter and began the first leg of the long journey home.

Chapter Twelve

The Cannondale Man

Alaska was a wisp of a memory by the time I hauled my belongings into my new home—a squat five-bedroom house on a large lot. South Shields Avenue separated it from the campus of Colorado State University.

It was good to be back. I shared the place with Bryan, Shane, and two other buddies from the dormitory. I had the feeling from day one it was going to be a year to remember, or better yet, a year I'd forever endeavor to remember. I wasn't proved wrong. In an astoundingly short span of time "The Shields House," as it was soon dubbed, became a legendary party house among the university's thousands of students.

We'd been sitting in the same two lawn chairs for hours.

"When did this happen?" I asked.

"Beats the hell out of me," Shane answered.

Earlier, sitting in the backyard with a full keg of beer between us, we watched the sunset peacefully put an end to another day. Now we were surrounded by a sea of screaming lunatics, many of who were wildly dancing to the lyrics of Mötley Crüe, which blasted from speakers that had somehow ended up on the roof.

"I only made two calls. I swear," I shouted.

"Me too. That was the deal."

We were the only two at the house that night, and we had found ourselves in the rare position of having too much beer. So we agreed that we should each ring two friends and invite them over to lend a hand. Apparently, that's exactly what we had done, but the house's reputation preceded us. There were now dozens upon dozens of people kicking it up in the backyard.

"More kegs on the way!" a random guy exclaimed as he rolled past, a skimpily dressed girl in tow.

"Guess we're having a party, man," Shane deduced.

"Guess so. I better go check on the pooch."

A week earlier, with no particular forethought, I swung the Mustang—after it's dip in Fish Creek, it underwent major surgery and had been hanging together ever since—into the Humane Society parking lot and went inside to have a look around. Every corner of the place was crammed with cages of barking, whining animals. I'd never been into one of these places before, and I wasn't sure why I was now. After a few minutes of being subjected to the mild stench and incessant noise, I resolved to make my exit. Working my way back to the front door, I passed a pen housing three puppies. The sight of the little puffs of fur tumbling about stopped me dead in my tracks. The largest of the three, which had the markings of a German shepherd, was busy chewing on the ear of the runt. Executing a far from flawless front roll, he twisted his fluffy white body free and tore circles around the enclosure, his larger brother giving pursuit. With no interest in joining the folly, the third puppy bounced over to where I was standing. He sat down, looked up at me, and let out one very small yap.

"How you doing, little guy?" I grinned.

My goodness, this was a cute puppy. I bent over the low barricade and gave him a scratch behind the ear, which wasn't easy since my hand was about the same size he was. He stood up and wagged his miniature tail.

"You can go in there and play with them if you want."

I twisted around. A woman, who obviously worked there, was standing behind me.

"Aren't they just gorgeous," she said.

"They're awesome. I can't keep from laughing."

"We don't get puppies like this very often. I've been fighting the temptation to take them all home myself."

"How long have they been here?"

"A man brought them in two days ago. Frankly, I'm amazed they haven't been adopted by now. I'm sure they'll be gone by Friday though."

"What breed are they exactly?" I asked, watching the small white one steal a sock from the largest pup.

"We can't be totally sure of course, but everyone here agrees they must be half husky and half German shepherd. I mean, it's pretty obvious. Well, I better get back to cleaning cages. If you want to go in, just sign the sheet there first."

"Okay, thanks."

"Looks like you've got yourself a friend," she said before exiting through a nearby door.

I looked to where she had pointed. The black-and-white pup was seated directly in front of me, quietly staring into my eyes.

"I suppose you want to come home with me, huh?"

He wagged his tail. Then his brothers ran over him. The three combined into one small ball as they spun about the enclosure, barking and nipping at each another.

Two hours later, I walked out of the building with the black-and-white one. I named him Hank on the drive home.

"Come on, dude, wake up. Come on, man!" I felt someone shaking me and heard the threads of a human voice. "Garrison, wake up! Where's Bryan's bike?"

I forced my eyelids open a crack and, through beer cataracts, detected the blurry figure of Doug hovering over me. "What?" I coughed.

"Dude, I need Bryan's bike. Where is it?"

"How the hell should I know?" I grumbled. I was now conscious enough to realize I was no longer sleeping.

"Well, I don't know either, and I need it."

"You need to piss off before I smack you."

I rolled over and experienced a huge stabbing sensation in the base of my skull.

"Get up, man!" he insisted.

My roomy wasn't getting the picture. I very reluctantly pushed myself into a sitting position and asked him to clarify what the fuck he was going on about.

"Look, I need to get to Shannon's place, and I can't find Bryan's bike."

"So go ask him where it is?"

"He's in Oregon, remember?"

"Oh, yeah."

Bryan had decided to give himself a beginning-of-the-school-year holiday and drove out to Hood River to indulge in his latest passion—windsurfing.

"Did you check his room?"

"I've looked everywhere. It ain't here. Boy, you and Shane had a hell of a party last night. The place is trashed."

I was having problems establishing what species I was, let alone the memories of the previous night. "Just give me a minute, dickweed."

I got up slowly and searched the floor for some clothes, gradually ceasing when it dawned on me I was fully dressed. "Go," I said, following him out of my room with one sock on, my pants unbuttoned, and my beer-stained shirt on inside out. It must have been a pretty good night.

It was a painful fifteen minutes, trailing Doug around the property, looking for the stupid bike, but then, I had become used to painful mornings. I was coping until it became apparent that Bryan's bike really was missing.

"See, man. I told you it's gone!" he said in a tone I wasn't all that receptive to at the moment.

"That sucks." Holy cow, talking was difficult at the moment. "Hey, take mine, okay? I'll go wake up butthead. I shouldn't be the only one enjoying the moment."

With Doug merrily pedaling my bike down the road, I shuffled to the living room and filled up a dirty pitcher from a flat, warm keg. I took a few sips off it while I made my way to Shane's room.

"Wake up, loser!" I upended the pitcher over Shane's peaceful body.

What happened next happened at just under the speed of light. In a blinding flash, I was lying on the carpet, cupping my throbbing testicles. As my watering eyes refocused, I watched Shane beat the hell out of his desk with a bike lock. Note to self: wake Shane with a beer shower, and your sperm count will be permanently lowered.

After a while, he calmed down, sort of, and the aching in my stomach eased off, sort of. I peeled myself off the floor, and, hobbling, I followed him down the stairs and into the kitchen. I had deserved the punishment I received, so there was no use discussing it. Instead, I simply asked him if he was okay—in a slightly higher octave than I normally speak.

"Do I look okay, you piece of shit?"

"I think we've got a problem."

"Yeah, like you pouring a pitcher of beer on me!"

"You'll dry out. No, I mean Bryan's bike got stolen last night."

At that he froze. The sugar-encrusted cereal he was eating dribbled out of the box as he slowly brought it down from his face.

"No kidding?"

"No kidding."

We duplicated Doug's search with no more success.

"Nada, dude." Shane voiced the obvious.

We picked up our lawn chairs and sat back down where we had been roughly five hours earlier. This wouldn't have been such a drama if Bryan's bike had been a piece of junk. But it wasn't. He had used a fair portion of his summer wages to buy it. We were missing a brand-new, top-of-the-line Cannondale mountain bike with all the bells and whistles. We were out an easy grand.

It wasn't acceptable.

Hangovers faded as soon as we returned inside and began formulating a war plan. With a swipe of his long arm, Shane cleared a spot on the living room picnic table, and I grabbed a pen and notepad. We sat there for the better part of fifteen minutes trying to recall anyone we knew from the party. It amounted to a list of sixteen names. After putting a phone number to the majority of names, I poured us each a nasty beer, and Shane set to work dialing.

"She don't know shit." Slamming the phone into its cradle, Shane motioned for me to cross Helen Wise off the list. Well, we still had half the names to go, I thought hopefully. My hope was justified when a few of the remaining names proved fairly productive. We now had some decent prospects.

"All right, I'll look up the addresses; you get the bikes," I told Shane. "Oh hey, Doug's got my mine, grab Clint's."

As we headed out of the littered yard, Shane jumped off the Schwinn, ran back inside, and returned with a sawed-off hickory baseball bat.

"We've got a green light, ghost rider," he said.

I couldn't help but wonder where and why he had gotten a sawed-off bat.

"Knock lightly," I whispered. It was still before the general waking period on a Sunday morning in the dorms, and whispering seemed the prudent move.

"Open up, bastards!" Shane screamed.

Nice.

After some muffled bustling from within, the door hesitantly cracked open. Before I could utter our intentions, Shane pushed through the opening, knocking a kid to the floor in the process. Stepping over him, he stuck the bat in the face of his roommate who was still in bed, cowering beneath a Denver Broncos comforter.

"Where the hell is it? If I don't see a bike in ten seconds, I'm gonna trash me some dorm rats!"

I wasn't sure if I should run or laugh. I did neither. I opted to do my best to calm the situation.

"Listen, guys, we had a party last night at The Shields House, and we're missing a bike. All we want is to get it back."

"We don't have it!" the pale kid on the bed squeaked. "We weren't even there!"

"No, I'm pretty sure I remember you." Shane scowled. He pressed the bat hard against the kid's blanket-covered groin.

What is it with Shane and nutsacks today?

"Okay, okay! Yeah, sure, we went to a couple of parties last night. We might have been at yours. But we don't know anything about a bike. Honest."

Shane replied, "Fine. Here's what we're going to do…"

We left the room with an updated list and a cup of coffee in our stomachs to boot. I was awestruck. Subsequent to his blazing-guns approach, Shane switched to a gentle yet mildly threatening tactic and finished off with the you're-my-best-buddy, ya-want-to-hang-out-sometime approach. By the time we left, those two nerds worshiped Shane. It was masterful. Maybe I should talk him into cruising over to Denny's; he might be able to schmooze us some free eggs and bacon. Sadly, that would have to wait. We had to track down our newest lead.

This time I shoved Shane back and politely knocked.

A good-looking, short redhead with pleasantly wide hips answered the door. She was wearing skin-tight shorts and a halter top, which consisted of roughly the same amount of fabric as a sock. My mind went blank, my tongue numb. Shane, however, spoke up immediately.

"We want the bike back from last night," he half-heartedly yelled, listlessly raising the bat. God love him. I started to intervene, but there was no need.

"Come on in, guys," she said.

I admired the view as we followed her into the apartment. We took a seat at the kitchen table.

"You're Dan, right?" she asked.

"Um…" I unnecessarily coughed and fought hard to keep my gaze from drifting lower than her face. "Yes, that's right."

"I know you."

"Really?" I found it difficult to believe I would have forgotten her…features.

"Yeah, my friend Alisa introduced us once."

"Oh?" Alisa, who the hell was Alisa?

"You probably don't remember. We just stuck our heads into the darkroom; you were developing some pictures that she needed."

Oh, Alisa, one of the editors at the college newspaper, right.

"She says you're a pretty good photographer. You guys want some coffee?"

"Love a cup, thanks."

It turned out we didn't need to go Denny's after all. Kate and her roommate, Stephanie, fed us some kind of vegetarian mush, which was surprisingly edible, while they related everything they remembered from our party.

"Um, Kate, I was just wondering why I didn't see you at the party? It sounds like you guys were there for quite a while," I asked.

"I saw you," she said.

"You did? You should have come over and said hi or something."

"I don't think I would have gotten much of a response. You were passed out in a chair."

Blood surged into my face.

"It's time we get going," Shane said. "Thanks for the eats."

They responded that it was their pleasure and escorted us out. Slowly, Stephanie closed the door, but not before Kate gave me a big wink.

"We now have the target in sight!" He was jacked. The girls had provided us with vital information. I couldn't give a shit less. I was still staring at the closed door, hoping it would reopen.

"Maybe I should apologize about last night." I raised my fist to knock.

Shane grabbed my arm. "Come on, lover boy. We work before we play."

Four miles and many burps of water chestnuts later, we arrived at our next destination. It was a wreck of a building, obviously a student house. I was preparing to make our presence known when Shane put a finger to his lips and opened the ratty screen door. I followed him inside, suppressing my anxiety.

Stumbling over an empty Jack Daniels bottle, I trailed him down the dark hallway to a door. He pushed it open with the bat, revealing a chaotic but unoccupied room. We continued down the passageway to the next door, which was covered with Black Sabbath posters. Before Shane's hand reached the handle, the door flew open with a bang, and a madman rushed through, throwing himself squarely into Shane's chest. In the blink of an eye, the pair hit the floor. Shane was trapped beneath his attacker, desperately trying to shield himself from a rain of blows. As I prepared to charge into the melee, I noticed the bat lying on the floor a few feet away. I scooped it up and gave the guy the good news. Within moments, he was still. I pushed him aside with my foot and towed Shane from the house, forcing him to mount his bike. Seconds later, we were cycling down the street.

"Your face doesn't look so good. Come on, man, we're far enough away now; let's stop for a second. Dude, hold up!"

He was on automatic—pumped full of adrenaline, mindlessly pedaling, and most likely feeling no pain from his injuries. I had a hell of a time getting him to calm down a notch and pull over.

"It's all right. There's some blood, but it's not as bad as it looks." I ripped off one of my shirt sleeves. "Here, let me wipe the blood off. Hold still! Dude, I'm serious; just quit squirming, will ya."

It took a few minutes, but I cleaned him up the best I could. I tossed the bloody rag in the bushes and did a quick inspection. A small cut on his nose, a couple of lumps on his forehead, and a good chance of a beauty shiner. Yeah, he'd live. "Come on, let's go home."

"Hell no! Let's go back."

"Dude, I pummeled that guy pretty good. I am *not* going back."

"Fine."

Good, we're not going back.

Shane pulled the crumpled list from his pocket, studying it with one good eye, and I knew we weren't going home either.

"What's up, brother?" Standing on the rotten porch, which was attached to a decaying two-story house, the white guy greeting us wore a Rastafarian shirt and sported a head full of greasy dreadlocks.

"We're looking for a bike, bitch!" Shane yelled.

Guess he hadn't calmed down as much as I had hoped.

"Yeah, it looks like you could use a new one," the pale Bob Marley said, eyeing the Schwinn. "How 'bout a toke instead?" He passed Shane a smoldering joint. "Come on in, guys. We got tons of bikes."

That was my last accurate memory of the day. I have vague recollections of listening to Pink Floyd and eating some kind of foul-tasting mushroom. I'm fairly certain at some point I was sitting in a homemade hot tub in what I took to be the backyard, surrounded by hippies of all shapes and colors (and I mean rainbow colors). And I have fragments of retention about voicing my thoughts, seemingly the deepest I'd ever had, on everything from black holes to the superb qualities of Little Debbie Nutty Bars.

A shoe was tapping me in the head. "Let's go."

Shane managed to rouse me from my stupor, and I immediately knew this was going to be yet another unfun morning to be alive. I wobbled to my feet and followed him out the front door. My senses were about as sharp as a basketball, which explains why it took a moment to realize that Shane was wearing only a T-shirt, his tighty-whity underwear, sneakers, and a knitted cap with several peace buttons pinned to it. We dug our bikes out of the front hedge and rode home in silence.

It was Tuesday, and I returned from class to find Shane, Clint, and Hank sprawled out in the living room watching an infomercial.

"Ticktock, ticktock," Clint taunted, scratching Hank's back with his toes. "I was just reminding Shane that Bryan is supposed to be back on Friday."

The bastard was getting a big kick out of our dilemma.

"Looks like you two are gonna be owing him some big bucks."

"It's the hippies, man, they…" Shane didn't complete his thought. He was too consumed by the infomercial. "Right, like your curtains are gonna look brand new just by steaming them with that piece of crap."

"Fine, then let's go back. Back to the hippie place."

"What?" He picked up a ski pole and knocked the TV dial to a different channel. "I can't remember where it is."

"Whad'ya mean?"

"Can you? Can you remember how to get back there?"

"Uh, yeah, I mean…well, not exactly."

"Man, you guys gotta lay off the drugs." Clint laughed.

"So are we just giving up then?" I asked. "I mean, I don't have that kind of cash just to flush. Do you?"

"Nope, but hey, we gave it the old college try. Besides, I ain't all that enthused anymore."

He was right. I mean, the meatless lunch with Kate was nice, but getting beat up, threatening people, and hanging out with hippies heavily tipped the scale toward giving up.

"Why don't you just ask for it back?" Clint asked.

"Shut up, loser," Shane said, jabbing him with the pole.

"Keep it up, and I'll reopen a few of those scabs on your face," Clint teased.

"I'll give you some scabs!"

"Wait a minute, morons!" I shouted. "What do you mean, Clint?"

"I mean, you're the wannabe journalism dude, so why not write him a message and put it in the paper?"

"That's not the stupidest thing you've ever said, Clint."

The next morning, I sat on a bench outside the offices of the student newspaper and wrote an ad. Once finished, I took it to a nice-looking brunette girl who processed the classified ads from a cubbyhole.

"Hi. How soon can I get this in?"

"For five dollars, it will go in next Monday and run a week. Or for ten dollars, it will be in tomorrow and run for three days," she informed me with a smile that didn't even seem fake.

"Okay, I'd like it in tomorrow please." I pushed the form across to her.

She glanced it over and then, with a changed look of concentration, really read it.

"Uh, I'm going to have to get Paul to approve this. I'll be right back."

She slipped behind a metal door, leaving me and my pessimistic thoughts alone. A few minutes later, she slid back into her seat and stamped my form, neatly dropping it into a box labeled Ads Received. With a grin, she requested my ten dollars.

Thursday morning, I managed to pry myself out of bed relatively early. I was eager to ride to campus. Wheeling up to the student center, Hank perched in a milk crate I had lashed to the handlebars, I found a stack of morning newspapers and grabbed one from the top. Sitting down next to my bike in a patch of dew-covered grass, I quickly flipped to the classifieds. Yes, hot damn, there it was! It read:

> From the guys at The Shields House to the Cannondale Man. Do the words intensive care mean anything to you? If we ever made a promise we meant to keep, it is to find you. We will stop at nothing until the bike is back or Batman has discussed it with you. We are really, really close.

It was a complete last-ditch effort. The odds were long, but it made me feel better anyway, perhaps because it was the only thing I'd ever written that had been published.

The next morning I awoke to what initially seemed like a recurring nightmare.

"Dude, wake up!" Doug screeched.

I cracked open my eyes and rolled over with a thud.

"Garrison, get up, man! The bike's back!"

I sat up at once. "You better not be messing with me, Doug."

"Come on, come on."

He yanked me out of bed, and we jogged out to the front yard. Shane was already there, like me, dressed in nothing but his underwear. Making my way to his side, I discerned what was holding his attention. There, leaning against a tree, was Bryan's bike. All the stickers Bryan had put on it had been removed and the seat had been lowered, but other than that, it was in perfect shape. Before we could rejoice, a car turned off the street and pulled into the driveway a few feet behind us. We turned in unison. Bryan climbed out of his Ford Escort.

"Damn, guys, what's happening?" He slid his sunglasses onto his forehead, staring at the scene before him. The three of us, two being virtually naked, huddled around his bike a mere ten feet away from morning traffic. We wheeled the bike into the living room and confessed.

The following week, I was sitting in the library, procrastinating the research I should have been doing by flipping through the day's classified ads, and came upon this:

> From the Cannondale Man to The Shields House. I do believe you guys owe me a big Thank You. Next time, I'll keep it.

Chapter Thirteen

Summer Heat

It was a dusty, noisy place to work. Surrounded by gravel pits, conveyor belts, rock crushers, and two concrete plants, the hub of this scar upon the earth was an immense paved square. It was the only ground for miles that was safe from being dug up, torn apart, and crushed. On one side of this haven of asphalt sat the company offices, housed in a nicely maintained two-story building. On the opposite side leaned a hodgepodge of battered buildings, surrounded by tires, vehicle parts, fuel pumps, and forklifts. I worked on the latter side, the mechanics side, entering the opposing air-conditioned offices just once every two weeks to liberate my paycheck.

Hank and I spent three sweltering months at Walkman's Gravel and Concrete Company of the greater Seattle area. Hank whiled away the majority of the summer, sniffing around the barren landscape, hoping to find something a bit more interesting than dust and rock. I had to use my time more fruitfully. It was actually a pretty cool job. Once again, I had Phil to thank. This time he called in a favor with a friend who was in a business that was, thankfully, far removed from the sea.

During the days, I worked with Jeff, the company tire guy. We repaired and changed tires on everything from handcarts to colossal front-end loaders. In the evening, I drove cement mixers across the wasteland to the reclamation plant where I dumped any remaining concrete and thoroughly washed out the barrels.

Jeff and I worked out of a little hovel that was haphazardly attached to the side of the much larger mechanics shop. There were so many tires stacked inside that it was difficult to squeeze through. Out front, the stacks continued up a slope, eventually petering out near two diesel pumps. Even though our shop provided a small degree of relief from the summer sun, I preferred working outside. So on Monday morning, I was happy to learn I would be spending a portion of my day in front of the shop.

"I've got to go in to the Tacoma offices, got me pushing paper today," Jeff said, his calloused fingers fidgeting with an unaccustomed tie. "I want you to mount these on those rims, and don't forget to balance them. That pile of flats there, go ahead and move them around back."

I followed him outside. "All these need to be branded." He motioned to a row of roughly eighty new tires.

He must have noticed my puzzled expression for he added, "Oh, that's right. I never did show you how to do that. It's easy. Here's what you do…"

After a five-minute crash course, he climbed into a company truck and was gone.

I decided to tackle the branding first, since the instructions were still fresh in my mind, and besides, it sounded like fun. I eyed the apparatus. It consisted of a large propane tank and a torch, like the weed-burning kind, with twenty feet or so of rubber hose connecting the two.

Welded to the front of the torch was the brand—it spelled out *Walkman G & C* in little metal letters. The idea was as simple as the device. By branding each and every tire, the evil plans of the wily tire rustler were thereby foiled.

Following Jeff's instructions, I grabbed the lighter, cranked the valve open on the tank, and lit the end of the torch. Within seconds, the large flame reduced in size, turned bluish, and immediately began heating the brand. It didn't take long until the little letters were red hot, and I was ready to begin stamping my rubber herd.

I leaned on the torch and melted a hole right through the first tire. Oops. I might have to hide that one somewhere. My second attempt went better, and I was off and running.

After an hour, I was nearing the final stack, but the taut hose wouldn't reach any farther. I was about to head back to the tank to see if I could gain any more length when an unexpected sensation hit me. I looked down and, to my surprise, beheld a two-inch wall of water striking my boots. The current of the little river ebbed when it hit the front wall of the shop. Quickly the parched area began filling up. I was so fascinated by the miniature flood that several moments passed before I considered where it had come from. Turning to investigate, the fumes and the answer hit me simultaneously. It wasn't water. It was diesel! And then I identified the source. A truck was sitting at the pumps, filling up. For whatever reason, the nozzle hadn't automatically shut off when the tank was full. The driver was nowhere in sight. Gallon after gallon spewed forth, forming a small petroleum geyser. The liquid had traveled down the slope until it had been momentarily stopped by a low dirt embankment, which had given way moments earlier. Instinctively, I clutched the torch with both hands, frantically inspecting it for an off switch.

"There isn't a shut off on the torch. You have to do it at the tank." Jeff's earlier statement ran through my mind.

"Hey! Hey! I need some help here!" But my cries were useless. Before they traveled ten feet, my words were drowned out by the constant drone of machinery.

I felt lightheaded. The fumes were strong. I was beginning to think I might pass out. Panicking, I ran a few steps toward the much-too-distant propane tank. My heavy-footed tromping splashed fuel in all directions.

I froze.

My imagination whirled; all I could concentrate on was fainting and the fiery explosion that would ensue. The flame jumped back and forth, producing an evil hiss, hypnotizing me.

"Move, Dan! Get to the tank. Walk! Do it now! Do you want to be cremated?" I yelled.

It worked. The spell of overwhelming fear was momentarily broken. I clutched the torch hard enough to drive the blood from my fingers and lifted it over my head like a soldier crossing a river with his rifle. Slowly I tiptoed, concentrating on the movement of each foot, each step.

"Righty tighty, lefty loosey," I chanted, as I finally reached the tank.

The flame reluctantly died as the valve sealed shut. After triple checking that the flame was truly extinguished, I leaned the torch against the building and sat down on a tire. With a trembling hand, I lit a cigarette.

Just kidding.

I never mentioned my close encounter with incineration to anyone, just the fact that there was a pond of diesel threatening to turn into a lake. It turned out there had been an ongoing problem with one of the fuel nozzles; every so often, it wasn't shutting off properly. The guys in the air-conditioned building promised to get it fixed after the appropriate paperwork had been filled out.

It was Friday morning, and I had gotten to work earlier than usual. The place seemed deserted, but the door to the mechanics shop was ajar, so I went in and headed to the break room. Light shone through the crack under the door. Maybe someone else is here? Entering the room, I found I was correct—someone was there, but he wasn't reading the paper or drinking coffee.

"What in the hell?"

Frank was standing side-on to me next to the communal table. His overalls were down to his knees along with his boxer shorts, his pecker in an empty coffee mug. I was too bewildered to utter anything further. I just waited for some sort of reply to my question.

All Frank said was, "Hang on just a second."

I diverted my eyes while Frank finished up his penile hula dance with the innocent mug and dressed himself.

"Have a seat, Dan," he said, taking a seat himself.

"Jesus, Frank, you some kind of pervert or what?"

"Take a seat."

I warily obeyed.

"How long have you worked here?"

"A couple of months."

"You ever noticed how me and Ralph don't quite see eye to eye?"

"Yeah, I guess so." It was no secret—Frank and Ralph hated each other with a passion.

"Well just sit tight, and I'll tell you a little secret."

I was all ears.

"I hate that scumbag. Hate him like some sort of crotch rot I can't rid of. God knows I do hate him. Do you understand true hate? Probably not, and Mother Mary help you if you ever do. I've put up with him for sixteen years. Every day, he sucks a bit more life out of me. But every night when I drive home, I'm not frowning; no, I'm smiling. You know why?

"It's because I know that bastard is getting the sharp end of the stick. For the last ten years, I've gotten up at five in the morning. And let me tell you something, Dan. I'm not a morning person. But I do it happily. I do it so I can be the first one here. Every morning, I go over to the rack there and take down Ralph's cup. And then with more pleasure than I can put into words, I wipe my dick in it. I wipe it thoroughly."

My eyes were as wide as a deer's.

"And sometimes, just to mix things up, I piss in it."

My mouth dropped open.

"And, oh, there have been a few special occasions, when he has really done something rotten to me," he said with a ghoulish smirk, "I bring in a Playboy."

A minute ticked away in utter silence while Frank just stared at me through tired, triumphant eyes.

"Ten years?" I checked.

"Yep."

"No one has ever caught you?"

"Nope."

Except me—why me?

"Look, Frank, this is none of my business, really. I mean, I didn't see or hear anything."

"You're a good kid. I'm certain you'll keep your mouth zipped."

"Yes, I will. You can count on that."

"Great," he said. "Now how about I buy you a cup of joe?"

"Uh, I'll pass on that, thanks."

Chapter Fourteen

Missteps

Another summer break had come to a close. Yet, I didn't rejoin the intoxicated paradise of Colorado State University. God knows I had every motivation to do so, but I didn't. I was trying to be responsible, grown up even. If I was really serious about becoming a newspaperman, then it only made sense I should attend the best school possible, and Colorado State certainly wasn't it. So I transferred to a college in a state I had never visited and knew very little about. The University of Missouri, which boasted one of the nation's top journalism schools, had accepted my application, so that's where Hank and I went.

The fall semester commenced in a week, and I was completely unprepared. Lost in a strange town, without so much as an acquaintance or a place to live, I was a bit dubious my decision had been the correct one.

Over the next few days, battling the sopping-wet heat, Hank and I shared our misery in a cruddy hotel room, leaving intermittently to buy textbooks and food and search for a place to live.

"I've taken us to hell, Hank." I leaned back into the sweaty chair.

He didn't respond. He was sprawled out on the bed, his muzzle inches away from the whirling fan I had bought earlier that day. Fur drifted about the room. I had a quick daydream about making naked snow angels and then refocused on the classified ads spread before me.

"No Pets…NO Pets…NO PETS!"

It was becoming evident that this was going to be an uphill battle. I had responded to over thirty ads, either in person or over the phone, and no one would give us a break.

"It seems like folks here in the heartland might be a bit prejudice against you."

Hank opened his eyes, gave me a hateful look, and went back to trying not to die.

I scanned the paper again, crossing out ads I had already crossed out before. Then it just popped right out.

> Roommate wanted. Nice place, three
> bedroom, two bath, no smoking, pets
> ok.

"Wow, where the hell did this come from?" I'd been scrutinizing the small print all evening without observing the ad.

Way to pay attention, pal.

I prayed the blunder hadn't cost me a shot at the place. I nabbed a near-boiling can of beer off the floor with one hand and the phone with the other.

After the sixth ring, "You asshole, I'm going to kill you!" blasted through the receiver.

"Pardon?"

"Who is this?" she demanded.

"Ah, sorry for calling so late, but I saw your ad for a roommate."

"Oh, I thought you were someone else."

Who would that be—your mother perhaps?

"I'm really interested, that is if you haven't already found someone."

"The ad's still in the paper, isn't it?"

Nice.

"I've got a big but extremely well-behaved dog; is that okay?"

No sense beating around the bush.

"That's fine."

"When can I come by and look at it?"

She was an attractive, short brunette with spooky black eyes. She was about the right weight for her height, but her chest must have accounted for just about half of it. She would have been a great candidate for the breast-reduction poster girl.

"Come in. This is the living room. The kitchen is back there, the bedrooms are"—with a snap of her heels, she turned and stormed down the hallway—"I told you to smoke outside, goddamn it!"

I had no idea who she was talking to. I continued to hold my position on the six square feet of brown linoleum that defined the entryway. I heard muffled arguing while I surveyed what was possible to survey.

The living room was devoid of any furniture. It looked starkly unlived in. The carpet looked dirty, and the walls weren't much better. I caught a glimpse of a skinny white guy, tattoos covering his bare back, crossing the passageway. A door slid shut, and immediately the girl returned.

"Don't be shy. Take a look around," she barked.

I followed her to the rear of the place and found myself standing in a bare cubbyhole of a kitchen. There were no dishes to be seen, just some crumpled-up Burger King bags and empty soda cans littering the countertop.

"Take a look upstairs. Let me know when you're done. I've got to check on dipshit out there." She used her head to point at the creepy-looking guy who was enjoying a smoke on the tiny, moss-covered balcony.

Upstairs, I found a bathroom the size of a cereal box and three bedrooms. The largest contained a bed and a few clothes strewn in a far corner; the other two were empty. My brief tour complete, I returned to the lower level and found tattoo man still outside, working through another cigarette. She was standing in the kitchen staring at a wall.

"Uh, all done."

"So do you want to rent it or what?"

"Um, I'm sort of confused. I mean, who are you exactly? Do you live here, or are you just renting the place out?"

"I'm Lana."

"Oh, okay, but do you live—"

"I rented this half of the duplex a month or so ago," she interrupted. "The other two backed out on the deal, and I got stuck with it. I hope they get hit by a train."

Gee whiz, why wouldn't anyone want to share a place with you, darling?

"So you live here then?"

"Duh, I've got the big room upstairs."

"Yeah, I noticed all the clutter. So what's the rent?"

"You'd have to pay half the rent until I find a third roommate."

"And what is that?"

"Three hundred a month plus utilities."

I thought I saw her flinch as she said it, like the amount was physically scary.

"And my dog is okay, right?"

"I told you that on the phone."

"How long is the lease?"

"There's about four-and-a-half months left. After that, I'm out of this shitty deal."

"You are quite the saleswoman." I took a deep breath. "Where do I sign?"

The first two weeks at the duplex were bizarre, and the feeling only intensified the longer I lived there. I hadn't seen Lana since the day I signed the lease and she gave me a key. Not that I was missing her, but it was odd, and I was beginning to feel very isolated.

Classes had commenced, and it was proving difficult to get to know anyone. It turned out, much to my dismay, the majority of students were Greek—that is, they belonged to a fraternity or sorority. These were generally tightknit organizations that weren't overly hospitable to nonmembers. Fortunately, I had Hank to keep me company during the evenings, which typically consisted of flopping down on the secondhand sofa I had purchased and watching reruns on a small black-and-white TV.

It was Friday evening, so I stopped off on the way home from school and picked up some ice-cold beer and a couple of steaks—one for each of us. After taking Hank for a short walk in the monotonous heat, I cracked a brew and was unwrapping the meat when I heard the front door open. Hank rushed down the hallway barking.

"Hey, get your dog off me!"

"Hank, come here."

He left her alone and returned to guard his steak.

"Hi, Lana. Didn't think I'd see you again."

"Been over at Rick's." She took a seat on the couch. "So what are you doing tonight?"

"Just gonna have dinner and a few beers. Watch some TV. Nothing really."

"You don't have any friends, do you?"

Surprisingly, I didn't find the question offensive, just obvious. "No, not here."

"Why are you here anyway?"

"I'm beginning to think the only answer to that question is stupidity."

"You need to get out, meet some people. Let's go to a party."

"Wow, uh, where's Rick?"

"Hey look, I'm not offering to shine your weasel or anything like that. If you must know, Rick pissed me off, all right. So come with me, okay? I don't want to go alone."

"Sure."

The entire time I lived in Columbia, Missouri, I was lost. I couldn't seem to grasp the layout of the town. I'd never been great at finding my way around new places, and without the Rocky Mountains as a constant reference point, I was hopeless. So as Lana drove us through the perpetual countryside in her titanic Lincoln Continental, I only hoped she wouldn't ditch me, for I hadn't a clue where I was.

After many miles of dusty traveling, we pulled up to a farmhouse that was obviously in the grip of a huge college party. I timidly followed Lana into the rocking house and immediately found myself in the valley of the giants. Randomly spaced between groups of chattering girls were some of the biggest men I had ever seen. I grabbed Lana's shirttail before I lost her in the throngs and yelled over the noise, "These guys look like the Denver Broncos!"

She laughed. "Close, this is the invite-only party for the Mizzou football team." She tore free and jiggled her way into the mob, leaving me alone to mull over that statement.

"Hey, buddy, what's your deal?"

I stared up into the face of a behemoth. At minimum, he must have been six-foot-six-inches tall and weighed around 350 pounds. I swallowed hard.

"Uh...um...I uh...I came here with this girl named Lana and uh..."

"You don't have a beer." He closed the gap between us with one mighty step. I fought the urge to run.

"Uh, no, I guess I don't."

"Come on, little man, let's find you a beer!" He effortlessly picked me up and handed me to one of his gargantuan brethren. "Pass the little guy to the keg! He ain't got a beer!"

Subsequent to being passed around like a saltshaker at the dinner table, I found myself next to the keg where I was immediately and repeatedly challenged to chugging contests by most of the offensive line. Needless to say, I lost and lost and lost.

"You can't chug for shit, but you can hold some beer, little dude!"

"Thanks, giant dude," I slurred.

Somewhere in the house, the dial on the stereo was turned up several notches. AC/DC's "Back in Black" boomed from the speakers. The beer splashed out of my cup as I was once again lifted off my feet by a pair of arms that felt like steel I beams.

"Go deep!" the owner of the arms yelled. The next second, I was sailing through the air, plucked to safety by an immense black guy.

"Blue diamond, blue diamond. On two. Hut, hut."

I found myself airborne yet again. Several others joined the impromptu football game. It ended abruptly after an incomplete pass left me in a heap on the floor.

"Let me help you up, guy. You're all right. Here, have a beer."

Things were starting to drift out of focus. I shuffled around in a stupor for an undetermined amount of time. The next thing I remember, I was holding on for dear life on the back of a really fast motorcycle. Some more time was unaccounted for, and then I found myself stumbling around a massive outdoor party that was being held somewhere in the original business district of Columbia.

Fuzz and brain spins.

There were thousands of swirling bodies packed tightly around me. I couldn't deal with it. All I wanted was a bed. No, a bed was too much to ask for. The concrete would do. My butt thumped down on the sidewalk, and I crumpled to my side. Sleep, beautiful sleep. Several shoes kicked me. Someone stepped on my face.

Time to sit up!

"I've got to stay…staying awake…okay now."

I hung in there, just. I labored to my feet and battled through the crowd, looking for a quieter spot to plant my mailbox. It was difficult to make any headway through the horde, but eventually I stumbled across an unoccupied doorway. I plopped down and stared out, trying hard to find something steady to focus on. All I saw were hundreds of blurred legs. Occasionally, one would knee me in the head as it whirled by. I welcomed it; it helped me stay conscious.

I was quickly sliding into nothingness when the crowd erupted in a roar of cheers. Something was obviously happening—better see what it is. It was a good excuse to get off the ground anyway.

Forcing myself into a swaying stance, right away I understood what the fuss was about. Directly in front of me, maybe forty feet away, some drunk lunatic was climbing a pole that supported a set of traffic lights. He made it to the top and swung out to the horizontal bar, making his way, hand over hand, toward the center of the intersection. With feet swinging high above the spectators, he screamed something unintelligible and then, whether by design or accident, he let go. Like a frightened school of fish, the horde instantly parted, leaving me with an unobstructed view of his body crunching into the hard pavement. Cheers turned to screams, and people ran in all directions. I was in no condition to join the frenzy, so I just stood there gaping at the motionless body in the street. From the way his right leg was abnormally bent and the weird position of his bloody head, I was pretty confident his partying days were at a permanent end. There wasn't anything I could do but leave, so I did.

It took the rest of the night and part of the morning to stumble clear across town, but eventually I somehow located home, where I curled up with Hank and slept the weekend into history.

A long and lonely fall semester was drawing to a close under an icy, gray winter sky. I guess hell does have seasons.

Not long after my introduction party to Columbia, Lana suckered in a third roommate. Her name was Alice. Getting to know her was toilsome, for she was permanently in some state of drunkenness, taking a break from the bottle only to pass out or swerve down to the liquor store in her rust-adorned El Camino. I avoided her as much as possible, which wasn't difficult since I spent nearly all of my time either studying or working at a factory where I stood in front of a conveyer belt, packing bullets and explosives into wooden crates for minimum wage. Grudgingly, I had to leave Hank at home much of the time where he was in his own private hell with Alice's three near-feral cats. Life was sucking, and I was at a loss at how to make it better.

Then, the week before Christmas break, I got lucky. During the semester, I had gotten to know a sophomore who sat next to me in Russian history class. I can't say I knew him well, but sadly, Hank aside, he was the closest thing to a friend I had. Mike struck me as a decent guy, and I liked him even more for resisting the overwhelming pressure to join a fraternity. He and his roommate were tired of dorm life. Consequently, they had found a place to live off campus the following semester. They had one problem, however. They needed to come up with an additional roommate to bring the rent down to a reasonable level. Without much hope, I explained I was interested, but I had Hank. The following day, before the final exam was passed out, he related the phone conversation he had had with the landlord the previous night. A dog didn't seem to be a problem. I was in! We shook hands, and I told him I'd catch up with him and his roommate, Dave, after the break.

It was cold, really cold. It was exactly the wrong type of weather to trek across the better part of three western states in an aged car with a busted heater. Nevertheless, I was on a mission to escape, at least for a little while. I was going to make it to Dad and Annie's house for Christmas come hell or high water.

The day before we left, I engaged in one of my many epic but fruitless skirmishes with the Mustang. Something was always falling off or breaking on the damn thing; presently, it refused to make hot air. Armed with a half roll of duct tape and a spool of wire, I set to work. Three irritating hours later, I chucked a screwdriver as hard as I could at the fence, kicked a tire, and retreated into the warmth of the duplex in defeat.

The next morning, heater or no heater, it was time to hit the road. The last thing to do was load up my things. Yet I found myself stymied with even that simple task. The trunk wouldn't open. I dropped the pile of clothes I was holding on the icy ground and fiddled with the key. Try as I might, it wouldn't turn the lock. I applied more force and...snap. I was left holding half a key. Son of a bitch, are you kidding me? In disgust, I chucked everything, snow-covered or not, onto the back seat and returned inside for the remaining items and Hank.

On the way back, I noticed a gallon of antifreeze sitting below the front steps. It seemed like a good thing to have on a long, frozen drive, so I chucked it in the car. With that, Hank and I roared out of town.

My feet were the first to go numb. Another fifty miles rolled by, and the life drained from my hands, nose, and ears. I pulled to the shoulder of the interstate, hopped around for a couple minutes, and tugged my way into another layer of everything. It was to become a routine of driving, freezing, pulling over, trying to warm up, and driving a bit farther. It was miserable. I was envious of Hank, curled up on the seat beside me, apparently nice and warm—warm enough to sleep anyway.

By the time we reached the outskirts of Topeka, Kansas, I was so stiff with cold it was becoming dangerous to drive. I spotted an off-ramp ahead and took it. I pulled into the parking lot of a fast-food restaurant.

I seized a change of socks, another pair of thermal underwear, and a better pair of boots.

"I'll be right back," I informed Hank.

Shivering, I changed in a bathroom stall. It had a bit of a warming effect but not nearly as much as the large coffee I ordered. Guilt over leaving Hank in the car got the better of me, so I unenthusiastically left the warmth of the restaurant and returned to my wheeled icebox. Hank was sitting up, patiently awaiting me.

"Okay, buddy, I feel a bit better. Let's keep going."

I was about to fire up the car when I noticed everything in the back had shifted; some of the clothes were on the floor. I twisted around and began straightening up the mess. Near the bottom of the pile, I found the container of antifreeze. I lifted it up, and it felt strangely hollow. I sat there for a moment, dumbfounded. I inspected the cap. It was still tightly screwed on, and the factory seal hadn't even been broken. My heart began to race as I glanced at Hank. I brought my face closer to the container and there along the bottom edge were several punctures.

"Oh, Hank...you...you didn't?"

I felt the floor. There were damp patches, but it definitely wasn't soaking wet.

"Oh man, oh man, this *cannot* be good. Jesus, Hank, why? Okay, okay. Just stay put for a second."

I dove out and sprinted back into the restaurant. I had no idea how much he had drank or how much would kill him, but I knew time was not going to be kind. I ran to the pay phone and quickly ripped through the phone book until I reached the Vs. The first vet I called could barely speak English, so I hung up. I rang the next one.

"Hello. Mercy Animal Clinic," a woman answered.

"I'm on the freeway east of town, and my dog has swallowed a ton of antifreeze," I yelled at her.

"Did this just happen?" she calmly asked.

"I think so." The truth was I didn't really know since I hadn't looked at the antifreeze since we left home.

"You need to get him here as fast as you can. Do you need directions?"

"Yes."

Without a pause, she gave me concise and exact instructions.

"What kind of dog is he, and how much does he weigh?"

"He's half German Shepherd and half husky. He's about seventy pounds."

"Okay, we'll be ready for him. Hurry."

"Hang on, man, shit, just hang in there, pal. It's going to be okay." I brought the Mustang to life and laid rubber across the parking lot. Within seconds, we were flying down the interstate at over a hundred miles per hour. Luckily, there wasn't much traffic. I had never driven that fast before, let alone on a freeway, entering a city. I was panicking. Sweat dripped down my face and dripped under my arms too. How quickly things can change!

I flexed my leg and shoved the pedal to the floor with as much force as I could; the speedometer needle climbed. The landscape, man-made and otherwise, screamed past. I just barely glimpsed the sign I was waiting for. The exit was a mile farther. We came upon it before I could adequately slow down, and I perilously swung the steering wheel to the right. I locked up the brakes and shoved it down into third. Smoke bellowed out the rear, but the Mustang managed to stay its course, and the transmission remained in one piece. I blew by the stop sign at the top of the overpass, swerved out of the way of an oncoming truck, and punched it again. Flying down the hill, I saw the road stretch out before us. It was a long, straight boulevard full of traffic lights and intersections. I had a decision to make. The lady on the phone said it was two miles down this road; do I obey every goddamned red light or just tuck my head and punch it? I didn't have to make the decision that instant, for the first two lights were green. The next was solid red, however. I slowed from eighty miles per hour to fifty, switched to a lane that was void of cars and bolted through the light. I repeated this suicidal stunt through the next four lights. When we cleared the seventh light, I spotted the Mercy Animal Clinic sign. I pulled up on the sidewalk, grabbed Hank by the collar, and ran him in the front door. Two ladies adorned in light-blue doctor's coats were waiting for me.

"You're Dan, I take it?" the older one asked. The younger one snapped a leash onto Hank.

"Yes, yes…" I was half a thump away from a heart attack.

"Cindy, get him into the back," she directed. Hank

was whisked away. "My name is Debbie. Doctor Hubbard has prepared for him. Do you want some water?"

Maybe a paper bag, I thought. I was on the verge of hyperventilating. "No, no thanks. I'll be okay."

"I'm going to go help with Hank. You can join me or stay here and catch your breath. Joanne can make you some coffee if you like."

"I want to go with you," I said between gasps.

I trailed her through a couple of short corridors and into a large examination room. Hank was on the other side of a sliding-glass door, pacing around a small fenced outdoor area. Three women were bustling around, carrying out the vet's orders, which seemed to be spewing forth nonstop. I drifted into a corner, feeling lightheaded. I really thought I might faint. The vet gave a look of subdued shock as Hank vomited up several big pools of bright green antifreeze. When it became apparent there was nothing left in his stomach, one of the assistants brought him inside, and the doctor injected him with a giant syringe loaded with a clear liquid.

Everything went fuzzy for a moment.

Gradually, my eyes refocused, and I witnessed the doctor threading a small tube down Hank's nose. My legs were buckling. I weaved my way back down the hall and fell into a chair. I was still feeling woozy when the doctor appeared.

"Hi, Dan. My name is Steve." He shook my hand. "You saw what I saw back there, and I'm not going to sugarcoat anything. To be blunt, I've never seen an animal with that much antifreeze in its system. He drank a lot."

My heart sank, and I felt tears welling up in my eyes. He continued, "We purged his system, so the bulk of it is out, but we just have to cross our fingers that a significant amount hasn't been absorbed by the digestive system yet. You see, the reason antifreeze kil...umm, gets an animal in trouble, is that as the ethylene glycol is metabolized...sorry, you don't need this lecture right now. To be brief, it causes, among other things, kidney failure. The good news is that you got him here quickly."

"Is he going to make it?" The tears wouldn't be held back any longer.

"He's okay for now, but we'll have to do blood tests in the morning. Do you want to see him?"

"Please."

We made our way down the corridor back to the same room. There, in the middle of the room, was Hank, sprawled out on a medical table; one of the assistants stood near, petting him.

"How you doing, buddy?" I gave him a big hug. His eyes were open but droopy and glazed over. He gave a very slight flick of his tail in response to my hug. I asked Steve what was wrong with him. He didn't respond right away; instead he walked over to a shelf and returned with a bottle of grain alcohol.

"Well, among other things, we injected a fair amount of this into him," he said.

"So he's...he's drunk?"

"I'd say he's really drunk."

A slight chuckle sprung forth between my tears as the staff quietly left us alone. A bit later, an assistant returned and informed me Debbie would like to speak with me. I followed her out to the waiting room.

"How are you feeling?" she asked, staring into my swollen eyes.

"I'm hanging in there. It's been one hell of a day."

"Yes, it certainly has, but I think you got him here in time. Try to relax a bit and don't worry too much. Where were you headed when this happened?"

I related my story, how I was headed to my father's in Colorado for the holidays.

"I wanted to let you know that Doctor Hubbard will need to see Hank first thing in the morning. Do you have a place to stay tonight?"

"Um, I'm sure I can find a hotel. Uh, I hate to ask this, but do you have any idea of what this is going to cost?"

"I'm not sure. Let me check. I'll be right back." She left me standing there with one of the assistants. The entire afternoon was a blur, but I remembered seeing her throughout it, petting Hank and calming him as best she could.

"Hank's a lucky pooch," she stated. "By the way, I'm Cindy."

"It's nice to meet you. I always thought I was the lucky one...the way he sort of found me. I suppose we're both lucky to have made it here without dying in a car accident."

"Yeah, we were amazed at how fast you got here. Have you ever been to Topeka before? I mean, do you know your way around?"

"No, she, I mean, Debbie, gave me great directions over the phone. I just drove as fast as I could. Uh, no, though, no I've never been to Topeka before. I mean, I drove through it once before."

"It's a great town; it—" Just then Debbie returned, and Cindy cut herself short.

"Well, it's going to be a bit expensive. Doctor Hubbard said he will reduce the bill as much as he can, but it looks like it will be in the neighborhood of $350," she said apologetically.

"Oh, he doesn't need to do that, knock any off the bill I mean; that's very nice of him. I mean, he has to make a living." I was rambling because I only had four hundred dollars, and my brain was scattered in too many directions at the moment. Debbie excused herself again, and Cindy picked up where she had left off.

"Topeka is really nice once you get to know it. I love it…"

I wasn't listening. I was wondering how I was going to pay for a hotel room, the bill, and buy gas for the rest of the trip.

Debbie rejoined us.

"Dan, I just got off the phone with my husband, and we would like you to stay with us tonight. Hank's been through an awful lot today, and this way you both can get a good meal, and I can keep an eye on him."

What an absolutely fantastic lady, I thought, the tears rolling down my cheeks yet again.

By five o'clock closing time, Hank was only sober enough to attempt a sitting position, so I gently carried him to the car, situating him snugly on his blanket on the passenger's seat. I followed Debbie's dark-red truck for half an hour, leaving Topeka behind and traveling into the barren, windswept plains. The terminus of the commute was a tidy yet modest farmhouse.

"Dan, this is my husband Robert, and this is Sarah and Amy. Sarah's the one in pink."

"Nice to meet you," Robert said, pumping my hand. "It sounds like you've had a heck of day."

"Where's your dog?" the twins chimed.

"He's in the car."

"Come on, girls, let's get inside. You'll catch your death out here," Debbie said.

"I'll help you in with your things, Dan. From what Debbie told me on the phone, sounds like you might need a hand with Hank as well."

"Thanks. Thanks for everything. I really appreciate it."

We had just finished dinner. Debbie was in the living room checking on Hank and making up the couch for me while I sat at the table, sipping a cup of coffee and listening to Robert explain the trials and tribulations of being a small Kansas farmer.

"Prices were pretty crummy this year, but we got by. Of course, there's always perks to having your own plot of land." He plucked the last bit of ham off his plate just as Amy cleared it away.

"That meal was divine," I said.

"Can't say that was the best hog I ever raised, but Debbie has a knack of turning even the worst cut into something special. Actually, I think she switches it for that fancy store-bought stuff when I'm not looking."

"Mind your tongue, Rob. We've got a visitor," Debbie said, ushering her friend into the kitchen.

"Well, hello there, Cindy. I didn't hear you come in." He pushed his chair back and stood to face the women. I followed suit.

"I snuck through the back window." She smiled. It was a nice smile. She was really quite pretty. It wasn't something I could have appreciated earlier that day.

"Actually, she's been here for a few minutes. We were looking after Hank," Debbie said.

"How's he doing? I should probably go be with him," I said.

"He's fine, Dan. Really, he is," she said and then turned to Cindy. "I've had a terrible time convincing him of that. I nearly had to have Rob carry him to the supper table."

"Maybe I can help." Cindy blushed. "I was wondering if you'd like to see a bit of Topeka?"

"Oh, that's really nice of you," I said, "but I really shouldn't leave Hank."

Robert leaned over and whispered in my ear, "Are you blind, man? A pretty young girl asks you out, you go!"

Now *I* was blushing.

"Rob, behave yourself!" Debbie scolded. "I just gave him another injection. He's going to be out to the world all night, and I promise I'll keep an eye on him the whole time."

"I really couldn't ask you to do that."

"I'm going to be in there watching TV anyway. It's no hardship, really."

"The hardship will be if you don't escape before she makes you watch her shows with her."

"Hush, Rob!"

"If you really think it's okay…" I looked over at Cindy's deep-blue eyes.

"Get, you two."

Robert, Debbie, and the twins shepherded us to the front door and waved good-bye as Cindy steered her truck back toward Topeka.

"Dan, time to wake up."

I peeked through crusty eyes. It took me a moment to realize where I was. Debbie was leaning over the couch, gently shaking me.

"Cindy sure knows how to show a guy a good time I see. I set out a towel for you in the bathroom. You'll be happy to know Hank got up all by himself this morning and did his business. When you're ready, there's a bit of breakfast waiting in the kitchen."

"Thank you." I got up and made my way over to Hank. Jesus, my head hurt. I kneeled down and gave him a scratch behind the ear. His tail flopped back and forth. He certainly looked more alert, but I could tell he was still drunk. That made two of us. What a night.

Cindy and I had really hit it off. Of course, the dozen or so beers she refused to let me pay for surely aided matters. I was nervous and felt terrible for leaving Hank for the first few hours, but around the time we entered the third bar of the night, I was really enjoying myself. It was the best night I'd had in a very long time.

"Thank you so much for looking after Hank last night. And I'm sorry about coming back so late." I was feeling better, thanks to a hot shower and a delicious country breakfast.

"I doubt there was much you could have done about it; that girl has a bit of a wild streak in her," Robert said. "Debbie will be ready for work in a minute. We better get you and Hank loaded up so you can follow her in. She's not one to be late."

With a bit of help, Hank managed to get into the car under his own power. I closed the door and turned to thank Robert once again.

"We can't send away a weary traveler empty handed." He presented me with a very full bag and a five-gallon bucket sealed with a plastic lid. "We've got more ham than we can eat, and Debbie made you some biscuits last night, thought you could make up some sandwiches on the road. As for the bucket, there's a new jug of antifreeze in it. I figured you could use another one, seeing how the last one went missing."

"Wow, Robert, I can't thank you enough. This whole thing is just unbelievable. I wish I could repay you."

"You can. Keep the lid on."

They had done everything under the sun to alleviate my worry—babysit Hank, make me feel welcome, show me the town—and it had worked, but back at the clinic, sitting in the same chair as the day before, my anxiety was back in full force. They drew blood from Hank shortly after we arrived. Since then, there had been nothing for me to do, other than sit quietly, pet Hank, and wonder how I was going to handle the inevitable, horrific news. It just didn't seem possible the news could be anything but bad. *"I've never seen an animal with that much antifreeze in its system,"* kept replaying, over and over, in my head.

"Dan," the receptionist said, "they're ready to see you two. Would you like a hand to the examination room?"

"Uh, no thanks. It looks like he can walk okay." The question was, could I? My whole body felt like it was getting stabbed with needles. This was it.

I was completely taken aback when I entered the room. Steve, Debbie, Cindy, and two other assistants were there. It was wall-to-wall grins. I tried to speak, but the words stuck in my throat. My eyes felt watery.

"They say a miracle happens every day. Well, today it happened here," Steve said, slapping me on the shoulder. "The tests showed no damage whatsoever. I wanted to be sure, so I ran them twice."

"And I ran them a third time," Debbie said. "Sorry to keep you waiting."

"I…I…thank you, thank you!"

After several big hugs and a few tears, the room slowly emptied, leaving me and Hank alone with Cindy.

"I'm so happy things turned out all right."

"I still can't believe it, any of it. Debbie and Robert, Doctor Hubbard—you." I was simply overwhelmed.

"I wish you didn't have to go, but I understand. I just wish, well, you know."

"I wish that too."

I felt a spark of confidence as we rumbled past one tired house after another. Admittedly, it was a mean-looking neighborhood, but the landlady had sounded desperate to rent the place. Pulling into the driveway, my hope died a quick death. The bedraggled old house was huge. Dilapidated or not, I could never afford to rent a place this size on my own. Oh, what the hell, I'm here.

"Hi, I'm Dan."

"Ethel. Come on in." The heavyset, silver-haired woman ushered me into the front room.

"Like I said on the phone, I'm sorry about the other guys backing out on you."

"Looks like I'm not the only one they run out on."

"Yeah, they told me they were totally serious about moving in. Mike even said he'd already given you his and Dave's deposit. I thought it was a done deal."

"Maybe so, maybe so, but after Mike's father phoned me up, telling me his boy was staying put where he was, I gave them their money back. He sure wasn't too friendly 'bout it neither."

"I just wish I had known all this a few weeks ago. I would have stayed put at the duplex." She gave me a quizzical look, so I added, "I just got back from Colorado. I was at my dad's for Christmas. Before I left, Mike told me about this place and that everything was set, so I gave notice at the place I've been renting. Anyway, I'm in a bit of a bind. I really need a place to live, but I don't want to waste your time. I don't think there is any way I can afford this place all by myself."

"Are you telling me you're homeless?"

"Well, not at the moment. But I guess I might be on Tuesday. That's when I've got to be out of my place."

"Hmm, you are in a pickle, ain't ya? We might be able to work something out. But first I gotta ask—do you know where you're at?"

"Pardon?"

"Bet you didn't see too many white folks like yourself when you drove here, did you?"

Come to think of it, I hadn't.

"What I'm trying to tell you is, you won't be seeing too many of your college buddies 'round here. No doubt that's why Mister Barns jerked the plug on his son's plans. He probably found out where he was movin' to. So you still want to talk about a deal?"

Wow, she was right. I didn't have a clue where I was. "Yes, I sure do."

It was certainly a less-than-ideal plan, even if it was affordable. Ethel was going to rent the upstairs, which included two bedrooms and a full bathroom, to her cousin, Sean. She said he was getting out of a halfway house the following week, but not to worry, he had a job and kept to himself. Swell. Keeping things in the family, her nephew Jamaal was going to move into the basement. She didn't explain how that situation had come about, and I didn't ask, afraid she'd tell me he was just released from prison or something. As for me, the living room, a small bathroom, and bedroom on the main level were all mine. The kitchen would be communal.

That afternoon, I unloaded my belongings from the Mustang in a mild daze. The stupid half of my brain was ticking along nicely, as it generally did. It was the relatively intelligent half that was mute, shocked it had agreed to such an arrangement.

I placed my bike against the front-porch railing and returned to the car for the last box. "This is another fine mess I've gotten us into, eh, Hank?"

He was leaning against the side of the car. I swear he looked scared.

"What's the matter?" I spent a few minutes petting and talking to him, but it didn't seem to have much effect. He was not happy about his new surroundings. I knew how he felt.

I slammed the trunk lid down and replaced the bungee cords that held it in place (the new locking system). I picked up the box and coaxed Hank to follow me inside.

"See, buddy, this isn't so bad." I dropped the box onto the floor alongside the rest of my meager belongings. "We'll make it livable and—" Hold it a second!

I rushed back to the porch. Oh man, it really *was* gone. I ran down the steps and circled the house, scouring the lot and the nearby streets. No pedestrians, no nearby cars, no barking dogs—nothing. Baffled, I went back and took a seat on the steps.

Scratch one mountain bike.

I switched on the kitchen light. I don't know who was more startled, Sean or the cockroaches. Waves of the black insects scurried for cover, and Sean followed suit. Clutching his plate of greasy food, he scooted past, leaving behind a faint aroma of Jim Beam. I'd been sharing the house with him for approximately two months, and he had yet to utter a word. To say he preferred his own company was like saying Jamaal enjoyed a cup of tea with a friend or two in the evenings.

I flicked a dazed roach off the counter and prepared my lunch. It was crazy—the filth, the bugs, and even Sean were no more than annoyances compared to Jamaal and his basement drug emporium. The rooms below my feet were busier than a florist on Valentine's Day.

I bagged up the sandwiches and brought them into the bathroom with me. I did things like that now. I gazed in the mirror through tired eyes. The angry red welt on the side of my neck appeared to be abating at last. One morning, a week earlier, I had woken up with the wound. I wasn't exactly sure what had caused it. It could have been anything from a rat to one of the Frisbee-sized spiders that darted around the place. I scrubbed the hell out of it in the shower, got dressed, gathered my books, and retrieved my wallet from a plastic bag that was hidden behind the refrigerator crisper drawer. Like I said, I did things like that now.

"I'm sorry, pal. I filled your bowl. And, hey, look, even a new ball to play with!"

He wasn't interested in the lame ball. He was geared up for what was coming next. He knew the new routine well enough. I gave him a guilty little pat on the head and closed the gate behind me. Walking down the driveway, past the Mustang, which had fallen into disrepair, I heard Hank's low whining. I knew he was staring through the chain link fence, watching me. I turned the corner with a terrible feeling in my gut and walked the five miles to campus.

My days were long and joyless. I was enrolled in the maximum number of classes allowed, and I was finding every one of them beyond challenging. The journalism school deserved its reputation as one of the best. It had swallowed me whole, and I was just waiting to drop out the other end. Between classes, I spent the vast majority of my time in the library. I found a forgotten corner on the upper level, where I could study and cry in peace. The hours of each week passed painfully slowly, but thankfully they did pass.

"Next week we will be discussing the early partisan newspapers. I highly recommend brushing up on chapters six and seven, paying particular attention to the history of the *Gazette of the United States* and John Fenno's role in it, as well as the pages regarding the *Connecticut Courant* and the *Aurora General Advertiser*. There will be a quiz on Monday, so I suggest you do some reading this weekend."

The professor began stuffing papers into his briefcase, signaling that the lecture was at an end. I flexed my cramped hand, stowed my notes in my backpack, and followed the crowd out of the sterile building. The majority of students drifted toward the parking lot while I split off and headed for home.

I really hate that class, I thought, walking past the dark and vacant student rec center. It was bad enough it was so boring that I had to chew the inside of my cheeks bloody to remain conscious, but it was a night class to boot. I sorely missed the use of my car; I wished I had the money to get it fixed. Oh well, at least it was Friday—for whatever that was worth.

Halfway home, I talked myself into popping into a liquor store and buying a six-pack. Standing in front of the cooler, trying to decipher the best deal, I found myself surrounded by a group of rowdy students, getting geared up for a night of partying. I shelled out six bucks for a twelve-pack instead.

Making my way down the neglected sidewalk, I waited for a car to pass before I cracked open a third beer. Putting the can to my lips, I noticed the car had stopped in the middle of the quiet street. The reverse lights came on, and it quickly backed up to where I stood. This is probably not good.

"Hey, boy, whatcha drinkin' there?"

Three shadowy faces stared at me from the dark car. It was hard to make out any details. The city didn't waste money lighting up the streets on this side of town.

"Pardon me?"

The door swung open, and out climbed two very large black guys.

"He asked you what're ya drinking."

"A beer."

"He wouldn't just be having the one," the driver shouted.

"Give 'em over."

Goddamn it! I have just about had it with *everything*. The fear I felt a second earlier was swamped beneath an emerging tidal wave of anger. These bastards think they can just pull up and relieve me of the one small pleasure I've had all week? The hell if they will. "Go fuck yourselves!"

There was no immediate response. I had shocked them into silence. Oh boy, oh boy, was that stupid. Run! Run! Run! I didn't. I just took another sip of beer.

"You crazy or something?"

I knew there was no going back on what I had said, and anything I added to it now would just make things worse, so I gave no response. Instead, I upended the beer and chugged. I might as well face whatever was coming with a buzz.

"Give me that!" The larger of the two grabbed the beer out of my hand and threw it into the gutter. "Let's spare tire this asshole."

A moment later, I was hugging my backpack, bouncing around in the darkness of the car's trunk.

They hadn't hurt me, not yet anyway, but it still felt like I had been slapped in the face several times. It all happened so fast, just like the panic that was sweeping over me. My God, what had I done? Where were they taking me? This is just how it happens on those TV shows. Someday a farmer will unearth my skull with his plow. The cops will show up with a bunch of shovels and bag up what's left of me. I'll end up scattered across a steel table. A bunch of guys in lab coats will test my crushed bones and teeth, but they won't be able to identify me. They'll just shove me in a box and...

The car came to a stop. I heard one of them mutter something, and then the doors clunked shut. The lid to my prison sprang open, and four hands reached in and hauled me out, onto my feet. Even though I was about to fall over with fear, I managed to take stock of my new surroundings. As inconceivable as it seemed, I knew precisely where I was.

"So...so you were just screwing with me?" I let loose an odd-sounding laugh. "So you guys want to come in? Have a beer? You guys want a beer, right? Of course you do. I mean, that's what this is all about, huh?"

"This is one crazy-ass white boy!"

"Maybe we should just cut him loose, Dwayne. It ain't right messin' up a retarded kid."

"No, we're taking him inside." He seized my arm and roughly pulled me through the gate and into the backyard. The other two reached the door and pummeled it with their fists.

"Hey, Jamaal, open up, man! Come on, open up!"

Without warning, Hank shot from the darkness and attacked the guy standing next to me.

"Aaaah! Shit, man! Get off! Get him off me!"

Hank clamped down on the back of his left ankle. With a ferocious growl, which frightened even me, he violently shook his head back and forth, knocking the guy off balance and sending him reeling to the ground.

He sank his teeth into the screaming man's leg a couple more times before positioning himself directly in front of me, tail low, hackles up.

The other two were pressed against the door and nearly fell into the house when Jamaal jerked it open.

"What the hell is going on? Dwayne, what are you doing on the ground? What's wrong with Hank? Dan, is that you? Shut your dog up!"

I straddled Hank and pinched his jaws shut. I was going to do anything Jamaal asked and pronto. He had a pistol.

"Shoot that fucking dog, Jamaal. He tried to tear off my leg. See, look at that, I'm bleedin'. Ah shit, these were new pants and everything."

"What's going on, Dan?" Jamaal asked.

"Uh…easy, Hank…uh, I was just coming back from class, and these guys gave me a ride. I forgot to warn them about Hank. Sorry about that, fellas." I was just praying Jamaal had some influence over the bumbling gang—with that gun I thought he might.

"What up, Dwayne, that right?"

He picked himself up and dusted off his pants, flashing Hank a malevolent look in the process. "Yeah, sure, man, that's right; we was just givin' the kid a lift."

"Whatever," Jamaal said. "Get downstairs. For your sake, I hope you got the stuff. And don't be bleedin' all over my leather couch, Dwayne."

They vanished without a word.

I relaxed my grip on Hank as Jamaal tucked the gun in his waistband and took a seat on the top step. He whistled and Hank tentatively walked over to him. "That's a good boy." He gave him a scratch around the scruff of the neck. "This here is a good dog. Guarding the place, weren't ya? Yeah, we's friends, ain't we."

I forced my legs to cross the yard and took a seat next to the pair. I was having a much harder time calming down than Hank. Of course, no one was telling me how brave and great I was—no, I figured Jamaal was going to take a different tack with me.

"You 'member when I moved in?"

"Yes," I quietly answered.

"You 'member me saying that if you didn't cause no problems and let me do my thing, I'd do my best to protect your Casper ass? And if things didn't go smoothly, well, we were gonna have some problems, right?"

"Yeah, I remember."

"We got us a bit of a problem now, don't we? The deal's all gone to shit, huh?"

"Look, Jamaal, I'm sorry. I really am. But it wasn't my fault. "

"You're sorry?"

I really thought he was going to pull out his gun.

"*You're sorry?*"

He took hold of my chin, forcing me to stare into his eyes.

"You're not the one who needs to apologize. I am. I don't know what those fools thought they were doing putting you in the trunk like that, but I do know them niggers picked the wrong white boy to fuck with—my white boy. But I can tell you this, it's all good now. Ain't nobody going to mess with you anymore, not in my neighborhood. That's straight up from me to you. That's the new deal." He knocked a fist on my shoulder then disappeared into the house.

The school year had finished, and it was back to the molten heat of summer. I survived my first year in Missouri. It had been a rocky beginning, but then, quite unexpectedly, things had begun to look up. I suppose the night I went for a joyride in Dwayne's trunk was the watershed. Subsequently, Jamaal began spending more and more time upstairs, watching TV, sharing dinner, and playing with Hank. Astoundingly, Sean would leave nut-ball tower occasionally and join us—although he never added much to the conversation. The drug dealer, me, and mentally unstable grandpa—it sounded like a really bad TV sitcom.

Added to my newfound domestic delight was my recent employment as a bartender. Decent tips and pretty girls, I liked it, and it earned me enough to fix my car. I had even managed to pass most of my final exams.

As the summer wore on, I gradually began to put some serious thought into my life after school, perhaps for the first time. It seemed my entire life was devoted and tied to one single decision. I had decided I wanted to be a journalist. As ridiculous as it sounds, I couldn't quite remember why I had chosen to pursue that field of study. I guess during the second year in college, a person needs to focus on something, choose a major. Being far from gifted in mathematics or the sciences, I think I sort of gravitated to journalism by default. I liked photojournalism, but I wasn't very good at it. I guess I could hold my own when it came to interviewing people and writing stories. But until I came to the University of Missouri, I had little idea of all that a career in journalism encompasses.

Every day there would be a deadline. Editors, who all seemed fairly egotistical to me, would be clamoring for an article and then cut it to ribbons when it materialized. The pay wasn't great. The competition was fierce, and the hours were generally bad. What the hell was I thinking? This was the prize I was struggling to win? It looked like I was forcing myself down the wrong road. Still, unless I wanted to stay in school for another couple of years, it was a little late to change my major. That was okay. I couldn't come up with an alternative subject I was dying to pursue anyway. But there was a change for the better I could make.

Chapter Fifteen

Brick Courses

I was home.

This time, Bryan, Shane, Hank, and I shared a small three-bedroom apartment several miles away from the campus of Colorado State University. It certainly wasn't a repeat of the virtual anarchy of The Shields House, but that was probably a good thing. We were seniors. Classes were more advanced and projects more time consuming. Don't get me wrong—we still allotted a decent amount of time to football games in the park, camping in the mountains, and general beer drinking, but it was a calmer, perhaps a bit more serious, time.

That year, I earned my degree. My proud parents were on hand to watch me receive my diploma. Lacking a plan, I intended to stay put at the apartment for the summer, picking up more hours at the Pancake House where I had been working the night shift as a cook. But all that changed when my dad handed me a wad of cash, and my mom surprised me with a plane ticket to Europe.

Way to go, Mom! Way to go, Dad!

A couple of weeks later, after boxing up my belongings and taking them, Hank, and the Mustang to Dad's, I boarded a plane for Paris.

I was a bit anxious about traveling alone, but it turned out to be one of the greatest trips of my life. Leapfrogging from hostel to hostel and train to train, I traveled through country after country, including those on the other side of the recently abandoned iron curtain. Sometimes I went it alone, and sometimes I teamed up with other people my age that I had met along the way. I made it all the way to Turkey before my funds ran dry. It was time to head back to reality.

Reality was bleak. I returned to Dad and Annie's house with three hundred bucks, no job prospects, and no plan. Dad wasn't overly impressed with me. This I understood. At the moment, I wasn't overly impressed with me either. After a couple of apathetic days, I loaded up my things and Hank and drove to Fort Collins. I told Dad I had lined up a job and had a place to stay with a friend. Both were lies.

After an uncomfortable night's sleep in the car, I resumed my search for Bryan, Shane, and numerous other friends, but I was having little luck. Eventually, I made contact with Justin. He was a buddy from high school who apparently had recently bought a house in a small town north of Fort Collins. Sitting in his living room, we popped open a couple of beers, and I told him what I had been up to recently and, more importantly, the situation I was currently in.

"I'd love to help you out, but as you can see, this place is small. There's only the two little bedrooms, and Danny is living in one of them."

"No, I totally understand, man. I thought you may have some ideas. I mean, I just got back, and you know, end of summer and everything, I have no idea where anyone is."

"I think Bryan is back in Oregon surfing or whatever it is he does out there. Clint went back to California for the summer. Doug just disappeared, sort of like you did. And Shane is working in Denver I think."

"Half the guys we know are still in school; some of them have to be coming back to town and getting places to live, right?"

"I guess so. I doubt any of them are going to let you move in without forking over the money for the deposit and first and last month."

"Good point."

"Hey, I just thought of something. I doubt this is a good idea for you or for me, but you do seem to be pretty screwed at the moment."

"Yeah, what is it?"

"Come have a look."

I followed him into the cramped kitchen where I watched him pry up several loose floorboards in one corner. He grabbed a flashlight off the top of the refrigerator and shined it into the hole.

"I didn't even know this was here when I bought the place. I guess it's some sort of root cellar or something."

It was roughly eight foot by eight foot. The walls were rough concrete and stone, and from the dirt floor to the underside of the cobweb-encased floor joists measured about six foot I guessed.

"If we built you a ladder to get up and down and maybe got an old chunk of carpet to throw down on the floor—"

"Yes! Oh, man, you are saving my bacon right now. Yes!"

"Hold on a minute, champ. This would only be temporary. Only until you got back on your feet; then you have to find somewhere else. Okay?"

"Sure, you bet."

"Also, you have to kick in a hundred bucks a month. I know you don't have it right now, but I reckon with that college degree of yours, you'll find a good-paying job quick enough, and we can settle up then."

Justin's prediction was partially correct. I did find a job quickly, and the pay wasn't bad, but it had very little to do with possessing a college degree. There wasn't even a job application to fill out. One day, I spotted the ad in the local newspaper; the next, I found myself hiding behind a dump truck on the verge of passing out from fatigue.

The first week of being a hod carrier was brutal. College life hadn't left me in the best of shape. However, my new job quickly rectified that as I soon became acquainted with the duties of a hod carrier. It was pretty basic really. Masons laid the brick, concrete block, or stone. A hod carrier did the rest. I set up and took down the scaffolding. I shoveled mountains of sand. I carried ninety-four-pound bags of cement. I mixed endless batches of mortar in the cement mixer. I pushed an overloaded wheelbarrow for miles each day. I carried and stocked all the bricks, block, or stone. And with three masons to keep up with, the work was endless, and every bit of it was extremely physical.

Much to my surprise, I really enjoyed it. I was finding out I was a pick-and-shovel kind of guy. And the fifteen bucks an hour really added up since we worked a fifty-hour week. Much to Justin's delight, it wasn't long before I was able to come up with the cash to move out of The Hole and into a small apartment in Fort Collins.

Nearly a year had passed. And it was a good year. I liked my snug, comfortable abode. I was still enjoying my work and so was Hank, as he got to explore a new construction site nearly every week. Plus, I even managed to save up a bit of money. Yet, I just couldn't shake a restless feeling that had been steadily growing within in me. I suppose it was a combination of things. A lot of my friends had graduated and left town to pursue their careers in larger markets. The rest of them would, no doubt, follow suit shortly. Through the grapevine, I heard the girl I had dated on and off over the years was getting married. It just seemed as if everyone else was racing past, while I plodded along aimlessly. I guess there was nothing wrong with my life; still, there was so much else out there—the trip to Europe had taught me that.

Mulling things over one day, I had a eureka moment. What about heading back to Alaska? Why not? It was beautiful, nearly limitless, and seemingly full of opportunity. At least that's what I believed it to be. With a total lack of further consideration, I made the decision then and there. I would try my luck in the last frontier.

Chapter Sixteen

Admission Fee

It was mid-October, and the progressively declining temperature was compelling the rain to turn to snow. An hour passed; still I was unable to muster the courage to roll out of my sleeping bag. It was the twenty-seventh consecutive day my dreams had given way to this dreary reality. Every fiber of my being begged to stay put. I marshaled up a shred of determination and mentally prepared for the jolt I was about to receive.

"Ready to get up, pal?"

Nothing moved.

"Okay, one, two, three!" I lay there, gazing at the crystallized condensation hanging from the canopy. "Shit." I pulled a frosty pillow over my head. A few more minutes passed.

"Okay, let's go, Hank. Ready? One, two, and three."

This time I did it. I sat straight up and wiggled out of my toasty cocoon. Son of a bitch, it was cold! I fumbled for the same dirty outfit I'd worn for the past few days. I was fully dressed in seconds.

"H-h-h-ow-w y-y-yaa do-ing?" I asked Hank.

He stood up and executed a long, relaxed back stretch. Oh, how I envied that thick fur coat of his. I unlatched the warped tailgate and crawled out. Standing there, rubbing my arms and legs, I stared at our home—a slightly dented gray pickup truck with a flimsy metal topper mounted on the bed. The jury was still out on whether it had been a good swap for the Mustang. There were three inches of wet snow covering everything in sight.

Swell.

I began my morning routine of feeding Hank, dousing my head with ice water, and heating up some instant coffee over the camping stove. While I busied my body, my mind wondered exactly when it was that this existence had completely lost its appeal. Juneau perhaps? It rained without interruption the six days I camped there. Maybe it was the Canadian border, when customs officials exhaustively, and unjustly, searched me and the truck, accusing me of hiding drugs? Or it could have been two weeks ago when the truck broke down a hundred miles from the nearest town, and I was reduced to fixing it with a Crunch 'n Munch box and duct tape. So many options...

At least most of the journey through Canada had gone well. There had been plenty of places to camp, and the weather had been decent. Approaching Alaska, I decided to head to Juneau, it being the nearest large town. That proved to be a mistake. There didn't seem to be any work and very few places to rent. So we continued north, stopping at the few small communities we came upon. But no opportunity presented itself. Wherever we went, I received the same advice, over and over. "Go to Anchorage. It's a big place. That's where all the work is."

Five days ago, we arrived at this small campground outside of Alaska's biggest city. Every day, I desperately searched the rental section of the *Anchorage Daily News*. I followed up likely prospects with a phone call and drove all over the place meeting with wary landlords. Each day, the results were the same—a newspaper covered with scribbles and a cold truck to sleep in. It didn't make any sense. Based on what I saw, there was a dog on every corner in Anchorage, yet, no one would rent to me because of Hank, and, well, possibly my appearance had a bit to do with it too.

"You know what, Hank? The hell with this. I've had enough of Anchorage," I said, sitting on the frosty tailgate, finishing off my second cup of coffee.

Even though I was leading a grubby, pathetic existence that was going nowhere fast, I refused to retrace my steps south. Returning to Colorado on borrowed money with both our tails tucked between our legs was not an option.

I pulled the tattered map from the glove box and confirmed what I already knew. There was only one road north, and it led to Fairbanks and the end of the line. I made a brief count of my remaining money—$987.11.

As soon as Hank did his business and finished off his breakfast, we were off.

"We're just getting in deeper and deeper, huh?" I waved good-bye to the little campground with my middle finger and steered a course straight for the Arctic Circle.

An hour into the estimated six-hour drive, we rolled into Wasilla. I was surprised. I assumed it would simply be a wide spot in the road, like so many other places marked on the map had turned out to be, but this had the promise of civilization. I stopped at the gas station and purchased the local paper and a drink. Back in the warmth of the idling truck, I pulled out the very thin classified section. The first ad listed under Rentals gave a very brief description of the property and stated, "Pets welcome."

Fucking amazing.

I jogged back to the store and rang the number from a pay phone. A throaty male voice answered, and within seconds, an immediate appointment was arranged. Following his curt directions, I soon found myself parked in front of what could only be described as a shack. Stoney's Real Estate was hand painted above the door.

I told Hank to stay put and slid across the ice.

Inside, I found a very large man crammed behind a desk that filled nearly half of the small structure. He was chatting on the phone, a lit cigar stuck in the corner of his mouth. He motioned for me to have a seat as he continued his conversation. "Sally, look, you just have to get your butt over there and evict them. Yes, I know, I know. But they'll be in jail before you know it anyway. Okay, just get it done."

He slammed the phone into its cradle, pushed his immense bulk deep into the large leather chair, and stared at me.

Finally, I cleared my throat and broke the silence. "I'm Dan. I just spoke with you on the phone."

"Yeah, sure you are," he said, nestling his cigar into an overused ashtray. "You look pretty rough around the edges. You a junkie?"

Completely taken off guard, I quietly answered, "Uh, no, not that I know of."

"Yeah, maybe. You have a job?"

"Um, no, not yet. I just moved here." An expression of disapproval flashed across his red face, so I added, "But as soon as I get a place, I'm going to find employment, first thing."

"How much money do you have? I mean total, all up. Don't lie, or I'll ask to see it."

I gambled. "Around three thousand dollars."

"I'll tell you what. I'm going to take a chance on you because I like you, and you caught me in a good mood. But you have to promise me three things." He returned the wet cigar to his sausage lips.

"Okay?"

"First, you have to get a job pronto. Second, you have to sign the lease right here, right now. It will save me from going clear the hell out there this afternoon and showing it to a couple of boneheads. And third, you got to get off the dope. Do those things, and the place is yours."

"Sure."

Thirty-five minutes later, Hank and I arrived at our new place. Astoundingly, it actually looked okay. It was a small, isolated house situated at the base of a treeless mountain. I unlocked the front door with my new key and found the inside to be quite livable. I returned to the truck for my gear and Hank.

After I had taken care of Hank's needs, I curled up in my sleeping bag in a corner of the living room and slept for sixteen hours.

A few days after we moved in, the clouds spat out two feet of snow. Everything seemed to be closing in around me, including my finances. I needed work and fast.

Eking by on gas fumes and my remaining camping food, I spent the week visiting just about every shop in Wasilla. Initially, of course, I checked the classifieds but to no avail. So I was trying the direct approach. I went to business after business; I didn't care what it was—

supermarket, secondhand store, head shop, gas station—but nobody was hiring. It became apparent I had moved right into the center of an economic sinkhole. Things were looking grim, and I found myself at a total loss.

For lack of a better plan, I aimlessly drove around the area. I felt guilty wasting precious fuel indiscriminately, but I was bouncing off the walls at the house. At some point, I found myself thoroughly lost and ended up following signs that promised a lake would appear at the end of the road. A peaceful place to mull over my predicament sounded like a good idea; besides, I could quit burning fuel. However, when the road ended, I didn't see a lake, just what appeared to be a fairly large lodge. Things certainly weren't going my way. I couldn't even find a solitary spot to think. I circled the parking lot and was about to head back the way I'd come when the obvious hit me—here was a possible job opportunity! I cleaned myself up the best I could and went in.

I spent the next thirty minutes talking with a tiny Japanese woman. It turned out she and her husband had recently purchased the lodge and were in the midst of having it renovated.

"There are a few positions to fill yet. Is there anything on this list you have training in?" She slid the paper across the table.

I quickly looked it over. Food and beverage manager—well, yes! No, I doubted my title at Marine World when I was fifteen would hold water…guest service agent—nope…head housekeeper—a definite no…housekeeper—hmm, probably not…waitress—no…cook—well yeah, that could be a maybe! It was my only shot, so I stretched the truth. I told her I had considerable cooking experience. (Flipping flapjacks and burning toast at the Pancake House had to count for something, didn't it?) I fudged my history a bit on the application, and she hired me on the spot. There was only one hitch, and it was a big one. The job wouldn't begin until the remodeling was finished, which was estimated to be another eight weeks. I'd be dead long before that, and as delicately as I could, I told her so. She suggested I speak with the general contractor, Wayne.

It wasn't much of an interview. He sized me up, apparently deciding I was fit enough, had me sign a couple of things, and I was carrying lumber. I was elated.

The work continued for two months as promised, and then came the day when it was time to lay down the hammer and pick up an apron. It was the grand opening, and I found myself floundering around the kitchen, cremating everything in sight. I weakly carried out my bluff for another two days.

"I'm sorry, Dan, but business is business, and I have to be blunt here—you are a terrible cook. I'm going to have to let you go. But hey, from what I heard during the remodel, you are a pretty good laborer. Maybe you should stick with that."

I couldn't disagree with her. Regrettably, the general contractor couldn't afford to hire me back. At the moment, he said, work was scarce, the holidays were just around the corner, and things were always slow this time of the year. I should just enjoy the time off, he advised. I wished I could. After paying rent, the bills, and purchasing much-needed parts for the truck, I was far from setting up a bank account.

It was Christmas Eve, so I splurged. I bought a case of good beer for myself and two packs of hotdogs for Hank. Sitting on the floor of the completely unfurnished living room, building a pyramid out of empty beer bottles, and throwing chunks of hot dogs to Hank, I wondered how in the hell I was going to get out of this unchanging mess. A few days later, the phone rang, and my problem was solved. Just not the way I had hoped.

"Dan, it's Frank."

"Who?"

"Frank Stoney. From Stoney's Real Estate?"

"Oh, hey, Mr. Stoney. What's up?"

"Remember when you moved in I told you the place was for sale, right?"

"Yeah, vaguely."

"Well, it's been on the market for forever and a day, so I didn't figure it'd ever sell. But an investor who looked at it several months ago called me up last week and told me he had decided to buy it. So it's a shitty deal, but you got to be out by the end of the month."

"You mean the end of this month? Like in *five days?*"

"Afraid so, kiddo. It's going to take a month to get the place up to scratch, and he wants his tenants in there by February. Listen, I feel really bad about this, and I'll do my best to find you something else, but it being this time of year and all…"

"Wasn't there something in my lease about you having to give me notice or something?" I pleaded.

"You didn't really read the lease, did you? Hey, don't feel bad—no one ever does. The answer to your question is no."

"That sucks."

"Yeah, it's a raw deal, but that's life, huh? I'd appreciate it if you would drop the key off next week."

"Yeah, okay, I guess."

"Hey, happy holidays anyway."

I was at a loss. Sadly, it was a very familiar feeling. In times past, when I had found myself in such dire straits, I could always count on the support of friends and family. That didn't exist here. The only family I had was Hank, and I didn't have any friends. I hardly had any acquaintances. Let's see, there was Mr. Stoney, for all the help he had been. There was Anzu, the lodge owner, but the mess I made of her kitchen hadn't exactly endeared her to me. And, of course, there was Wayne, but I had already barked up that tree. I had gotten to know a few of the other construction workers, but they all seemed to be older and married. Except for one guy...what the hell was his name? He was about my age, and I'm pretty sure he lived in the area. The problem was, I had never gotten to know him very well. He only worked for Wayne for a couple of weeks before he quit. I rifled through the piles of my scattered belongings. I was pretty sure he had given me his phone number. After a half hour of searching, I came across a scrap of paper with the name Jeff on it, followed by a local phone number. With nothing to lose, I picked up the phone and dialed the number.

"Hello," a girl answered.

"Hi, can I speak with Jeff?"

"Just a second." With the phone still near her mouth, she yelled, "Jeff! Jeff! Well, what do you think? Yeah, it's for you."

"Hello."

"Hey Jeff, this is Dan. We met working at the lodge." I prayed he would recognize me.

"How ya doing, man? Still working down there?"

"No, it's over." I related the story of my failed cooking career.

"Ha, that's funny. So what are you up to now?"

"Not a whole hell of a lot. In fact, the place I'm renting sold, and I have to move out, so I'm trying to find somewhere else. I was wondering if you had any ideas?"

"Wow, that's a trip that you just said that because me and Sandy were just talking about needing someone to move in. Making rent has been a bit tight. You interested?"

"You bet I am."

I took a meandering drive out to their place the following morning, and my enthusiasm quickly fizzled. Although it was a fairly new house, tucked back in the forest at the end of a gravel road, it was absolutely tiny. It couldn't have been much more than a thousand square feet. Worse, I found my assumption that Jeff and Sandy were the only occupants to be faulty, for when I entered the place, I was introduced to Sandy's two younger brothers, Royal and Chad. During the thirty-second tour, I noticed there were only two puny bedrooms. Sandy informed me that if I moved in, Chad and I could share one of the bedrooms, while she, Jeff, and Royal would gang up in the other.

"Your rent would be a hundred-fifty a month, plus your share of the power and phone," Jeff said.

"I have a dog; is that okay?" I asked, half hoping it would blow the deal and half hoping it wouldn't.

"Sure, we have three. They're outside somewhere."

Five people and four dogs in this house—this is going to be a nightmare.

"Sounds great. When can I move in?"

At some point during the first week, it fully sank in how incredibly dismal my new situation was. We lived twenty miles outside of Wasilla, basically in the middle of nowhere. The sun only illuminated the snowy landscape for a scant five hours a day. The mercury in the thermometer seemed to be permanently stuck at the zero mark. None of us had jobs. And everyone but me was stoned senseless every waking moment. It didn't take the passage of too many days before I was suicidal. It would be a mercy killing. If only...

At first, I whiled away the days in sullen silence, grasping at any task that would keep me occupied. I chopped firewood for the wood stove, crudely butchered half of a caribou someone had given Jeff, stitched up my clothes the best I could, and took Hank for short walks. The others passed the time creating perpetual clouds of pot smoke. One morning, I woke up and felt as though I'd go insane if I stayed there a moment longer, so I drove into town.

During the drive, my resolve to find a job renewed itself. I was not going to return empty handed! Five hours and twenty familiar stores later, I was as unemployed as ever.

With the sun dipping below the mountains, I found myself in a shop that sold tree-harvesting equipment. They weren't hiring either. Defeated, I rejoined Hank in the truck. I took out my wallet and made the daily count of my remaining funds—$1,152. I stuffed the money back into my wallet. Staring blankly through the windshield, I felt a tear travel down my cheek. And then I felt another. There was no stopping it now. Four months of misery poured from my eyes. I put my hands to my face and felt Hank's muzzle worming its way beneath my arm. Before I knew it, he had pushed his way onto my lap and was licking my face. I laughed through my tears and gave him a big hug.

"I'm sorry I brought us to this godforsaken place."

I took several deep breaths and slowly collected myself. "God, how am I going to get us out of this? There must be some way to make some money. Sell blood? Sign up for a few medical experiments? Hell, I don't know."

Just then, a light flickered, and suddenly the small parking lot was bathed in yellow rays coming from the Curt's Chainsaws and Accessories sign. As I stared at it, an idea took shape. Why not? I had nothing to lose. It was a product people always needed, and it wouldn't require much equipment to get started.

"Stay here, buddy." I shoved my wallet into my pocket and ran back into the store.

I returned thirty minutes later, cradling a well-kept used chainsaw. It cost $302, including two files, oil, an extra chain, and a gas can. For the first time in a long time, I felt happy.

Locating a place to legally harvest trees was by far the easiest thing about my new career. They were virtually in the backyard. After a bit of research, I learned the house was practically surrounded by public land, and obtaining a firewood permit proved to be very simple and cheap. Bundled up in my bulky snowsuit, boots, and earflap hat, I set to work.

The first order of business was finding the right-sized trees—too small and they wouldn't be worth the effort; too big and I wouldn't be able to handle them. Exploring a network of plowed tracks, it soon became evident that I had been preceded by years of woodcutters, and they, of course, had targeted the trees closest to the road. Disappointed but determined, I parked at a random spot, grabbed the saw, and walked into the woods. I made it all of twenty yards before I had to stop and catch my breath.

"This is absurd," I gasped.

The snow was deeper than I had expected. Punching through knee-deep powder is one thing, but this was hard, crusty crotch-deep stuff. I turned and saw Hank walking slowly and deliberately, like a stalking cat, in an effort to stay on top of the fragile layer. He made it a few more steps, and then the shell collapsed, and he was buried up to his neck.

"Hang on; don't panic. I'm coming."

After dragging him free, I threw him over my shoulder and fought my way to the road. After a few minutes of thawing out in front of the truck heater, I got my wind back.

"Well, that's certainly not going to work. You have any ideas?"

As if to answer, he vigorously shook his wet coat, covering everything in the cab with water and fur.

"Thanks." I wiped my face with the back of my glove. "I'll assume that was your vote for waiting for summer. I wish I could, but we need the money now. So how are we going to do this?"

Then, a simple answer occurred to me. Although, I wasn't overjoyed with the idea as it meant spending more money.

"Let's go to town."

The next morning, we were back. After a bit of practice on my newly purchased snowshoes, I grabbed the chainsaw and tromped into the forest, leaving Hank in the truck. A hundred yards from the road, I came upon a suitable stand of trees. Coaxing the cold saw to life, I steadied myself on the unwieldy footwear and cut into a thirty-foot-tall spruce tree, yelling in triumph as I watched it make a quick journey to the ground.

The next few hours were an absolute mess. Limbing a spruce tree on dry, solid ground can be a bit of chore, for a spruce tree has a lot of bushy limbs, but on snowshoes, in low light and freezing temperatures, well, it may not be impossible, but I certainly found it to be very impractical. I threw in the towel as the sun set and headed back to the house. Maybe my brain would thaw out next to the stove and come up with a solution.

The solution was more work. The next day, armed with a snow shovel, I found myself back at the fallen tree. My plan was simple—if there was no solid ground to work on, then create some. I spent the entire day and the next shoveling snow. There was now a thirty-by-ten-foot cleared area plus a path back to the road. I would snowshoe in, cut down a tree, slice it into six-foot lengths, drag them to the cleared area, limb them, drag them to the truck, and load them. Then I would drive to the house where I would unload it all and cut the logs into one-foot long rounds. Then I would split them with an axe. What could be simpler?

It took roughly two days to convert enough timber into one cord of sellable firewood. I spent the six hours of daylight working in the forest and another six at the house where the porch light provided just enough illumination. The only break in the routine was when a customer would respond to one of the ads I had posted around town. Then, I would load up the truck and deliver and stack a small hill of firewood. I charged eighty dollars a cord, which was thirty dollars below the going rate, as the wood was green.

Over the next two months, I waged my private war against the forest. At the end of eight brutal weeks, I had delivered and collected on twenty-five cords, which netted me two thousand dollars. By the time my expenses and bills were paid, I had $750 stashed in a coffee can, which I squirreled away safely under the house.

It was a bitter couple of months. Every morning, I woke up with yet another stabbing pain. But all the sore muscles, cuts, bruises, and touches of frostbite were sufferable; my place of residence, however, was not.

A description of any given day for my roomies was a description of every day for them. About the time Hank and I returned home to warm up and eat lunch, Chad would wake up on his side of the floor of our bedroom and saunter into the living room where he would light a joint. With the scent of pot wafting down the short hallway, Royal, Jeff, and Sandy would slip out of their communal bed and join Chad in a little wake and bake. The afternoon was wasted away in front of the television and checking the mailbox for Jeff's unemployment check. On the occasional evening, they would pile into Jeff's run-down Buick sedan and go somewhere. They were usually absent for a few hours, which wasn't nearly long enough for me. Upon returning, Jeff would tote in one, sometimes two, bulging trash bag. After Jeff dumped the bags out, a large mound of recently uprooted budding marijuana plants would cover the kitchen table. Jeff's unemployment check was the secondary source of income that kept them alive. By drying and sorting pot plants for local growers, he had managed to find his own form of self-employment. By this time, it was usually past my bedtime. Their laughter and shouts made a peaceful sleep impossible. However, sometime around 2:00 or 3:00 a.m., the place became quiet as they all finally stumbled to bed. Jeff's little clan was as happy as could be.

I was still pondering suicide.

❖

"Dan! Hey, Dan! *Hey*!" Sandy was standing on the porch, waving her arms. I killed the chainsaw. "Hey, you got a phone call."

"Okay, thanks. I'll be right there." I knocked the snow and sawdust from my boots and went inside. I hoped it was another firewood order.

"Hello?"

"Hi. Dan?"

"Yes."

"This is Amy down at The Pantry restaurant. I'm calling because I need a dishwasher, and your application came up. Are you interested?"

"Yes, I'm very interested," I excitedly answered.

"Do you remember where we're located?"

"I think so, right next to the snow machine shop, right?"

"That's right. Can you come down this afternoon?"

"No problem."

I landed the job. It was part time, but the money worked out to be about the same as I had been making; plus it had the added benefit of free food, and the risk of cutting off a limb was much, much lower. I never would have believed I would be so giddy to get a part-time dishwashing job. It was a sublime moment.

The food was great, and the employees were nice enough. One evening, while chatting with one of the waitresses, I mentioned I was seeking a new place to live. The following afternoon, she showed up to work with a friend and called me out front.

"Dan, this is Val. She has a place to rent, and I told her you might be interested, so here she is," she said. "I'll let you guys talk. I've got to get changed."

"So I hear you're pretty desperate to find a new place to live?"

"Pretty much, yeah."

"Listen, I have a trailer; actually my boyfriend sort of inherited it last year. Anyway, we haven't really thought about the rent. It's, well, it's…why don't you just come by after you're done here and see what you think."

"Is there a problem with me having a dog?"

"No." She chuckled. "That doesn't matter."

I met her later that evening at the trailer. It was situated in the heart of a chaotic jumble of other mobile homes. The dwellings I observed driving in could only be described as third world. The truck's headlights moved through a landscape of discarded appliances, abandoned shopping carts, rusty hot-water tanks, and wrecked cars. Maybe the one she is renting is one of the better ones?

It wasn't.

"It's unlocked. Go in and take a look. I have to get this kid changed. I'll be back in a few. I just live around the corner." She hustled the screaming child back to her car and drove away.

I stepped onto a very small rotten deck and managed to force open the sticking front door. I was in the kitchen, or what I gathered to be the kitchen. The horizontal refrigerator in the middle of the room gave me a clue. There were two windows. One had clear plastic stapled over it; the other didn't. It was just a big hole in the wall. Snow had blown in and drifted across the counter, partially burying the sink. Shaking my head, I turned to my left. There stood a wood stove, which appeared to be intact. It was upright at least. Farther back, I viewed the scattered remains of what I deduced was the bathroom. Beyond that was the back wall and a door. I counted four more windows as I strolled out of the entryway. They all had tattered plastic in their frames instead of glass. Stepping over a chunk of ice, I made my way to the remains of the bathroom.

It looked like a bomb had gone off. Taking note of the patchy flooring, I clearly saw where the walls used to be, but I couldn't even begin to imagine where they had gone, or why. A corner shower stall stood all alone. There was no sink or vanity. I kicked the remains of a toilet aside and turned the shower valve to the on position. Nothing came out. I wasn't surprised.

The rear area was full of empty boxes and miscellaneous garbage. I grappled with the door in the back wall until it snapped open and revealed the guts of a small lean-to. On the slanting floor sat a rust-splotched water heater and pressure tank. Both of them were covered with a dense layer of ice crystals. I shut the door and walked back to the kitchen. That about concluded the inspection, I reckoned. Just then, Val banged her way in.

"So what do you think? Do you want it or what?"

"Well…" I was dazed. It took me a second to locate my thoughts. "You want *me* to pay *you* for this?"

"Yeah, I know it's not in the greatest shape, but the roof doesn't leak, it has power, and there's a lot of land around it."

I laughed.

"Look, what you see is what you get. I thought you were in a bit of a bind. I was just trying to help you out."

"God, I must be completely off my nut." I hadn't meant to say that out loud. She shot me a dirty look.

"Well?"

"Oh hell." I closed my eyes and pinched the back of my neck.

"I don't have all night, you know."

"What's the rent?"
"How does a hundred bucks a month sound?"
"Make it seventy-five, and you got a deal."

Chapter Seventeen

Intestinal Fortitude

My shift from the domicile of dope to the trailer of trash was complete. The only stop I made during the move was the liquor store, where I sprung for a cheap bottle of whiskey. I'd never cared much for the stuff, but it felt like the right time to learn.

Sitting on the refrigerator in my torn-up coat and badly worn mittens, I watched Hank sniff out his new surroundings. I sure have a knack for finding five-star accommodations, I thought. I may have outdone myself this time. God, a pizza would be awesome right about now. I took another long, throat-burning pull off the bottle. How about a nice warm beach and a couple of palm trees...

"Stop it, stop it, stop it."

I had to stop myself before I was truly drunk. If I didn't, there was the real possibility of freezing to death. Although they say it's one of the least painful ways to die...

"*Stop it!*"

I screwed the cap back on the bottle and shuffled over to inspect the wood stove. The glass door was sound and shut tight. The firebox had been cleaned out. All the welds seemed to be holding, and the damper, well, it wouldn't budge. I removed a mitten and gave the flue a rap with my knuckles. It sounded solid.

"Shit."

Three hours and several nips of whiskey later, I had years of creosote buildup cleaned out of the pipes and the whole thing reassembled. I barely had enough energy left to chop up a handful of kindling.

It wasn't long before the logs stubbornly began to release their heat while I curled up in front of the stove with Hank and dreamed of a long white beach and native girls in grass skirts. I woke up five short hours later with the side of my face frozen to the carpet.

My newest nightmare was just beginning.

After my rude awakening, I reduced a pot of snow to water on the wood stove. (The kitchen stove didn't work, surprise, surprise.) I poured half of the steaming liquid into Hank's water bowl and used the rest to thaw my cheek. I rinsed my mouth out with a slug of whiskey and slumped down on my only piece of furniture—the fridge. As I surveyed the wreck before me, it was difficult to know where to begin. As if to answer, a gust of icy wind swirled through the kitchen.

"I guess the windows come first. The stove is next to worthless with a hole every three feet."

I threw another log on the fire and took Hank for a drive to the local hardware store.

I finished just before noon. I had removed the old, torn plastic and replaced it with six layers of new, thicker plastic, three on the inside and three on the outside. Before I completely tacked up the inside sheets, I stuffed the void with wadded-up newspaper. I finished off the crude repair job by firmly duct-taping the inside edges to the frames. Throughout the process, I took breaks and stoked the fire until the firebox glowed bright orange.

Adjusting to the heat, the rickety trailer groaned and popped. It was definitely warming up. Sitting on the floor, splitting a convenience store sandwich with Hank, I deliberated what my next project should be. Which was more important, the shower or the toilet? Neither, I realized, looking at my diminished pile of firewood. I shoved the last of the meal in my mouth, picked up the axe, and headed outside with Hank in tow.

Earlier, while I was outside nailing cleats over the plastic, I noticed a pile of logs sticking out of a drift next to the trailer. It seemed like a lucky break since the meager supply of wood I had brought with me was all but gone. I bent down and grabbed one, but it resisted. I tried another, but it wouldn't budge either. I cleared the snow away and discovered why they were being so stubborn. Over time, snow melt from the roof had dripped and refrozen, encasing the entire pile in a miniglacier.

"Great, just great," I yelled.

Somewhere close by, several dogs responded to my frustration with barks and howls.

Two hours of axe swinging yielded five medium-sized logs. I hauled them inside and dropped them next to the stove to thaw out.

With more than a night's worth of firewood secured, I decided my next task should be the toilet. The flange seemed to be intact, but upon closer inspection, I could see that the pipe connected to it was completely broken off just below floor level. It looked like I was going to have to go underneath. After locating the access hole, I found my flashlight and stuck my head down to have a peek. It was difficult to judge the height of the crawl space due to the thick ground covering of frozen garbage. Beer cans, cereal boxes, rusty scraps of metal, fast food containers, and a diaper, among other things, appeared from the darkness as I swung the beam of light in a circle. Curious about the hole in the floor, I heard the pitter-patter of Hank's paws above as he trotted over and dropped his head down next to mine.

He sniffed the air. Perhaps even through the deep freeze he could still pick up the odor; fortunately, I could not.

"It just keeps getting better and better, eh?" I moved aside the trash that had been deposited directly below until I reached dirt. "Damn."

I had hoped the layer of rubbish would have been deeper than a few inches, thus increasing the distance between the ground and the floor. What a twisted bit of wishing that was! The crawl space was all of twenty inches deep. Christ, let's get to it.

I zipped on my snowsuit, tied my hat strings tightly around my chin, and put on a pair of work gloves. Groaning, I slithered down into the narrow space, taking with me the flashlight, several large squares of plastic, and a half roll of duct tape, which were left over from the windows. Lying on my back, I wiggled my way through the frigid, confined space, dodging rusty nails, cobwebs, and exposed wiring. I collected and wrapped up items in the plastic that would have weakened even the staunchest of stomachs. With the flashlight resting on my chest, I pushed across the dirt toward the bathroom, the only patch I hadn't freed of debris. Beginning to feel the effects of claustrophobia and extremely anxious to finish the hellish task, I pushed too far too fast. The top of my head rammed into something solid. I rolled over onto my stomach, almost getting wedged sideways in the process, and lit up the area in front of my face.

"What the hell is that?"

I tapped it with the flashlight. It was rock hard. It looked like a foot-tall brown volcano. Protruding from one side was a large broken pipe. It was the toilet pipe. Which means this thing I nearly have my face pressed against is...

"*Aaaaaaah*!"

I propelled my body out of the crawl space in a frenzy, striking my face in the process, cutting a deep gash down my right cheek.

I was done working for the day.

I spent the remainder of the evening sitting in front of the fire, petting Hank with one hand and pressing a blood-soaked cloth to my head with the other, wondering if I shouldn't call my parents, ask to borrow some money, and fly back down to the sanity of the lower forty-eight states. If I had had a telephone, I'm quite sure I would have placed that call.

The next day, it was time to return to The Pantry and wash dishes for a few hours. I'd never been so eager to get to a job in my life. The constant seventy degrees of the restaurant felt like a massage. I washed every part of my body I could fit under the steaming hand sprayer and gorged on the half-eaten meals that slid past. But the bliss was short lived. My shift soon ended, and I was forced to go home.

My primary concern remained avoiding hypothermia. I pushed my back muscles to the limit hour after hour until I had freed virtually every log from the bastardly hill of ice. Once split and stacked, they amounted to nearly a cord and a half, enough to last the rest of the winter if I was very frugal.

Next, I attacked the kitchen. I reinforced the lower cabinets, reattached missing drawer faces and cupboard doors, set the refrigerator upright and plugged it in (and it worked!), replaced the ceiling light, scrubbed the floor, and whitewashed the filthy walls. Earlier, while shoveling snow, I uncovered a large propane tank, the weight of which suggested it was nearly full. So I cleaned it up and screwed the line onto it. I returned inside and lit the stove. Amazingly, all but one of the burners functioned. Now if I could get the sink operational, I would have a fully functioning kitchen, but that required going back down into the crawl space. That was certainly something I did *not* want to do. I suppose that's why I had started fixing up the kitchen in lieu of the bathroom. Unhappily, it looked like I had reached the point where I could no longer avoid it. So I mustered up all of my remaining courage and returned to the miniature hell that existed beneath my feet.

Aside from working a few hours each day at the restaurant, feeding Hank, keeping the fire burning, melting snow, and giving myself a nightly sponge bath, I spent all of my time over the next several days on my back, freezing, cussing, and fighting off claustrophobia. It was like a plumber high on PCP had done his worst. Every pipe, both supply and waste, was either broken, frozen solid, or hooked up wrong. The repairs would have gone much faster if I had known what I was doing, but I learned along the way, disassembling and reassembling the entire system, inch by inch, until at last I felt confident enough to open up a faucet.

Nothing came out, not even air.

I attacked it for another four hours with the same miserable results. Water should have been pouring out of the damn thing, but it wasn't. Then an original thought tore through my exasperated thinking. What if the line from the well to the trailer is frozen? Perhaps even the well itself isn't functioning? The only problem was I had no idea where the well was, and I sure as hell wasn't going to shovel hundreds of cubic feet of snow looking for it.

I decided to walk Hank over to Val's trailer and ask her. She never did mention exactly where she lived, but driving in and out of the impoverished neighborhood, I had noticed her beat-up Firebird parked beside a trailer only a few blocks away. As I passed the adjacent dwelling, the twenty or so dogs that were chained up around it went wild when they spotted Hank. Hank did nothing more than eye them and continue walking by my side. Before we could make our way past the wailing confusion, the door swung open and a wiry, unshaven guy popped forth.

"Shut the fuck up! Don't make me come down there and give you all a whackin'!" The pack simmered down a notch. "Hey, how's it goin'?" he hollered in my direction. "Are you the guy who moved in next door?"

"Yep, that's right."

"Hang on. I'll be right out." He disappeared back inside the ramshackle mobile home.

I straddled Hank and furiously scratched the scruff of his neck. He loved that. A moment later, the guy made his way to where we stood. He was wearing a pair of dirty trousers, Mickey Mouse slippers, and a T-shirt.

"Sorry 'bout the dogs; when they get goin' it's hard to get 'em to shut up," he said. "I'm Joey."

"Dan," I replied, sticking out a mitten.

"So when'd ya move in?"

"A couple weeks ago."

"Jerry and Val own that place, don't they?"

"Yeah. Actually I was just headed over there to try to find out where the well is." He looked confused, so I added, "I can't get any running water."

"Oh, the lines are probably froze up," he said in an experienced tone.

"Yeah, well, I spent a ton of time underneath that bastard, and all the lines are clear now. There's no water in them to freeze, so I figured the well was screwed or something."

"Nice dog." He reached down and gave Hank a pet. "I can show you where the wellhead is if you want."

"Sure, that'd be awesome."

We skirted around the outer edge of his four-legged prisoners and pushed into a large patch of willows that separated our two places.

"It's in here somewhere. Here it is, I think."

We kicked aside a couple feet of snow, me with my boots, Joey with his slippers, until we uncovered a large black pipe that emerged from the earth.

"That's it, I'm pretty sure."

"Cool, thanks, man. What's that hose coming out of the top?"

"Don't know. Could be the way they have it rigged. It's probably the line going to the house. Bet it's frozen, and that's your problem."

"Bummer."

"Just see if you can't get it loose and take it inside to thaw out. Then you should be good to go."

"Yeah, okay."

"I'm freezing my butt off. I'm goin' back in. If it screws with you, let me know. Becky and me probably got a spare hose somewhere."

"Thanks for the help."

"Nice meetin' ya." He hugged himself tight and jogged back through his dog pack, which went nuts again. "Shut the fuck up!"

I retrieved a shovel and started digging. I didn't have to remove too much snow to understand Joey's theory. The hose came out of the top of the well and then made its way to the trailer *on top* of the ground. I assumed it would be buried. I mean, why the hell wouldn't a person bury it? It's not like they wouldn't know it was going to freeze for seven or eight months out of the year.

"Somebody ought to be paying *me* to live in this dump," I grumbled.

It might have taken an hour—it may have been four. I was too pissed off to care, but at last, I had the hose uncovered from the house to the wellhead. In places, it lifted right off the ground; in other spots, it was trapped below thick pools of ice. I couldn't very well chip it out with the axe or I'd risk cutting it. So I devised another plan. It was to be the easiest chore I had done in weeks. I packed every pot and pan I owned with snow and sat in the warmth of the trailer, watching the stove slowly turn them into boiling water. Then I ran outside and dumped them on the ice and down the pipe, quickly refilling them and hustling back inside. It wasn't a quick process, and I was glad about that. Hank and I passed the time wrestling around on the floor and playing tug of war.

Ultimately, the thirty-foot length of hose pulled free, and I was able to drag it inside. I stoked the fire and called it a day. I cracked a can of cheap beer for myself and a can of expensive dog food for Hank.

"Who knows, maybe tomorrow we'll actually have running water."

The next day, I awoke with all the anticipation of an eight-year-old on Christmas morning. I felt my quest for an operational plumbing system was about to be realized. I coiled up the now-limber hose and lugged it outside.

I was back inside within seconds.

"Holy shit, it's cold."

It had to be at least ten below zero; worse, it was blowing a gale. I pulled on another layer of clothing and asked Hank if he was coming. He didn't move from the pile of clothes he was lying on. He wasn't stupid.

I dropped my head and pushed into the wind. The glacial air seemed to be injected straight into my flesh. Luckily, reattaching the hose only required a few minutes, and soon I found myself back in front of the toasty fire.

"Th-th-thaat w-w-w-wa-sn't very f-fun, H-h-hank."

Once my limbs stopped convulsing, I flipped the circuit breaker for the well and hot-water tank and went to the kitchen sink and turned on the faucet.

Nothing happened.

I gave it a few minutes. Still nothing happened. I gave it a bit more time. Nothing, nada, zip.

I was about to fly into a rage and rip the sink out of the counter, when I heard a spurt. All at once, ice-laced water gushed forth.

"*We have water! We have water!*" I felt the sting of joy in my eyes. "For the love of God, we have water."

The following morning, the monumental accomplishment was savagely erased when the tap refused to produce water. I was heartsick. The wind hadn't eased, and the temperature remained well below zero when I checked the hose. It was frozen.

Of course it was. How stupid could I be? You left a hose full of water out in this weather—what did you expect would happen, dumbass? But what could I do about it? It was just going to keep happening over and over. I was bamboozled. The only thing I could think of doing was asking Joey.

A petite girl with cropped brown hair and big, round glasses answered my knock. "Yes?"

"Hi, I'm Dan from next door. I was wondering if I could speak to Joey," I said loudly, competing with a noisy rush of wind.

"Oh hi. Come in; we're letting all the heat out."

I slipped inside and found myself standing in the middle of a bizarre zoo. There seemed to be animals of all kinds penned up in every corner of the place, but my attention was drawn away before I could take it all in.

"Hey, Dan," Joey said, appearing from some back room. "Is it cold out or what?"

"It's pretty damn chilly."

"Oh, uh, Dan, this is my girlfriend, Becky."

"Hi," she said shyly.

"Nice to meet you."

"So what brings you out in this weather?" he asked.

I explained how he had been right about the hose, and I had followed his instructions and managed to get the water flowing, but today it was frozen again.

"Oh," he said with a snicker. "Sorry, I figured you knew. You can't turn the water completely off once you get it going."

"What'd you mean?"

"Follow me."

We walked into the kitchen. It was a wreck. There were boxes stacked in front of the lower cabinets, and the countertops were heaped with dishes, empty food containers, and a couple of bongs.

"See, you've got to leave the faucet trickling like

this."

A steady line of water flowed out of the nozzle, cascading down the side of a mountain of dirty dishes.

"If the water is always moving through the pipes, they can't freeze. When it gets butt cold like this, you want to turn it up a notch, because if it's only dripping, they'll still freeze."

"So you leave it running all winter?"

"From October until April," Becky quietly chimed in.

"Wow."

"I don't know if you already thought about this, but"—he gave Becky a sideways glance—"you know the pipes underneath will be frozen now too."

I closed my eyes and rubbed my forehead.

"Fuck."

I was back to square one. I couldn't believe it.

In a mood as rotten as I had ever experienced, I slid back down into the pit. I didn't have to be at the restaurant the next day, so I worked through the night. Fuck it. Time didn't matter in the crawl space anyway. It was an uncaring black coffin of agony. Methodically, I disassembled the entire system, removed the ice, and put it all back together. I even carried on further, removing the remaining rubbish and the poo volcano under the bathroom. Why not? It couldn't get any worse than it was. When I finished at long last, I pulled myself from the hole and crawled into my sleeping bag, filth and all.

When I unhappily regained consciousness, I picked up some pipe insulation at the hardware store and forced my sore body to go through the routine of thawing out the line to the house. When I had it reattached, I wrapped the entire length with the insulation and buried it with snow.

I opened up the faucet and sat down on the kitchen floor until eventually the water began to flow once more. There was no cheering this time. I left a steady stream flowing and went back to sleep.

An hour or so into my much-needed and well-deserved nap, the front door nearly left its hinges as someone on the other side forcefully banged on it. The noise didn't startle me—the fact a person was actually knocking on my door did, however. Must be Joey, I thought. I thrashed my way out of my stinking sleeping bag, zipped up my coat, told Hank to stay put, and opened the door. At first, the huge bulk of a man who was wrapped up tight in a large green parka didn't register, but as he pulled the fur-ringed hood back, I instantly recognized his square jaw, bent nose, and bushy mop of brown hair. It was Wayne, the contractor.

"Wow. Wayne." I truly never expected to see him again, let alone at the rotten stoop of my door.

"Hey, let me in. It's frickin' cold."

"Yeah, sure, come in."

While he removed his gloves, he glanced around the place. For days I had felt so proud of my recent victories, but now, as we both gave my home the once-over, I was awash in waves of shame and embarrassment. It looked like a homeless person had broken in and was squatting for the winter. I wished like hell I hadn't opened the door.

"Hey, Hank, come here." He trotted over and was rewarded with a scratch. "You're a tough guy to find."

"Uh, yeah, haven't quite gotten to the point of getting a phone yet," I said, staring at the brown-stained socks I had on. "How'd you find me?"

"I had Jeff's number on file, and he told me where

you worked, and I called there. A girl gave me directions. She sounded good looking." He flashed a brief smile.

"Oh."

"I've got quite a bit of work happening at the Dimond Center, and I could use your help. You up for it?"

"Yeah, sure, you bet."

"It's twelve bucks an hour. We start at six in the morning."

"Okay."

He reached inside the flap of his jacket and produced a palm-sized tin. The type cigarettes were sold in ages ago. He pushed aside a couple of empty dog-food cans, set it down on the countertop, popped open the lid, and lifted out a small wooden pipe.

"Let's have us a puff."

He removed a small bud from the box and, using one of his large thumbs, packed it tight into the bowl.

There wasn't much I could say.

After we passed the pipe back and forth a million or so times, he said, "I've got to get home to Tammy. I'll see you Monday morning, chief."

I didn't respond. For the moment, I found it impossible to speak. I just stood there, leaning against the counter with a stupid grin plastered on my face, listening to my racing heartbeat. It seemed like an hour had passed since I had heard Wayne's voice. There were so many dog-food cans on the counter. Why hadn't I thrown them out? Boy, I could go for some gas station nachos right about now—

"Hey, I'm going. Here's my home number. I'll see you Monday."

"Yep, yep, that sounds really pretty good."

I, of course, spent the rest of the night stoned out of my melon. Watching flames dance around in the wood stove seemed to fill in the bulk of it. Eventually, I shut off the lights and turned in. Lying there, my brain whirled around, asking question after question. The last one I remember was, "What the hell is the Dimond Center?"

"I really hate giving you such short notice." I really did feel terrible about it.

"I've owned this restaurant for a long time," she said. "People come, and people go. At least you have a decent reason for doing so. You were a good dishwasher, but let's be honest—it isn't much of a career path. If this construction gig doesn't pan out, let me know; there's always a place here for you."

"I appreciate that."

After exchanging good-byes with the waitresses and cook, I made my way across the street to a public phone and dialed Wayne's number.

"Yeah?"

"Hi. Wayne? It's Dan. Hey, I forgot to ask you how to get to the Dimond Center."

"It's in south Anchorage…" And he explained how to get there and also clued me in that it was a large shopping mall.

I spent the weekend devoted to my ceaseless hobby. The enemy this time was the shower. After the trials of the plumbing system, I found it to be a pathetic opponent. I was jubilant. By Sunday afternoon, I had a working shower. The drain was leaking below, the handle was held on with wire, and the curtain was a couple of trash bags taped together, but I could easily remedy those things later, for at the moment, I was having the best shower of my life.

The only dire project now was the toilet, and without the use of the restaurant's facilities, it was even more so. But the bucket-and-bag method would have to suffice for a while longer. I had to be in Anchorage in the morning. It was still a city that was virtually foreign to me. I wasn't even sure how long it would take to get to the south side. I had a look at my shredded map and decided it would be at least an hour-and-a-half drive. But first impressions and everything, it would probably be prudent to add a half hour to that. I set the alarm clock, checked the fire, and went to sleep.

"*Beep, beep, beep, beep!*"

"Shut up! Shut up!" I fumbled in the dark until I was able to silence the evil contraption. I stretched and tried to come around. God, I hate mornings. This wasn't morning—night was more like it. The glowing-red numbers of the clock read 3:45. I forced myself out of my sleeping bag, disturbing Hank in the process.

"Oh shit, it's cold." (If I had a dollar for each time I had muttered that…)

I flipped on the light and noticed the wood stove looked dark and empty. I hustled to swap my long johns for a clean pair, threw on my army pants, boots, and three shirts.

As I opened the front door, a waist-high cloud rolled in and engulfed the kitchen. I had never seen anything like it. It was like some special effect trick out of a cheesy horror movie. I snatched the keys from the countertop before the fog swallowed them, hurriedly put on my parka, mittens, and hat, and followed Hank out.

What I saw was truly beautiful. A thick layer of hoar frost covered everything in sight, even the top of the snow. In the completely silent landscape, everything seemed to produce a bluish-white glow amid a patchwork of frozen vapor. The enchantment of the spectacle was short lived, however, as I spent the next ten minutes hacking ice off the truck.

I finally managed to get the driver's side door unstuck and crawled in. A film of ice coated the inside of the windows as well. Once I got the truck idling, the defroster would melt it. I turned the key. The motor repeatedly turned over, but was unable to do anything more than that. I gave it another try with the same results. The only thing I seemed to be accomplishing was draining the battery. I *really* didn't need this problem. In the past, I had found that priming the carburetor had done the trick in similar situations.

I ran back inside, returning with the chainsaw gas can. I popped the hood latch, but the hood remained frozen in place. I put my back into it, but it wouldn't budge. Frustrated, I grabbed the axe from the wood pile, and gave it several good whacks. It flew open, flinging ice chunks in all directions. I shed my mittens, climbed onto the front bumper, and removed the air cleaner assembly. I set the metal housing aside and hopped down. Inexplicably, the housing came with me. Stunned, I lost my balance and ended up on my back. When I pushed myself into a sitting position, I noticed the top of the housing was glued to my right hand. I couldn't let go of it. Taking a closer look, I found three of my fingers were bonded to the top of the large metal disc. Alarmed, I held it down with my left elbow and ripped my hand loose. Two small patches of flesh remained, stuck to it. I turned my hand over and inspected it. Two fingertips were bleeding, but I didn't feel any pain. In fact, I barely had any feeling in either hand. Covered in frost and snow, I got to my feet, grabbed the gas can, and poured a bit of the mixture down the carburetor. I sat back down on the rock-hard truck seat and turned the key.

The engine rumbled to life.

When I was certain it wouldn't die, I jimmied the air cleaner back together and jogged inside, taking Hank with me. I ran cold water over my hand. A mixture of blood and water swirled around the sink before heading down the drain. I glanced at the clock—4:21. Dammit. I had to get going. I dried my hands, jammed my mittens back on, made sure the faucet was running, and left.

Aside from two snowplows I scooted past, I seemed to be the only one traveling down the icy highway. It was a white-knuckle trip as I attempted to stay on schedule by traveling at a speed higher than I probably should have. You're okay; just don't hit the brakes, I reasoned, curling my fingers into a fist in an attempt to stem the bleeding.

After a wrong turn or two, I pulled into the mall parking lot. A large clock on the side of a bank across the street read 6:18/-14°. I arranged Hank's bedding, gave him a quick hug and a couple of dog biscuits, and hurried inside.

Wayne gruffly excused me for being late and within minutes had me hauling sheetrock up three flights of stairs to a space he and several other workers were methodically turning into a dentist's office. When lunch break arrived, Wayne called me into a backroom where half a dozen guys were sitting around, digging into their meals. I had completely forgotten to bring a lunch, so I quietly slinked into a corner and took a seat. When everyone finished eating, Tom, one of the carpenters I had briefly met earlier, lit up a pot pipe and began passing it around.

I didn't fancy carrying drywall the rest of the day on an empty stomach *and* being stoned, so I excused myself. After quickly rebandaging my fingers in the public restroom, I brought Hank some water, to replace his ice bowl, and took him for a very brief walk before returning to work. It was an exhausting day, and I was pleased when I heard the mall's imitation clock tower chime out six bells. Two hours later, we were home.

Without a fire burning all day, the temperature inside the trailer nearly matched that of the outdoors. But water was still trickling out of the faucet, bringing a slight, if fatigued, smile to my lips. After starting the fire, I fed Hank and fixed myself a long-overdue meal. As I was finishing up my third tuna fish sandwich, I went over and checked the fire. It had gone out.

Swell.

It was going on nine o'clock, and all I wanted to do was crash. I didn't have the energy to fight the stove for the next hour, so I went to the kitchen and dug out a cup and filled it with chainsaw gas. I looked in the stove carefully, even poking around with a stick to make certain the fire was definitely out. When I was satisfied, I stuffed a few sheets of newspaper in and flung a handful of kindling on top. I stood back and tossed in the gas.

"*Shiiiiiiiit!*"

With a flash, I was engulfed in flames from the waist up. Instinct took over. I flung myself to the floor, wildly rolling across the living room carpet. The fire was merciful and died with relative ease. I sprung to my feet and rapidly scanned the room. Two walls were on fire. The one directly in front of the stove appeared to be the bigger of the two, so I snatched a blanket off the floor and ran at the flames with the blanket stretched out before me. I pinned it against the wall with my hands and knees until the heat forced me to drop it and step back.

It didn't work.

It was still on fire, and now, so was the blanket. Nearly hysterical, I searched for something else to fight the blaze with, when a picture of a fire extinguisher bolted through my mind. There was one next to the hot-water heater!

I sprinted to the rear of the trailer and ripped open the lean-to door. It was there! I grabbed it and ran back, tearing out the safety pin as I went. I took aim and pulled the trigger. White powder shot forth as I doused the area. When I was confident the fire was out, I ran outside, coughing, and threw myself into a snow bank. While I finished hacking up a lung full of chemicals, Hank appeared, laying his head on my chest.

"Is this day over yet?"

Over the next week, while my eyelashes, an eyebrow, and the hair on my forearms began to regrow, I continued the routine of waking around four, driving to Anchorage, putting in a hard day of labor, and returning home by eight or so. It was grinding, but being in a heated building all day helped. Still, I was quite relieved when Friday ended, and I had two days off.

I had managed to scrounge up some building materials around the job site, including a worn but functioning toilet. So I spent the weekend painting the scorched walls and tackling the rest of the bathroom. By Sunday afternoon, the fire damage had been largely erased, the bathroom now had walls, and best of all, I had a working toilet. It was truly a joy-filled occasion. Hank wolfed down a pack of lunchmeat while I sat on the toilet drinking a beer, flushing it every so often, just so I could hear the happy little noises it made when the water circled down.

That evening, I decided to utilize the new back room the bathroom walls had created. It would be nice to actually have a bedroom. Besides, the days were getting incrementally warmer, and I didn't see the need of sleeping next to the stove anymore. It was an exciting day. I paid a visit to the secondhand shop and went on a spending rampage. I bought a used mattress, a small table, a bookshelf, and a toaster. On my way out, a piece of furniture caught my eye and stopped me dead in my tracks.

I do believe it was love at first sight.

It was the coolest couch I'd ever seen. It was also one of the biggest. It must have been ten-feet long, and it was covered with a tightly woven, grass-green material. It had four big cushions along the back and a smaller one on each side. It didn't appear to have any stains, tears, or holes, and best of all, it had an eighty-dollar price tag stuck to it.

It was an endeavor getting Big Green (the name seemed to fit) into the trailer. At one point, I considered getting out the chainsaw, but thankfully Joey happened by and helped me wrestle the monster into the living room. He made several flattering comments about my shrewd purchase.

That night, Hank and I sprawled out on Big Green, marveling at our reborn home. We had heat, water, a shower, a toilet, a bed, and one hell of a couch.

Life was sweet.

March capitulated to April, and life eased into a routine. Work was arduous, but I made no complaints—it was the steady income I had been lacking for so long. Even the weather was beginning to cooperate. The sun stayed in the sky longer each day and even attempted to produce a little heat. However, before the spring thaw could gain a toehold, winter reasserted itself one last punishing time.

Lately, with nightly temperatures seldom falling below twenty degrees, I had become slack about getting up in the middle of the night and feeding the fire. Instead, I simply stuffed the firebox full before I went to bed and let it burn out during the course of the night. In the morning, the bedroom was chilly but tolerable.

One night, after brushing my teeth and tending to the fire, I retired to the bedroom and made the decision that the time had come to forgo wearing clothes to bed. So I crawled in naked. For the past six months, my body had continually been wrapped up in layer upon layer of clothing. Over time, it had become claustrophobic, so lying there in nothing but my own skin, I felt more free and relaxed than I had in a long time. I was asleep in an instant.

It was a strange dream I was having. It was a jumble of places and people; nothing about it made sense except the one idea that ran throughout it all, like a needle pulling thread, stitching all the disjointed pieces together. And that idea was that I was dying. It was frightening. What an odd dream. There's no light at all, only the sound of someone weeping. Perhaps it wasn't that I was dying but already dead? I'm in a coffin, mourners wailing at my funeral? A constant, dull thumping sound began to rouse me. At first I thought I was still dreaming, but very slowly my conscious brain spoke through the darkness, and I realized I was the cause of the noise.

My body was violently shaking, making the mattress thump and squeak with each jerk. I still thought I must be dreaming, yet some small part of me began to doubt that I was. Things still weren't making much sense. I couldn't seem to fully wake myself up. I knew my whole body was shivering wildly, but I felt little concern. In fact, I felt fine. Then, for reasons I didn't understand, a command blasted through my brain.

"Get up!"

I sat up on the edge of the bed, but no sooner had I shifted my weight to my legs than I collapsed into a heap on the floor. I began to laugh as Hank stood over me, licking my face. I tried to say something witty, but I couldn't seem to work my mouth right. A wave of panic seized me.

Adrenaline shot into my system, and my hazy thoughts quickly sharpened. I was lying in a fetal position on the floor. I could hear my teeth chattering and vaguely sensed my convulsing body. I just couldn't feel anything. I was numb. I attempted to get to my feet but couldn't seem to do it. Jesus, I must be in serious trouble.

"You have to move now!"

I straightened out and rolled over onto my belly. Reaching for carpet, I heaved the weight of my paralyzed body forward, an inch at a time. Hours seemed to pass before I cleared the bathroom doorway. And then my body shut down, refusing to obey me any longer. I swung my arms and legs around, trying to get them to cooperate but to no avail. I'm going to die here! I let out a few wild sobs.

Hank was at my side, whimpering. I tossed an arm around him, and he lay down beside me. I pressed my naked body tightly against his and robbed some of his heat. We remained that way, motionless, for what seemed to be an eternity. I was slipping into dreamland again. I had to snap out of it and try again.

This time I didn't try to drag myself, I simply rolled sideways until I smacked into the base of the stove. I fought my way into a sitting position, raised one of my dead arms, and dropped it on the stove latch. It popped loose. Then I pinched the latch between the knuckles of each hand and pulled the door open. I flailed around in the darkness until I located the stack of newspaper, the lighter, and the pile of kindling. I picked up a few sheets of the paper by pinching them between the back of one hand and the opposing thigh. I managed to awkwardly get most of the sheets to my lap and from there shoved them into the stove. It took a few tries, but finally I was able to scoop up the lighter in my paralyzed fingers. But operating it was hopeless. I had to warm up my hands.

Hank continued his vigil beside me, and I decided to take advantage of his warmth once again. I stuck both hands on his belly and began rubbing them furiously back and forth. I did this for minutes. He never moved a muscle.

The tactic seemed to work, for a stabbing pain shot through both hands. I fumbled the lighter a few times, but eventually my thumb made the right movement, and it spit out a flame. I guided it into the stove. A corner of the newspaper caught. Within moments, it was blazing. I dropped the lighter, scooped up a large handful of kindling, and chucked it in. The flames took hold. I had a fire.

For the rest of the night, I sat in front of the stove, grinding my teeth, as sensation painfully returned to my body. I had plenty of time to wonder how I had reached this state. The temperature had unexpectedly and rapidly dropped that evening. By the light of the fire, I could just make out the thermometer hanging on the kitchen wall. It looked like it was reading ten degrees. Cold, but it sure wasn't the coldest of nights. Somehow I must have rolled out of my covers. That was odd. Stranger still, I hadn't woken up. I just lay there naked, sleeping until I nearly died of hypothermia. I couldn't figure it out. One thing I did know was I would have died if it hadn't been for Hank and that marvelous fury body of his. He was lying next to me, snoring, under several shared blankets. I lifted up a corner and inspected myself. My legs and arms were pure white, like every drop of blood had been drained from them, and the rest of my body was as red as a fire engine. I shifted back under the blankets and rested my head on Hank's back.

"God, how I love you."

A month later and the nightmares of winter truly seemed to be at an end. The Arctic sun increasingly refused to leave the sky, and the numberless snowflakes covering the land lost their grip, slowly trickling into the earth. It felt like spring, and it was about bloody time too.

The dentist office was finished, and it was on to another project at the Dimond Center. This time it was expanding a pet store. A steady paycheck, shorts weather, everything was swimming along nicely. I even got invited to lunch by a cute native girl who worked at one of the many clothing shops. Yep, things were certainly looking up. I only had one small complaint. I'd been having dull stomach pangs on and off over the past week, but I just figured I'd been living off crap food for too long. So I ignored them. Unfortunately, over the next few days, whatever had a hold of my stomach didn't take kindly to being neglected.

One night after work, I was sitting on Big Green watching a fishing show on my newly purchased TV, when out of nowhere one of the most intense pains I had ever experienced tore through my gut. It felt like my stomach was being shredded with a dull knife. The air was instantly sucked out of my lungs. I clutched my belly and doubled over. Seconds later, my bowels expelled the contents of my intestines in a violent fury that should not have been humanly possible. I slid off the couch and staggered in agony to the toilet. My guts exploded again. I bent forward and threw up on the floor.

The rest of the night was spent suffering over the toilet. I drank as much water as I could, trying to replace the volumes of fluid that were jetting out of me. Eventually, I went to bed and woke up the next morning feeling much better. Thankfully, I didn't experience any further outbreaks that day and optimistically surmised it had been a nasty bout of the stomach flu. If I had to have it, I was at least grateful it hit me when it did. For today, I had my first date since the sun was formed.

I shaved, scrubbed myself clean, and went to work dressed in my best set of work clothes. I met Liz promptly at noon at McNewman's—the nicest restaurant the mall offered.

"Hi," she said enthusiastically.

I slid into the bench across from her. "Hi. I hope you haven't been waiting long?"

"Oh, no, I just got here."

And so lunch progressed in a fairly predictable fashion. That is, until I was halfway through my burger and fries. Liz was telling me what it was like for her to grow up in a small village in northern Alaska, when all of a sudden I felt water dripping down my leg. Thinking I must have knocked something over without realizing it, I slyly looked at my lap and to my surprise found only dry pants. Before I could investigate further, my anal sphincter let loose, and a stream of raunchy fluid cascaded down the back of my trousers. It had come with absolutely no warning.

Mother of God, I just shit my pants!

"…and Mom would walk with the other mothers in a group around us kids along the way. Just in case another polar bear did the same thing…"

Okay, she's still talking…good. Oh man, oh man. Oh my God, what the hell am I going to do? Just get a grip. Fuck you! I just shit my pants! You have to get the hell out of here right now!

"...so it was pretty different"—there was a long pause—"growing up there and all."

"Oh, sure, sure, I'm sure it was."

Shifting my weight I could tell it had soaked clear through my jeans and was now working into the fabric of the booth seat. I totally freaked out.

Grabbing my jacket, I said, "Um, you're going to have to excuse me. I have to go now."

While still sitting down, I slipped my jacket around my backside and firmly tied the sleeves around my waist. I got up and ran straight out the back door, weaving through the parking lot.

I dove into the truck. Interrupted in the middle of his nap, Hank sprang to attention.

"Fucking A! I don't think it's the stomach flu."

It was a hellish week. Although the stomach cramps were mild, I had almost no control over my bowels and the waterfalls of liquid that sporadically poured out. I called Wayne and offered an excuse as to why I didn't return to work after my date with Liz, but over the next three days, after bolting off the jobsite ten times a day, I leveled with him and Tom, who was standing nearby. "How long has it been going on for?" Wayne asked.

"I don't know, awhile."

"I can't believe you let loose right in the middle of lunch!" Tom laughed.

"Thanks. Your compassion is overwhelming."

"No wonder Liz has been avoiding all of us," Tom continued.

"Yeah, I reckon that relationship was grounded

before it ever had a chance to fly. I really don't know what to tell you. I've never heard of the stomach flu lasting more than a couple of days. Maybe you just have a really bad case of it," Wayne said, untangling the cord on a router.

"Maybe you have beaver fever," Tom said.

"Beaver what?"

"You know, beaver fever. It's when you drink bad water, water that's got bacteria in it that makes you sick. Like Montezuma's revenge in Mexico. You can get it out of some of the rivers up here."

"Yeah, well, I haven't been to Mexico or been drinking river water, so I don't know how—" I stopped midsentence. "Oh, that goddamn trailer!"

I had the entire weekend to investigate, but as it turned out, I only needed about five minutes to find the root of my illness.

First thing Saturday morning, I hacked my way through the budding willows until I found the wellhead. The disgusting sight smelled terrible. A small stream had cut its way through the soft ground, carrying with it seven months of fecal matter from Joey and Becky's dog pack. It drained off their property to the low spot that just happened to be the dead center of my well. Even though Joey was most likely oblivious to the situation, I was still furious with him. I had lost several pounds over the past ten days. And I was still sick. After all the work to get the plumbing going, only to have it poison me!

I tried to compose myself. It wasn't Joey's fault, not really. It was just this hellhole of a trailer. It was cursed. "I should have let it burn down that night."

I pushed through the bushes.

"Hey, Becky. Is Joey here?"

"Hi, Dan. Yeah, come in."

Joey set down the bong he was smoking. "Hey, cowboy, what's up?"

"Well, Joey, it's like this…" And I strongly expressed my concerns.

"Oh shit, man. Sorry about that. Tell you what, why don't you go down to the store and get four or five gallons of bleach, and I'll get to work on diverting the runoff."

All the fight was drained out of me, along with most of my bodily fluids, so I simply replied, "That sounds good."

I spent another two months in the trailer without it trying to kill me. The brief Alaskan summer had arrived at last, and so far, it had rained every day. Even so, the days were warm, and all my winter worries melted away. The pipes could no longer freeze. My engagements with the wood stove were history. Mountains of dog poop were no longer flowing into my water supply. It was a real treat. Yet I knew I'd be right back in the same situation if I didn't find somewhere less threatening to live before the rain returned to snow.

I continued to work at the mall with Wayne until we completed the pet shop in July. Even though he constantly reminded me he was trying to pin down the next job, it had become apparent the schedule was blank. I was soon to be unemployed. Most likely, I would have been if a bit of slave trading hadn't taken place.

Riding in Wayne's mammoth screw-the-planet truck on our way to the lumberyard, he mentioned that Tom wanted me to call him. I was intrigued. I hadn't seen him in weeks. I had learned he wasn't just a carpenter working for Wayne but a general contractor himself. Work had been slow for him the past winter, so he had been lending Wayne a hand periodically. I called him later that evening from the phone I had finally gotten hooked up in the trailer.

"Hey, Tom. It's Dan. I got a message you wanted to talk to me?"

"Danny!" Tom's friendly voice shot back through the receiver. "How you doing?"

"Good."

"Good. Hey, listen, I talked to Wayne last week, and it didn't seem like he had much work coming up, so I asked him if I could borrow you for a while. I've got a remodeling job starting in a couple of weeks, and I could use you."

"That's great."

"The thing is, it's in Anchor Point."

"Where's that?"

"It's down near Homer."

"Oh." Vague memories of the Homer airport rippled through my mind.

"It's a pretty extensive master-bedroom-and-bath remodel. It should last two, maybe three months. How does fifteen bucks an hour sound to start? Oh and I'll give you a weekly allowance of say a hundred bucks, for food and whatnot. "

I just about fell off Big Green.

"That sounds excellent!"

"There's just one more thing. I couldn't find a place to rent for that short of time, so I'm going to pull my camper down and stay at the campground. It's a great spot, right next to a salmon river. You fish, don't you?"

"I do." I was trying to jump ahead and figure out

what kind of deal-killer bomb he was about to drop.

"So you'll need to get a camper, unless you already have one?"

"No. No, I don't."

"Well you can pick up a used one pretty cheap. You know, the kind that would fit on the back of your pickup?"

"Oh, yeah, right." There went my life savings.

Two weeks later, I was set. My meager possessions were neatly stowed in my new home—a bright-orange-and-blue 1978 truck camper. The only loose end was Big Green. I just couldn't bear the thought of returning her to the secondhand store. As a first and last attempt, I asked Joey and Becky if they would store her for me. To my surprise, they were more than happy to keep the beast in the back of their woodshed.

With that task completed, I left the despicable trailer behind forever. I was headed toward better days.

Chapter Eighteen

Mental

"Looks like it's salmon for dinner again," Tom declared.

I slapped the large fish down on the picnic table. "I caught it, and you know what that means—*you* fillet it."

"Gladly."

The past few weeks had been fantastic. We had the best two spots at the campground, and twenty steps away was a small river teeming with salmon. While Tom began cutting it up, I ducked into my camper to get us a couple of beers.

It was cozy, there was no denying that, but the compact design contained just about everything I could ask for. There was a spacious bed over the cab, a small booth (Hank's bed) and table, and a countertop, which housed a sink and stove. The only thing it lacked was a bathroom, but the campground had those facilities. I dug the beers out of the icebox and returned to the table.

"Beer?"

"Thanks. Hey, this is better beer than I can afford. I

must be paying you too much."

"I think the pay is about right for what we're putting up with."

"She does seem a bit crazy, huh?"

"Yep. But it's only for a couple more months, right?"

The river was frozen. I was not a happy camper, literally. Winter had arrived, and there didn't seem to be an end to the job.

The house we were working on was huge, more mansion than house really. It was an oddity in this out-of-the-way place. Anchor Point was just a wide spot in a road that stretched nearly 250 miles from Anchorage to Homer. There was a general store, a bar, a few small homes, and the campground. I had no idea why the couple we were working for built here; maybe it was because the husband, who was continually at sea captaining cargo vessels, had compromised with his wife—you can build your dream house, but we're putting it near one of Alaska's port towns. Whatever the case, it was clear that Nancy's interest, hobby, and job were the house. Six months after it was completed, she decided to remodel the master bedroom and bathroom. In step me and Tom.

"I can't believe we're tearing out this beautiful fireplace." I was complaining a lot lately. I handed down another bucket of mortar-coated river rocks. "I mean, is it just me? Doesn't this seem just a little bit weird to you?"

He dumped the rocks into the wheelbarrow and handed the bucket back up to me. "Look, we've been over this and over this. This is what Nancy wants, okay? We are here to do a job."

"Yes, to remodel the bedroom. We finished that three weeks ago."

"Hey, work is work. You're making money, so lay off the bitching."

"I'm grateful for the work. I really am. It's just that living at the campground is getting old, and Nancy is driving me nuts. She's always hovering over me, freaking out about something. Did I tell you she started crying yesterday? One minute, she's talking about how she doesn't like the wallpaper in the study, and the next, she just starts bawling her head off."

"Really?"

"Yeah, really."

"Just try to ignore it. As far as the campground is concerned, I've got it covered. It shuts in two weeks, but Nancy turned me on to a local guy who has a place he'll rent us. I'm going to take a look at it on Wednesday."

"I hope he rents it by the week," I griped.

"This just tastes *so* good." She moved a banana back and forth in her mouth, imitating a lewd action.

Tom was hiding behind the scaffolding. "Uh, I'm sure it does. Now, Nancy, I'd really like to discuss the final finish on this," Tom said.

I turned around and walked out of the room. It was easy to disappear in a house that size. She was getting worse. I almost wished she'd go back to the fits of crying. I'm sure Tom did. Lately, she had perked up. I mean, she had really perked up. Mercifully, I seemed to be too young for her, but Tom wasn't. I guess the fact he was married wasn't a problem. Maybe it shouldn't have been. Tom hadn't seen his wife for ages.

It was month seven. Seven months of tearing apart perfectly good rooms and putting them back together. It was truly insane. Every time we finished one project, Nancy immediately came up with another. Tom always acquiesced. Week after week was a repeat of the one before. Tom and I woke in the tiny three-room cabin we shared, ate breakfast in silence, drove five minutes to Nancy's, worked for eight or nine hours, and returned to the cabin where we grunted a few words to each other over dinner. Then the choice was either watch the one fuzzy channel the small TV received or go to bed. It seemed as though it would never change. That it would never end. But then one random day it did.

We pulled up to the house and parked next to Nancy's husband's company truck.

"John's here," I said.

"Uh-huh."

The last time we had seen him was over three months ago when he was home for a week. I let Hank out of the truck, and Tom and I made our way inside.

"Good morning," Tom called out.

"We're in here."

We followed John's voice to the large kitchen. He was seated at the table, stacks of receipts spread before him. Nancy was leaning against the dishwasher, tears streaming down her face.

"Hi, Tom. Hi, Dan. How have you been?"

"Fine, thanks," Tom responded. "It's good to see you, John."

"To be frank, I didn't expect to see you at all. I was quite surprised to find out you two were still here."

Tom didn't have a response.

"I know you were only doing what Nancy was telling you to do, but as far as I was aware, this remodeling business was done and dusted months ago." He shot Nancy a hard look. "I stayed up half the night going through this quite significant pile of invoices. It seems I have spent a small fortune lately."

Tom continued to hold his tongue. Nancy burst into wailing sobs and ran out of the room.

"I noticed you are in the process of redoing one of the basement bathrooms?"

"That's right. Nancy wanted the tile replaced and was unhappy with the vanity," Tom said weakly.

"Does she have you doing any other projects?"

"Dan is painting one of the upstairs bedrooms."

"And that's it?"

"Yes."

"How long will it take you to finish up those two things?"

"A week. Maybe two."

"Fine. I can arrange to be home for the next two weeks to project manage. After that, I'm afraid your work here is done."

Chapter Nineteen

Reunited

The atmosphere between Tom and I lightened a bit those final two weeks at Anchor Point. We were both relieved that our liberation was at hand. Tom was excited to return home to his wife, while I was thankful for the money I had socked away and also for the lessons he had given me.

I was beginning to get the hang of carpentry and a few other trades as well, like painting and taping sheetrock. I wasn't half bad either. Tom believed there was some merit in keeping me employed in the future and decided not to return me to Wayne. However, he thought some time apart first would be a good thing. I agreed. Over the phone, I had fortuitously lined up a pet-friendly rental in Anchorage and would need the time to get situated. I was especially eager to settle in, as Bryan was coming to Alaska. We had spoken on and off over the months, and I had slowly convinced him to leave Fort Collins and move north. I told him how great the place was. I lied a lot. It was selfish, I know, but it was going to be great to have him here.

After examining the place from the truck, I punched through two feet of snow and trudged to the front door. I knocked. An overweight guy, covered in a worn wool coat, greeted me by coughing in my face.

"Sorry, got some sort of bug," he said, dabbing phlegm from his chin. "You must be Dan?"

"Yes." I tried hard not to inhale.

"Come in. I'm Marv. Have a look around. The lease is on the washing machine. Read it over, and sign it if you want." He produced a few more violent coughs and made his way back to the kitchen stove, most of which was scattered on the floor. "Just replacing the element and cleaning it up a bit."

I made a quick circuit of the mobile home. It was outdated, by twenty years or so, with brown shag carpet throughout. Most of the walls were covered in dark paneling, and yellow-and-green curtains adorned with pictures of fruit, specifically pears and apples, framed the windows. Beyond the living room was a narrow hallway, off which were two good-sized bedrooms and a tidy bathroom. There was also a nook in the hallway containing a washer and dryer and a gas furnace, all of which seemed to be in good shape. It was a palace. I signed the lease after thoroughly reading it.

Not long after I moved in, Bryan turned up on the doorstep. He had survived the 2,500-mile journey. It was an impressive feat in a two-wheel-drive Ford Escort in the dead of winter. He told me about it over a meal of king crab and beer.

"The first part of the drive wasn't too bad. It was from Edmonton to Whitehorse that was hairy."

"There's a lot of snow out there, huh?"

"Tons and not much else," he said. "Okay, Hank. It's good to see you too."

He was all over Bryan from the moment he had stepped through the door. I think he was happier to see Bryan than I was. I didn't take it personally.

"One day I drove without seeing anything—no towns, no signs, no cars. It was spooky. I ended up sleeping in the car. I woke up the next day to a foot of new snow."

"What'd you do?"

"There wasn't much I could do. I drove about twenty miles an hour for the next four hours. Finally, I came to some Podunk town, and the road was plowed from there. It was a good thing that place was there; the Escort was running on fumes."

"Well, you made it in one piece. You're here now."

"Yes I am!"

"I know the place isn't much, but trust me on this, it's not so bad."

"It looks fine to me. We could probably use a bit more furniture though."

We were sitting on a couple of camping chairs with a beer crate serving as a table.

"Yeah, there's a Salvation Army store in town. We can head over there at some point and pick up a few things. I do own a pretty sweet couch though."

"Oh yeah? Where is it?"

"An old neighbor of mine is storing it for me. I gave them a call, but the number was disconnected, so I rang this chick who knows them, and she told me where they're living now. I'm pretty sure I can find the place."

"But they still have it, huh?"

"I guess so. Do you feel like going for a drive and finding out, after you've had a day or two to recuperate?"

"Sure, no problem."

I slid the truck to a stop, and we looked down into a depression in the landscape.

"This has got to be it," I said.

"Jesus, man."

The forest had been viciously removed and replaced with something out of a Mad Max movie. The narrow valley was littered with wrecked vehicles of all makes and sizes. Randomly strewn throughout the tumultuous parking lot were refrigerator doors, wood scraps, steel barrels, signs, hills of garbage, and a hoard of other items I couldn't even begin to identify. I estimated there were at least thirty abandoned vehicles, and chained to nearly every one was a dog. It seemed Joey's pack was alive and well—alive anyway.

Somewhere near the center of the carnage was a structure that must have served as the house. It was half buried under snow, but it appeared to be a poorly built shed with a few lean-tos tacked onto it.

"I *really* hope this is the right place," Bryan said.

"We'll soon find out."

Bryan was speechless as we walked down the embankment and into the mess.

The dogs went nuts. We picked our way through the maze, carefully avoiding the howling pack. As we neared the house, I noticed the front door was not a door at all but a thick blanket. Several extension cords ran underneath it. Suddenly it was thrust to one side and out popped Joey, wielding an extremely large handgun.

He didn't say a word, so I quickly broke the silence. "Hey, Joey, it's me, Dan. You know, your old neighbor, Dan?"

It took him a moment, but at last he replied, "Oh, hey, cowboy! I didn't know who was here. I just saw a couple of guys walkin' toward the house. Sorry, didn't mean to scare you." He lowered the gun. "Hey, Becky! It's okay; you can come out. It's Dan."

Her head and shoulders emerged from behind the blanket. "Hi, Dan. Long time no see," she said in that shy voice of hers.

"Yeah, it has been. This is my buddy Bryan; he just moved up here a few days ago."

"Nice to meet you, Bryan. Come on inside. Let's get out of the cold."

I noticed a shocked expression on Bryan's face as Becky made room for us to sit down in the cramped living room. The place looked a lot like their previous home. From floor to ceiling along nearly every wall was something. Scattered among the mundane boxes, dishes, and furniture was Joey and Becky's zoo. There were fish tanks of tarantulas, snakes, and turtles, and cages of birds, rabbits, and mice. Unlike Bryan, the scene didn't startle me, as I was somewhat familiar with it. However, it still amazed me that this odd assortment of animals, several of which should have been dwelling in the tropics, was living in the Arctic, in a shelter no better insulated than a mailbox.

"You guys wanna smoke a bowl?" Joey asked.

"No thanks, I'm good." I had a bit of experience with Joey's ultrastrong homegrown. It took a unique set of circumstances for me to partake. And this wasn't it.

He loaded his bong, took a long hit, and passed it to Bryan. "Smoke up, dude."

As the three of them passed the glass tube back and forth, I questioned Joey about his recent move.

"I got into a little bit of trouble," he said as he coughed.

"*A lot* of trouble," Becky corrected.

"Yeah, well, the short of it is, there's a couple of warrants out for my arrest, so I figured it was best to move somewhere where we could lay low for a while."

"This is my cousin's place," she added.

"No address, no phone, not very many people know we're here. Hey, how did you find us anyway?"

"Val."

"Oh. I knew I shouldn't have told her. That bitch just can't seem to keep her mouth shut."

I glanced at the pistol lying in Joey's lap. The conversation was edging toward the uncomfortable, so I decided to get to the point.

"I've been down on the peninsula for most of the winter, but we're renting a trailer in Anchorage now. We're a bit short in the furniture department and I was just wondering if you still had that big, ugly couch of mine?"

"You bet. I know right where it is."

A few minutes later, we escaped the smoke and odor of the place and followed Joey outside. He picked up a wooden club, and we made our way through the junkyard, Joey whacking a dog or two along the way. "Shut the fuck up!"

Battling debris-infested snowdrifts, we lumbered to the front of a badly rusted school bus. Climbing in, I spotted Big Green right away. She was clear at the back, entombed under a pile of old clothes, boxes, and liquor bottles. Overjoyed, I swiftly pushed my way through the mess, running smack into one of the nastier things I have ever seen. Tucked behind a large roll of carpet was a putrid, rotten chunk of flesh dangling from a hook. It was a marbled mixture of bright green and dull yellow, and it had begun to run liquid in spots, the ooze carving paths down the sides as it dribbled onto the floor. It was preserved, frozen, in this rank state of decay.

"Watch the moose there," Joey said.

He made his way past me and began flinging items off the couch. I wiped a few hairs from my face and joined him.

It took some doing, but we managed to wrestle her out of the bus, only brushing up against the rank carcass twice. Bryan and I carried her through the chaos and up the hill to the truck while Joey walked ahead, clearing a path through the howling dogs.

I shook Joey's hand. "Thanks a bunch for storing it. And for bringing it with you when you moved."

"Not a problem. Bryan, nice to meet you. You guys come back soon; just don't bring anyone with you."

"Sure thing."

As Joey made his way back, I waved to Becky, who was standing in front of the house. I got into the truck and turned to Bryan. His glassy eyes were bright red.

"Welcome to Alaska, buddy."

Chapter Twenty

Recreation

L ife in the new trailer was excellent. Everything worked flawlessly, and thanks to the furnace, it was always warm and dry. Bryan had found employment at a bookstore, and I continued my budding builder's career with Tom. Finally, I had stumbled upon a normal life. At first I found it difficult to adjust to having so much free time, but I soon found ways to occupy myself.

"You sure you don't want to go?" I asked Bryan one final time, stuffing my skates into a duffel bag.

"Not tonight. I'm really getting into this book. I think I'm just going to have a few beers and chill out."

"What about you?" I asked Hank, who was stretched out next to Bryan on Big Green. "You want to come, don't you?"

He didn't look very enthused to leave the warmth of the trailer.

"Okay, guys, see ya later."

When I arrived at the elementary school parking lot, I found, to my disgust, it was full of cars. A kid's hockey team was holding practice. I decided to try a nearby lake. I was in luck. There was nobody around, and it looked like the makeshift rink had just been cleared of snow.

I rushed down to a bench and quickly laced up my skates, inserted a Metallica tape into my Walkman, switched the volume to full, grabbed my hockey stick and puck, and went at it. Until recently, I had never ice-skated in my life. I really enjoyed it but had a lot to learn. That evening, I thought I would concentrate on practicing my puck-handling skills.

I zipped around the rink, knocking the puck back and forth, striving to keep control of it. I seemed to be doing okay, so I picked up the pace a bit. Back and forth the puck went, back and forth...

Without warning, everything ended in a fierce crash.

Lightning exploded through my eyeballs. My headphones and hat flew off, and my neck and back let out a crack as I was violently forced backward. My skull bounced off the ice, and I slid across the rink. When I came to a stop, I curled up into a ball and grabbed the back of my head. Tears formed in my eyes. I lay there for a moment, gritting my teeth and absorbing the pain. As the ringing in my ears faded, I could swear it was replaced by the distinct sound of clomping hooves. I gently rolled to my side and abruptly forgot the pain.

"Back off, man!" I screamed, clumsily getting back onto my skates. I retrieved my hockey stick and held it in front of me like a sword. "Go on, leave!"

I moved out of the way as a large bull moose trotted by and quickly vanished into the surrounding trees. I glided over to the snow berm and plopped down. Fingers of pain coursed through my neck, and my back throbbed. Still, I couldn't keep from laughing. Rear-ending a moose was pretty funny.

Chapter Twenty-One

Tenderfoot

"What do you think about this one?" I asked.
Bryan skimmed the page. "Yeah, that looks fairly promising."

He passed the Alaska fishing guidebook back to me.

"The lake contains a wide variety of species, including grayling, lake trout, burbot, and northern pike," I read.

"What the hell is a burbot?"

"I have no idea. It says there's a well-marked trail just off the highway. It looks like it's a bit of hike but not too bad. What do think? Want to give it a try?"

"Sure."

"Sucker Lake it is then."

The next day, the first of a week's vacation we had both managed to finagle, we packed up our camping and fishing gear at a leisurely pace. It was the middle of June, and the days were nearly endless. I loaded our backpacks into the Escort and told Hank to get in the back.

"We got everything?" Bryan asked, jumping into the driver's seat.

"I believe so. We just need to hit the liquor store and grab some lunch."

"Sounds good. We are out of here."

The two-lane highway leads in a northeasterly direction, hemmed in by the Talkeetna Mountains on one side and the Chugach Mountains on the other. It then rises out of the confined valley and cuts through a vast forested plain, continuing on to the small towns of Glennallen and Tok, ultimately reaching the Yukon border.

"Hey, get the map out. I think we should be getting close."

We had been driving for three hours.

"Let's see." I unfolded the map. "That sign we just passed said forty miles to Glennallen, hmm, so that should put us about here."

I mumbled a few calculations and decided I knew where we were. "Another ten miles, maybe? The book said the trailhead will be on our right."

Taking off his sunglasses, Bryan said, "You know those clouds we noticed earlier are getting bigger, darker too."

"Yeah, they're definitely headed this way in a hurry. I bet they just pass through though."

Twenty minutes later, the first drops of rain splattered against the windshield while we crept along the virtually deserted highway looking for any hint of the trail.

"Maybe we should turn around. We could have missed it."

"I don't think so. Hey, hey, I see something. Stop!"

I jogged down to the ditch, which ran parallel to the road, and inspected my find. Laughing, I held it up so

Bryan could see it from the car. It was a green metal sign, bent and heavily rusted around the edges and riddled with bullet holes. Sucker Lake, with an arrow below, was just discernible.

I got back into the car, wiping the rain from my face.

"So much for a visitor's center," I said, chuckling. "I suppose we're here, but I didn't see anything that looked like a trailhead. What do you think? You want to check it out or wait for the rain to blow over or what?"

"Hey, if we're here, we're here. I mean, it's just a bit of rain. I vote we grab the packs and at least have a good look."

After several minutes of stumbling blindly through the dense bush, we found a path of sorts. It was either a game trail or a long-forgotten human trail, probably both. But it headed in the right direction and kept us out of the worst of the wet brambles.

"It's decision time, huh?" I asked. "Ahead or back?"

"I'm as soaked as I'm going to get. Our gear should stay dry in our packs. I say we go for it. We still have hours of light before we have to find a campsite."

"Lead the way, ace."

Over the next couple of hours, the path grew fainter, until I noticed we were basically cutting our own trail through the dripping forest.

"You sure you know where you're going?"

"I'm just following Hank," Bryan jested. "Yeah, we're still on the trail; it's just really overgrown."

"You must have better eyes than—" The ground

disappeared from beneath my feet. In a flash, I was three feet shorter.

"Dude, help," I squeaked.

"Holy shit! Are you okay?"

I shook my head.

"Okay, okay, just stay still man. Try not to move."

I uttered an affirmative grunt.

"Can you reach my hand? No? Okay, okay. Hey, back off Hank! Look, I can't get any closer; I'm starting to sink. Uh, hang on and try not to move. I'm going to try and find a stick or something. I'll be right back, okay?"

Hank stayed with me, circling my position, whining. I felt like throwing up. I shut my eyes and attempted a few deep breaths. When I opened them again, Bryan was there, clutching a long branch.

"I think this will reach. Yeah, good. Okay, can you grab the end of it? Good. Maybe you can help. Can you push off the bottom with your feet?"

"There isn't one," I wheezed.

"What?" He was puzzled. "Never mind. I'm just going to have to pull like a son of a bitch, and you just hold on as tight as you can. On three, okay?"

I nodded.

"One, two, three!"

Bryan yanked me onto the forest floor.

"Are you all right?"

"I think so." My lower guts ached, and I was drenched from the chest down. "What the hell was that?"

"I don't know. Looks like you fell into some type of boghole or something. I didn't even see it. I must have walked right past it. You were lucky you didn't get swallowed whole. Why didn't you? I mean, if you couldn't feel bottom."

"There's a log in there." I rubbed my groin.

"What do you mean?"

"There's a tree or something stuck in there sideways. I was straddling it. It held me in place, but, God, did I rack the hell out of my nuts when I landed on it."

Bryan started snickering.

I pushed myself into a sitting position, and Hank licked my face.

"It's not funny."

"No, no, sorry, I know it's not," he said, still chuckling.

"Give me a minute. The pain's starting to ease a bit. I need to change my clothes, and then we can get going."

"Sure, sure."

"Man, I hope these bogholes aren't all over the place."

Bryan quit laughing then.

A couple of hours later, we hacked our way to the top of a small hill. We pitched the tent under a large tree where the ground was only damp and free from the undergrowth that engulfed everything.

"Son of a bitch! Is it me, or are the mosquitoes getting worse?"

"No, they're getting worse, a hell of a lot worse," he replied, slapping at the back of his neck.

I could barely manage to get Hank's food and bowls out of his doggy pack, the little bastards were annoying me so much. I stood up and spun in a circle, running my hands down my body.

"Get the hell off me. *Piss off!*"

Bryan slipped on a pair of thin gloves and threw a T-shirt over his exposed head.

"Here, put some more of this on." He tossed me the bug spray.

I doused myself, but it wasn't very effective. There were just too many of them. Hank, as protected as he was, had several drilling into his nose. I wiped them away in a bloody smear.

"Abort. Abort. Dude, just grab everything and chuck into the tent."

We ate our dinner cold that night and turned in early. I for one could use the few extra hours of sleep.

"Will you have a look at that," Bryan said.

It appeared as if the whole of Alaska was laid out before us. We stood at the crest, taking in the scene. The unbroken expanse of the deep-green forest would have gone on forever if not halted by a towering, ice-covered mountain range. The sky was devoid of clouds, and the sun's rays seemed to make the whole image glitter. There wasn't a trace of civilization.

"That is pretty awesome," I said, thoughtlessly scratching at the bites on my arms. "I don't see a lake anywhere though."

Bryan returned to our campsite, which we had packed up a few minutes earlier, and retrieved the guidebook.

"According to this, it should be directly in front of us. I'll bet it's behind one of those low ridges."

"Probably. Let's get going. These bugs are driving me crazy."

A few hours later, while picking our way through a low-lying, marshy area, we happened upon what were quite obviously vehicle tracks. They cut deep into the soft ground and were close together, much too close to have been left by a typical truck. They traversed the small valley and disappeared into the woods.

"Someone has been back here recently."

"And a lot. This looks like a well-traveled road," I remarked. "What do you think? Should we follow it? It would beat the hell out of this bushwhacking stuff."

"It seems to be going in roughly the right direction. Might as well."

It certainly did speed up our journey. The road had been well positioned. It skirted the swamps and hills and traveled along the spine of the ridges where possible. It was at one of these elevated positions we stopped for lunch.

As we admired the view and I finished off a second cup of soup, Bryan brought my attention to an object in the sky.

"What do you reckon that is?"

"I have no idea. Maybe a plane?"

Intrigued, we sat in silence, watching it draw ever closer. Gliding above the treetops, it quickly gained altitude, its unbelievably large wings gently beating the air.

The three of us rose to our feet.

"Damn. It looks prehistoric. That has to be an eight-foot wingspan."

"Minimum," Bryan whispered.

The eagle cocked his white head to one side and appeared to eye us with suspicion as he passed overhead. After a few moments, we realized that was the end of the show.

I was fairly certain we were lost. We continued following the track all afternoon. Periodically, it would wind its way south, which was the direction we were striving for, but inevitably it would curve to the east or west. I was about to voice my objections to continuing on when I heard a faint noise in the distance. Bryan stopped, and Hank's ears shifted forward.

"Sounds like an engine."

We stood listening for several minutes. The hum grew louder until the sound waves echoed loudly through the forest. An odd-looking vehicle emerged from the trees and wheeled its way down the hill facing us. It was cruising at a pretty good clip along the muddy trail, and it didn't take long before it was on us.

As the stubby six-wheeled machine ground to a halt, two small poodles leapt from the back and introduced themselves to a tail-wagging Hank. A man and woman remained seated in the canopy-covered contraption. He was dressed in a clean pair of Carhartt overalls and a black bowler hat, and she wore a frilly blue dress, a large sun hat covering her head.

The man pulled a lever and quieted the machine. "Good evening."

"How you doing?" Bryan replied.

"Sasha. Lucy. Come back here and leave that poor dog alone," the woman demanded of her dogs, who were orbiting Hank, turning him in circles. "Oh, you two are just getting filthy. Come."

They grudgingly left Hank and jumped back into the rear of the vehicle.

"Lovely evening for a stroll. You lads doing some camping I take it?" he inquired.

"Yeah," Bryan said. "We're headed back to Sucker Lake to do a bit of fishing."

"Does this trail lead to the lake?" I questioned.

"No, I'm afraid I've never gotten around to putting

in a road to the lake. It's quite a distance from here," he said.

"Oh." I knew we were lost. "So where does this go then?"

"It essentially makes a large loop around our homestead. How long would you say it is, my dear?"

"Oh, now let's see, from the lodge to Gold Creek and across to Caribou Lake, then back, hmm, I do believe it is twenty-six miles. Does that sound correct?"

"I believe it does. We're just out for our weekly drive, you see."

"Sorry, I didn't realize we were on private land," Bryan said.

"Quite all right. Happy for you to cross it. You'll be back on public land shortly if you intend on getting to the lake. You need to head that way." He pointed at the nearly impenetrable forest to our right.

"So are you sure there's not a trail we could follow?" Bryan asked.

"I'm afraid not. At least not one we've ever seen in the past thirty-one years," he said. "You lads take care; we better be moving along."

"Thanks."

The vehicle roared to life and lurched forward a few feet before coming to a stop and quieting back down. He turned and asked, "Have you seen any bears during your hike?"

"Uh, bears, no, huh-uh," I said. "Uh, why?"

"Just be careful. We've seen more so far this summer than we usually do in a couple of years. They are thick. Just make sure to keep one in the chamber."

Bryan and I shared a worried glance.

"You do have a gun with you, don't you?"

"Uh, no, actually we don't," I meekly replied.

"Well, just be on your guard and make noise. I doubt they'll bother you with that dog of yours around. But my advice would be to pick up one of these." He held up a mean-looking gun, a machine gun really. "It's an SKS Chinese assault rifle. The bayonet comes with it, but you'll need to purchase the thirty-round clip separately. I'd also suggest hollow-point rounds."

"Uh, good to know, thanks," I said.

He hit the throttle. They gave us a cheerful wave and continued on their way. Within moments, the forest returned to its silent state.

"Wow," Bryan said, echoing my thoughts exactly.

"I didn't like the sound of any of that."

"You're not giving up, are you?"

"Well…"

"I think the only thing we need to deal with at the moment is a campsite; it's getting fairly late. Why don't we continue up the hill and find some dryer ground for the night?"

"I guess so," I acquiesced.

"Things will look better after we open up the Jägermeister."

Bryan was right. Reclining in front of a warm fire with half a bottle of seventy-proof alcohol swirling around my belly made all the difference. We laughed at the notion of retreating. The lake would be ours! We'd be eating fish for dinner tomorrow night. Hell, it might even be a burbot!

I finished vomiting and pulled one foot after the other

from the ankle-deep gunk.

"Feel better?"

"That helped." I swatted at the ever-present cloud of bugs and slogged on, bringing up the rear. "The rest of the Jägermeister is all yours."

I have no doubt we were the first two human beings (and dog) to ever travel through this patch of hell. Hacking through the trees wasn't presenting too much of a problem, as the forest had thinned considerably. The hardship was what had replaced it. The countless stagnate ponds, bushes, and rotting logs made most of the terrain impassable. Sticking to narrow strips of soft ground seemed to be the only way through. But the water table was so close to the surface, it was like walking on a moss-covered swimming pool. Our feet drove into the mire several inches with each step. Mindful of our earlier experience with the boghole, we took no chances crossing the worst areas. Instead, we detoured and backtracked regularly.

By early afternoon, we made our way to the top of a low rise. The ground here was dry and solid, a very welcome oasis in the surrounding swamp.

"My God, this is fun." I shed my backpack.

"This will cheer you up. Come have a look."

I walked over to where Bryan and Hank stood. A smile broke across my unshaven face. "That's it, isn't it?"

"Yep."

It was big. It was hard to believe it had remained hidden from view until this point. It looked to be at least three or four miles long. The width was harder to judge. The water diffused into a white haze, blending in with several glaciers that seemed to be sliding off the rugged mountains and into the lake.

"Looks like we made it."

"We're not there yet. We still have to get through

that." I pointed.

We were standing on the last bit of high ground. Between us and the shoreline was another mile of marshland, and it looked even worse than what we had just battled through.

"I don't see any way around it."

"Me either," I agreed. "Back to the same old question—what to do?"

"It's right there, man. We can make it."

"What's that old saying, 'In for a penny, in for a pound?'"

"That's the spirit."

We weren't thirty steps from the base of our recent vantage point, and I knew we were in trouble. Being lighter and a quadruped, Hank was artfully picking his way through the landscape. Bryan and I, however, were not. Each time I planted a foot forward, it sank deep, the ooze clamping tight. It was like walking through a field of glue. Bryan was a few feet ahead, struggling to free his left leg, which was buried to the knee. All of a sudden, the ludicrousness of it all hit me, and I started laughing. In short order, Bryan joined in.

"This is crazy, man! Absolutely nuts."

"I can't..." He could barely get the words out between snorts. "I just can't...I *cannot* get my leg free!"

I totally lost it, watching him yank at his trapped leg with both hands. I was laughing so hard I fell over into a nearby bush.

"It just won't," he howled, "it just won't come free."

"Hang on." I was almost in convulsions. "Hang on.

I'll come and help."

I righted myself and stumbled over to his position. I locked my arms around his leg and gave it a feeble tug. I could barely breathe through the fits of laughter.

"Okay. Just a second. All right, all right. I'm going to pull for real this time. Ready?"

"Just do it, man," he said as he giggled.

I pulled a bit too hard. His leg shot from the muck with a sucking sound, sending both of us to our backs.

"We're gonna die out here," I roared.

Bryan was lying on top of me. Animated, Hank circled.

"No we're not." Bryan twisted off me, fought to his feet, and gave me a hand up. "You are fucking filthy, man," he said, still laughing.

"You should talk. Okay, Hank. It's okay." I gave him a pet and reassured him we hadn't gone mad. "So you really want to keep going?"

"It can't get much worse."

It was painfully slow and the hordes of mosquitoes had found us. We were suddenly at the center of a small galaxy of the bloodsuckers. With one hand, I prodded the nearly liquid ground in front of me with a long stick; the other was in constant motion, slapping my face and neck.

"I've changed my mind. I vote for retreat."

"The ground is getting firmer. I'm serious; it really is," Bryan shouted. He was well ahead. He waited while we caught up.

"See?"

We were standing in eight inches of stinking water, but the ground did feel solid. I was no longer sinking.

"Yeah, it feels like sticky clay or something."

"Come on. We're almost there."

Bryan continued in the lead, quickly outpacing us

again. The water rose with each step. After several minutes, I yelled at him to stop. He turned and looked back. The water was up to his waist.

"Dude! Hank is *swimming*." I waded over and helped him climb out of the water and onto a small island of grass-covered mush.

"But I can see the lake," Bryan shouted back.

"We are *in* the lake!"

He stood motionless for a few moments. Finally, he gave a slight nod of his head and pushed his way back toward us.

It was late evening before we had reclaimed the previous night's campsite. Our reeking, wet clothes and gear hung on a line over the fire. There wasn't much conversation that night.

The next day, it was back into the swamp. Back the way we had come. There wasn't any horseplay today. In fact, it had been a few hours since either of us had spoken, so I was a bit startled when I heard a shout of profanity from behind me. I turned. Bryan stood balanced on one leg, holding a sock-covered foot airborne.

"What happened?"

"The ground ate my boot."

We spent the next fifteen minutes pawing through the deep mud. Try as we might, we just could not find his boot. We searched for another ten minutes with the same results.

"Shit. What are we going to do?"

"Help me get a pair of socks out of my pack," Bryan said.

Leaning on me for support, he pulled them over the

top of the filthy sock he was wearing.

"It will have to do."

We didn't stop for lunch. We didn't stop for anything until we blundered onto the track made by the six-wheeler. It was definitely a different section of the road than we had walked before, but it didn't matter. We were out of the worst of it.

I looked at Bryan. His shirt was caked with mud. He was drenched from the thighs down, and his face was red and puffy from bug bites. I hardly recognized him. Hank wasn't looking much better. His normally shiny coat was brown and slick with marsh water and matted with bits from the forest floor. I'm sure I was looking pretty good too. We had been walking for nine straight hours.

"What's the plan now?" I asked.

"I don't know. Right now I have to check this foot."

We dropped our packs and collapsed onto the wet ground. I watched Bryan peel the shreds of cloth from his foot.

"Oh geez, man." The last piece had fallen away, exposing his raw, swollen foot. I couldn't help but notice several patches of blood. "Boy, that sure doesn't look good. I bet it hurts."

"Oh yeah."

"You know, we're going to have to go a bit farther. As soon as we get back up on dryer ground, I can set up camp, and you can get off that thing. Can you do a bit more?"

"Don't think I have much choice."

"Maybe we can rig up something a bit better than wet socks."

We set to work, and ten minutes later, we checked out our handiwork. It wasn't pretty, but hopefully it would help.

"Stand up on it; see what you think."

"That's not bad." He took a few steps.

"Do you think it will hold together?"

"I don't know, but it's the first time this stupid fishing book has been helpful."

Looking at our patch job, I had to chuckle. His foot was wrapped in the last pair of dry socks either of us had and surrounded by several pages of the guidebook. The front and back covers of the book served as the sole and the whole thing was bound together with fishing line.

"Onward, Hopalong."

"What, what, what?" I wormed out of my sleeping bag. "What is it, Hank?" I reached out in the darkness and tried to nab him, but he was having none of it. He darted back and forth in the confined space, growling loudly.

Bryan was awake and sitting up. "What the hell is going on?"

"I have no idea." I crawled across Bryan's legs and latched onto Hank. "Calm down, buddy."

He was clearly still ruffled, but he quit growling. When relative silence resumed, we could hear noises beyond the tent. A metal pot was making a clanking sound, and I swore I could hear the patter of feet.

"Oh shit, dude, there's something out there."

"What do we do?"

"I don't know."

Just then something brushed up against the side of the tent, causing the fabric to indent briefly. Hank went crazy again.

"We've got to get out of here! Let Hank out. Let

him out!"

I promptly unzipped the tent door, and Hank zoomed out. We followed. It was as dark as it ever got on a summer night, the half-light providing just enough illumination to glimpse the scene unfolding before us. At first I couldn't figure out where Hank was. There were too many of him. Yipping dogs were running everywhere. No, these weren't dogs. They were much too big to be dogs. Bryan started screaming something undecipherable and threw whatever he could lay his hands on at the swiftly moving creatures. I mimicked his actions, bellowing Hank's name. The pandemonium ended in short order as the wolves dispersed into the forest. I continued yelling, "Hank, Hank, Hank." He had vanished too.

I screamed myself hoarse over the next minute. Then we heard a yelp and the undergrowth rustled. Hank popped back into the campsite. We ran over to him. At some point during the fracas, Bryan had grabbed a flashlight. He shined it at Hank. My heart caught in my throat when I spotted the blood-soaked fur on the side of his face.

"Oh, Hank, what happened to you?" I ran my hand over his face. He winced. "Bryan, grab a rag or shirt or something and the water bottle."

I kept Hank seated while Bryan cleaned his face. The top inch of his left ear was gone, and he had a gash under his right eye. Both were bleeding freely.

"Is he okay?"

"I think so," I said. "His ear looks pretty bad though."

"What do you want me to do?"

"Um, what time is it?"

"Hang on." He ducked into the tent and returned holding his watch. "It's one thirty."

"All right, it will be light in two and a half hours. We'll leave then. In the meantime, I'm going to try and get Hank settled down and stop the bleeding. Maybe I can rig up a bandage for his ear. Why don't you start getting our shit together, and it wouldn't hurt if you made some noise. Maybe bang the pots together once in a while, and we should keep talking loudly. Shit, maybe first you should try and find some rocks or a big stick or something in case they come back."

They didn't.

By sunrise, I had Hank's wounds under control, and Bryan had everything packed up. We didn't linger.

By noon, we were completely exhausted, thirsty, and saturated. The only good thing about the downpour was it kept the bugs at bay. Hank seemed to be coping, but I knew he was in pain. Yet there was little more I could do for him. I could say the same about Bryan. At nearly every step he let out a low grunt. For the next seven hours, we traveled through the dank forest like zombies. Then, without any advanced warning, the accursed landscape ceased and we staggered to the edge of the highway. The Escort was nowhere to be seen.

"Aw, come on." Bryan moaned, limping to the center of the quiet road. "Where's the car?"

"Who the hell knows? I guess it could be either direction."

Bryan hopped back to the shoulder and awkwardly sat down on his wet pack.

"Give me the keys. I'll start walking, I don't know, that way I guess."

While I watched Bryan sluggishly dig through his

backpack, a motorhome appeared in the distance.

"Hold on, man, maybe we can narrow things down."

I walked to the middle of the road and waved my arms above my head. The RV rolled to a stop. I walked to the driver's side, noticing the New York license plate as I did so. An elderly man rolled down the window. I could hear the woman in the passenger's seat pleading with him to drive away.

"Sorry to bother you, but I was just wondering if you remember passing a gold Ford Escort on the side of the road?"

"Uh, are you okay, kid?" He had a stunned look.

"The car? Did you see it?"

"Don, just drive!" His nervous companion obviously wasn't happy with the sight of the three of us.

"Look, all I want to know is if you passed a Ford Escort. You know, a little gold-colored car parked on the side of the road."

"Uh, yeah, sure, it's back there about three or four miles." He quickly cranked up the window and sped away.

I staggered over to Bryan. "Give me the fucking keys."

Chapter Twenty-Two

Property Rights

I had lived in Alaska for over four years. Bryan, Hank, and I still shared our comfy trailer. I was still working with Tom, remodeling and building, and Bryan was now the manager at the bookstore. He worked with several other guys our age, most of whom we had become friends with. In the brief summer months, we fished and camped as much as possible (in sensible locations and always with the security of my new SKS assault rifle). During the winter months, we would frequently have sub-zero barbeques, poker parties, and impromptu hockey games at the elementary school.

The previous fall, as a group of us sat around the fire, enjoying what would probably be our last camping trip of the year, we entered into a conversation that would lead to one of the biggest undertakings of my life.

"Yeah, I've thought about it, but I don't know what I'd do with it," Jesse said.

"I know exactly what I'd do," I said. "I'd build a cabin and spend my days on the porch sipping margaritas."

"Easy to say when you're a carpenter. I can't even

build a sand castle. Besides, land is expensive," he replied.

"Land is cheap," Mike informed us. Unlike the rest of us transplants, he had been born and raised in Alaska. "Of course, it depends on where it is and if it has road access and power, but I think you can still find it for a thousand bucks an acre or so."

"Really?" That seemed incredibly low, but then I had never looked into it. "How come you haven't bought any? I mean, if for no other reason than an investment?"

"I don't need to. My dad owns tons of different plots here and there. I'll probably end up inheriting them, unless he sells them all first."

"He's selling some of it?" I queried.

"He mentioned a while back that he was. I can give you guys his number if you want to talk to him about it."

"Not me. Like I said, I'm broke," Jesse stated.

"Count me out," Bryan said. "I'm saving my dough for a house."

I gave him a curious look. His plans were news to me.

"It's not like we're going to live in the trailer forever," he explained.

I shrugged. "Well, I do have a bit in the bank, and I would be interested in talking with your dad."

I spent a lot of time that winter lost. It was a maddening exercise trying to locate the parcels Mike's father, Jack, was considering selling. Rural Alaska is not well signposted, and even if it was, it wouldn't have done much good, as everything is buried under hills of snow much of the year. Jack had done his best giving me directions and had even sketched several maps, but he cautioned that some of the information might not be very accurate since he had not visited many of the areas for a long time, in some cases decades.

All of the places I had been able to locate thus far were either too remote or too ordinary. Land bordered by a river or a lake, land you could drive to and maybe even had electricity, that's what I envisioned. I was asking for a lot, I knew, particularly with my limited funds. Yet there was one place on Jack's list that just might meet some of those conditions. The problem was I couldn't find it. I had tried once already, without success. But, armed with a bit more information from Jack and a better map, I decided it was worth a second try.

"Dammit, why can't I find this place, Hank?"

He really enjoyed our recent outings—sniffing passing smells from the truck, romping around in the snow, and chasing the occasional forest critter—he was on holiday. My festive mood, however, was quickly being nudged aside by frustration.

We were at the end of yet another desolate road. I executed a ten-point turn between the tall mounds of snow that hemmed the road and headed back the way we had come. Two miles later, the truck sat idling in the middle of a T intersection. Maybe Jack's right arrow here should have been a left one? With nothing to lose, I hit the accelerator.

A few minutes of driving brought us to yet another impasse. A tall, padlocked gate blocked the road. An attached sign read:

Hazardous Area
No Trespassing
<u>Approved Personnel Only</u>
Property of Pacific Rim Timber

"Dammit, Hank, where is this place?" I reiterated. "If the map is right, it has to be on this road. Hell, I don't know, maybe we passed it?"

I gave Hank a rub around the ears. After executing a tight one-eighty turn, we reversed course yet again.

Creeping along, I scanned the left side of the road.

"We have to be close…wait just a minute; what was that?" I stopped and reversed. "That sure looks like a clearing. It could be a road. Let's have a look."

We hopped out and scrambled up the tall snow berm that bordered the road without interruption.

"That is certainly a road."

A ten-foot-wide swath cut a straight line through the forest. After consulting the map one last time, I was fairly confident I had reached my goal.

"Time to get some exercise, buddy."

I strapped on my snowshoes and slung my backpack and rifle over one shoulder, and we went for a walk.

The narrow road held a straight course for roughly a mile before it abruptly ended, replaced by a mix of birch and spruce trees that gradually descended down the face of a thirty-foot bluff. Through the trees, I viewed what appeared to be a river that twisted through the sparsely treed plain below.

"This has to be the place."

It matched Jack's description perfectly. The land directly to the right of the road, five acres on top of the bluff and five acres below, must be his. We entered the forest and walked for a couple hundred yards, reaching a spot where the bluff protruded into the lowlands in a rough semicircle, creating an ideal platform for viewing the surrounding landscape in nearly every direction.

"Would you just look at that!"

Sunlight shone off the frozen river, beyond which the white forest spread forth to the base of the Alaska Range. Towering over the scene, Mount McKinley seemed to split the cloudless sky in half. Although I knew there were roads and homes out there, I could find no signs of human interference.

"Boy oh boy, if there was ever a spot to build a cabin."

"What's up, Hank?"

His ear and a half were cocked forward and his stance rigid. I shouldered my rifle and in a few strides was at his side. He didn't seem to notice me. Together we scanned the silent terrain. After a few minutes, I gave up. It was probably a beaver. It seemed they had colonized nearly every square inch of the marshy lowlands. I returned to the fire and my lunch of overboiled pasta. My meals were becoming less and less inviting as my stocks dwindled. Yet tasteless food, rain showers, and armies of mosquitoes hadn't dashed the elation I had been feeling for the past ten days.

Returning from the initial survey of the property, I immediately went to see Jack. After much discussion and a few revisions to his map, he concluded I had been in the correct place. I told him I was eager to negotiate the selling price; he, however, being older and wiser, advocated waiting for spring.

"Take a look outside, son. What difference would it make if you bought it now or waited for breakup? I think it would be in both our interests if you had another look at the place when it wasn't hidden under all this snow. Don't worry. I won't sell it to anyone else." He added that he could use the extra time to track down the legal documentation and plat.

He had made sense.

In late May, I returned with Bryan. Now that most of the snow was gone, we were able to locate the corner marker just off the road. Armed with the plat, a compass, a roll of survey ribbon, and a hundred-foot tape measure, we surveyed the three boundary lines (the fourth was naturally created by the river). It turned out that only about four of the ten acres were on the bluff; the remaining six were below. Although the lowlands were traversable, it appeared to be an ancient floodplain, dotted with ponds and dissected by a network of slow-moving waterways. It wasn't useable land, which was fine by me. It was an interesting environment, one that would be great to study from the deck of my cabin.

Two weeks later, the place was mine. Jack's asking price had been extremely fair and had left me with more than enough coins in my pocket to purchase food and supplies for a two-week stint at my new property.

It had been ten days of solitude and hard work. Stuffing the last of the sticky noodles in my mouth, I took stock of what I had accomplished so far. All of the trees, as well as the bushes and undergrowth, had been removed from roughly a fifty-by-fifty-foot area. Most of the felled trees were stripped of branches, which had created two large piles of brush, and I had cut nearly half the timber into firewood, neatly stacking it as I went. I had also hacked a trail through the woods from the freshly cleared cabin site back to the road where the truck sat.

"Unless I screwed up keeping track of the days, I guess I only have about three left to finish the firewood and clean things up. Don't know how I'm going to get rid of the limbs. Probably a bad idea to burn them."

The conversation I was having with myself came to an abrupt halt when Hank, yelping furiously, ran around the tent and struck me in the legs, nearly sending me to my butt. Before I could recover, an enormous brown mass stampeded through the campsite. What felt like a concrete wall slammed into my torso. The next thing I knew I was sprawled out in the dirt, stunned and gasping for air. My chest heaved; my vocal chords rasped with every shallow breath I took. My mind fought to comprehend. Painfully, I rolled to my side and through teary eyes caught sight of my rifle. I reached out and pulled my body toward it. Catching hold of the shoulder strap, I dragged it into my grasp. Gasping, I got to my knees, at which point my eardrums suddenly switched back on. Tremendous thuds and crashing explosions merged with Hank's nearly constant barking. Using the rifle as a cane, I wobbled to my feet and surveyed the area. The neat stacks of firewood lay in disarray. The tent had been half flattened, and the campfire had advanced well beyond the rock enclosure encircling it. I began kicking dirt on the spreading flames, simultaneously trying to muster up enough breath to whistle for Hank.

I didn't need to. Presently, he appeared in the clearing, running directly at me between the piles of brush. A second later, the undergrowth ruptured, and a huge, galloping bear emerged, only steps behind him.

Fear stung every cell in my body as I fumbled to get a round loaded. With the pair rapidly drawing nearer, I lifted the gun to my shoulder and pulled the trigger as fast as I could. Bullets zipped over Hank's head as he passed. Dirt and leaves erupted into the air as the rounds slammed the ground around the beast. The popping of the gun stopped him dead in his tracks. His head swung from side to side in a jerky motion, and his lip lifted like a curtain, revealing a massive set of teeth. After letting loose the scariest growl I will ever hear, he turned and loped back into the thicket. My shaking hands kept the rifle pointed at the far side of the clearing while I glanced over my shoulder, searching for Hank. I didn't have to look far. He was standing directly behind me, his head wrapped around the side of my leg, focused on the clearing. Continuing to scan the woods in front of me, I leaned back and ran a hand over his body. It was trembling, but I didn't feel any blood or obvious wounds.

Smoke began to obscure my vision, and I realized the fire was still burning unrestrained. As quickly as I could, I doused the flames with several gallons of water. No sooner had I finished than I heard the unmistakable sound of breaking branches behind me. I spun around and jogged to the edge of the bluff. Twenty feet below was the bear. He was ascending the slope in bounding leaps. Swiftly, I took aim in front of him and pulled the trigger. In an impossibly agile maneuver, his massive bulk twisted around, and without losing stride, he reversed his course down the hill and disappeared into the bushes. I randomly pointed the sights at the brush, continuing to yank away at the trigger. At some point, I realized the gun had become unresponsive. I was out of bullets.

I stood frozen. I was well beyond any form of panic I had ever known. My lips were forming words, or prayers, as I scrutinized the ponds and woodland below. A few squawking ravens took flight from a distant grove of trees. Everything else remained still. Over the heavy beating of my heart, I heard Hank whining. I lowered the gun and ran over to him.

"Oh my God, oh my God, oh my God…stand still…are you hurt?"

He wouldn't let me get a hold of him. Every time I got close, he'd dance away a few steps, turn in a circle, and let out a few restrained barks. After repeating this several times, I understood what he was so desperately trying to tell me—let's get the hell out of here!

"Okay, okay! Hang on! Stay put!"

I threw myself into the trampled tent and located the spare clip, swapping it for the spent one in the rifle. I hurriedly double-checked that the fire was out and then started running as fast as I could. Hank didn't wait for me. At the first sign I was on board with his plan, he leapt into the forest and headed toward the truck.

Branches slapped me in the face, and my shirt was nearly torn off in a fight with a bush as I pushed through everything in my path. At any moment I expected to be brought down and crushed by the monster. By the time I reached the truck, Hank was on his hind legs, his front paws clawing at the passenger's door.

I chucked the gun in the back, and we dove into the cab in a confused pile. I separated myself and pushed him to the other side of the seat, fished the keys from the ashtray, and fired it up. I didn't waste time trying to turn around. I jammed the shifter into reverse and slammed the pedal to the floor. We made it a hundred yards before I lost control. The driver's side mirror ripped loose as it clipped a tree. I brought the truck to a jerking stop.

"Get a grip, man." I took a couple of deep breaths, causing pain to shoot through the left side of my chest. "Just grab the damn mirror and get yourself out of here slowly. It's okay. You're alive."

As I opened the door, Hank went mad. With his ears laid back, he barked wildly at the windshield, nearly shredding the dashboard with his claws. I looked down the road. The bear was standing at the end, right where the truck had been parked.

I glued one hand to the horn and steered with the other, getting the truck centered in the road again. I stopped and looked. He was gone. I reversed down the rest of the lane, without losing any more parts off the truck, and quickly got us going the right direction on the connecting road that would ultimately take us to the paved road. From there, it was only 140 miles to the safety of the trailer.

Chapter Twenty-Three

Armed with Paranoia

"I thought your ribs were back to normal?" Bryan asked.

"What're you talking about?"

"You're grimacing."

"Oh." I dropped my overloaded backpack by the kitchen door and took a seat next to Bryan on Big Green. "Most of the time, they feel fine. Just every now and then, when I pick up something heavy with my left arm, they ache a bit. They're definitely healed or nearly anyway."

The souvenirs from my encounter with the grizzly had included three cracked ribs, a swollen left knee, a bruised hip, and one hell of a headache.

"You know you don't have to go alone."

"I know."

"Mike's got a ton of guns. With all of us armed, it'd be safer. Not that it's unsafe. I'm sure you'll be fine…you know what I mean."

"I've thought about it a lot. To be totally honest, I don't really want to go up there at all. The busted ribs have been a good excuse"—I sighed—"but I can't just leave all my stuff lying around with winter on its way."

"Yeah, sure, but we could go with you. We'll just drive up there, check things out, grab your shit, and be back here in time for a barbeque and beers."

"It's tempting, believe me. But say we did that? Then what?"

"What do you mean?"

"I mean, then what? What do I do? Never go back there alone? Or do I just say screw it and sell the place? Neither of those things is an option. I bought the place. I still want the place. And I'm going to build a cabin," I said firmly.

"Hey, don't let your pride get in the way."

"Why not? It has served me so well in the past."

I got off the couch and made my way to the door.

"When will you be back?"

"If you don't see me in a week, send the cavalry."

I was probably procrastinating. No, there was no probably about it—I was procrastinating. Even so, scouting the labyrinth of roads really wasn't the most foolish of ideas. The only time in the past I had done so was last winter when I initially tried to locate the property. At the time, most of the offshoots had been inaccessible. There must be someone living in the area, right?

One after the other, I explored the five tributary tracks. They all ended in less than a mile. The only evidence of civilization was a rusty, long-forgotten motorcycle lying in the woods and several empty beer cans strewn along the side of one road.

I drove on, reaching the T intersection, which Jack had mismarked on his map. There wasn't any point in turning right; I already knew that was another dead end. I turned left and headed toward the property. We really were all alone.

❖

"Don't go far."

Hank sniffed the base of a nearby tree while I geared up. I snapped a thirty-round clip of hollow-point bullets into the SKS, which now sported a larger bayonet and a compact scope. I loaded one in the chamber and slung it over my shoulder. I climbed into the truck bed, unzipped a duffel bag, and grabbed two more full clips, stuffing them into one of the cargo pockets of my army pants. Next, I put my new Rambo knife, which had an eight-inch blade, in the other pocket. Then I freed a pump-action twelve-gauge shotgun from the center of a rolled-up blanket and loaded it with copper slugs. Lastly, I fastened an ammo belt around my waist. It held twenty shotgun shells. It had been quite a shopping spree at the gun store. I only wished they sold grenades. I leapt off the tailgate and stared into the forest. Apart from the accelerated drumming of my heartbeat, all was quiet.

"All right, Hank, let's go."

Following the makeshift trail I had formerly hacked through the brush, I forced Hank to stop after about twenty yards. I stood completely still and listened. Nothing stirred. We continued forward. With Hank in the lead, I kept the shotgun pinned to my shoulder and scanned the forest, glancing back periodically. I brought us to a standstill again and listened. I thought I heard a very faint crunching sound in the distance, and then it was gone. We continued forward. I halted our walk several more times, straining to pick up any unwelcomed noises. Finally, his patience at an end, Hank trotted ahead and vanished into the undergrowth. I swiftly followed.

A few moments later, I joined him in the clearing. I skirted around a mound of firewood and cautiously made my way to the campsite. The chainsaw was resting on its side next to the blackened fire pit, and the tent was gone. A length of rope was tangled in the lower branches of a nearby tree. I wiped the sweat from my face and crept to the edge of the bluff. From top to bottom, the slope was littered with items—clothes, the cooler, dishes, the fuel can, bits of food packaging, a pillow, even my Walkman and headphones. It looked like the aftermath of a natural disaster. In a way, I guess it was.

It was a nerve-racking afternoon, to put it mildly. Even though I had had over six weeks to consider exactly what I was going to do when I was back at the property, I had never come up with a plan. I'm glad I hadn't promised myself I would simply straighten up the campsite and continue where I left off, because I would have broken that promise. There was no way in hell I was camping here again.

It took several trips to get all my belongings back to the truck, probably a couple more than it should have taken, as it's hard to carry much with one hand clutching a shotgun in a death grip. But they were certainly speedy trips.

That night, we slept in the cab. It was not pleasant. The next morning, I continued to sort through and examine all the bits and pieces I had recovered. The tent was ripped in several places, yet my sleeping bag, which had still been inside, was wet and a bit moldy but otherwise unscathed. My Walkman was way beyond repair, but the flashlight still worked. The cooler was missing its lid, which I never did find. Nor did I find a portion of my clothes. The most bizarre things were the fuel container and backpack. Not only was the backpack empty, but it was turned completely inside out and shredded. It looked like a banana peel. The fuel can looked perfectly normal—the cap was still screwed on, and it appeared undamaged. Yet it was completely empty even though it had been half full. Upon closer inspection, I found four equally spaced holes in the bottom corner—teeth marks. I smiled in spite of myself. I guess dogs love antifreeze, and bears love gasoline.

What I needed was a defendable position. At the very least, I needed a better view into the walls of wilderness lining the road. So for the next six days, I ripped into the forest with the chainsaw.

I felt relatively safe during the days. Since there was no electricity at the property, I knew, at some point, I was going to have to buy a generator. Even though it was an expense I would have rather put off, I went ahead and made the purchase. I didn't particularly need the power at this stage—what I wanted was the noise. It was loud. And so was the stereo I plugged into it. I figured between that and the rattle of the chainsaw, no critter, large or small, would want to hang around. Unfortunately, I couldn't feed the generator twenty-four hours a day. Hence, nights were quiet and spooky. I tried to protect us as best I could. I placed logs across the top of the truck bed, enough to support the weight of a small elephant. Then I covered them with the tent fabric and a thick layer of spruce boughs. I left a small opening just below the rear sliding window of the cab as an escape hatch. When it was time for bed, we slid under the logs, and I shut the tailgate tight. With one arm resting on the SKS, the other on the shotgun, and Hank snoring at my feet, I was able to get some sleep.

I also altered our eating habits. Much to his disgust, Hank had to make due with dry dog food. I ate packaged and canned food and was careful to keep the waste in tightly wrapped garbage bags. Nothing was cooked. It seemed prudent to eliminate those odors.

As I thinned the surrounding brushwood, I heaped the tangled branches in long piles along the edge of the bluff. It was a weak defense, but it might just slow down my adversary long enough for me to react.

By the end of the week, I was exhausted, filthy, and riddled with bug bites. But my efforts showed. Standing by the truck, I could now see into the forest more than twenty yards in all directions. I felt a bit better. It was a toehold. Yet, I wondered if any amount of precautions would ever be enough to cure my anxiety.

I guess I'd have another winter to think about it.

Chapter Twenty-Four

Holiday

"Hey, buddy!" We embraced in a manly half hug. "You're a bit overdressed."

I grinned. "Guess I am. But it was eight below when I left." That was ten hours ago.

"Let's go get your bag. When we get back to my place, you can change into shorts and a T-shirt."

Shane had done very well for himself. Admirably, and somewhat surprisingly, he had emerged from the anarchy of our college days with an engineering degree and had put it to good use. While I was living out of the back of the pickup somewhere in Canada, he was settling into his own private office, complete with a view of San Diego Bay. He had been pulling himself up the company rungs ever since.

"Looks like you're thawing out nicely," he said, tossing me a cold beer.

"Oooooh, sunshine, sunshine, sunshine. I hardly remember what it feels like."

"I don't know why you live in that Arctic wasteland."

I wasn't able to explain it to myself, let alone him, so ignored the statement. "I can't believe *you* live *here*. This place is awesome."

We were sitting four stories up on the balcony of Shane's three-bedroom apartment. Below, a few kids splashed around in a palm-tree-framed swimming pool.

"Yep, it's not bad. The neighbors are quiet, and there's plenty of parking. The best thing about it is it's close to work. Traffic in this city is a nightmare. Speaking of that, were do you want to go? Is there anything Eskimo boy is dying to do?"

"I hadn't given it any thought. I don't know. I've never been here before. What's there to do?"

We were having an excellent time. Every morning, after a dip in the pool, we went out for breakfast and proceeded to hit another attraction. One day, it was the world-renowned zoo. The next, a drive north to Los Angeles found us zipping around on the big-kid rides at Disneyland. We cruised through Beverly Hills and then had our picture taken with Darth Vader and several other characters as we strolled up and down Hollywood Boulevard. Back in San Diego, we spent a day at Mission Beach boogie boarding, after Shane patiently convinced me the waters were shark free. At night, we either hung out at his place or shot pool at a local bar.

"How do you like your steak?" he asked, hovering over the same rusty barbeque he had had since The Shields House.

"Completely dead." I popped open another beer and gingerly settled into a deck chair, cussing a bit as I did.

"Oh man, oh man"—he chuckled—"you are one cooked lobster. I told you to put on more sunscreen. Your pasty-white body was just asking for it."

"I know, I know. I wasn't thinking. God, this hurts. I don't think I've ever been this sunburned."

Shane disappeared inside, returning shortly with a bag of frozen peas. "Here, maybe this will help. Buck up, little trooper. We still have a couple of days left. And unless you have something else you'd like to do, I think I've got the perfect way to end things."

"Oh yeah? What's that?"

"How 'bout a little trip south of the border?"

"Wow, this place is…different." I was transfixed by nearly every sight that drifted past the window.

"What'd you expect? It's Mexico."

"I don't know. I guess I thought it would be similar to San Diego, only smaller."

"Nope. It's a shithole. But a fun shithole!" Shane inched his car through the disorganized traffic and pedestrians, pulling into a large parking lot. The sign in front of the well-maintained four-story building read, Hotel Tijuana Aztec.

"Geez, this looks pretty nice," I said.

"Better than you expected, eh? Yeah it's supposed to be one of the better places within walking distance to the happenin' part of town. I booked us a room with a couple of queen beds. That's all they had left."

I tried to pull my wallet from my back pocket without touching myself.

"Don't worry about it; it's on me. But I would keep your wallet in your front pocket from now on."

After a late lunch at the hotel restaurant, we joined the crowd and wove our way to Avenida Revolución. Shane explained that this was entertainment central. It certainly was entertaining and weird. There were people, shops, and vendors everywhere. A mariachi band blasted away on their horns while merchants beckoned us to buy their wares. Shop after shop offered racks of brightly colored blankets, tacky figurines, shot glasses, and pottery. From a street hawker, you could purchase anything from a fifty-cent taco to a hand-carved chess set. I opted for a brightly colored sombrero. It was just the thing to keep the sun off my roasted skin.

With dusk approaching, a man, sporting the largest mustache I had ever seen, talked me into having my picture taken with his zebra-painted donkey. Afterward, I bought Shane a sopapilla as a way of apologizing for being such an idiot tourist. There were nearly as many nightclubs and bars as there were shops, and we soon found ourselves sitting at a table in a crowded room. The music was quite loud.

"I can't understand a word he is saying," I yelled.

"It's cool. I'll order." Shane shouted something at the waiter, and he returned a minute later with an ice-filled bucket overflowing with bottled beer.

"Hope you're thirsty, brother!"

It should have taken twenty-four hours to consume that much beer. We did it in three.

"Right on time, señor!" Shane smacked the bottle-covered table with a heavy hand as the waiter set down a half dozen shot glasses full of tequila. "Drink up, matey!"

"Dude, where did those come from? Oh shit, man, I'm pretty wasted." I burped loudly a few times. "None for me, thanks."

"If you come all the way to Mexico and don't slam some tequila…then…then…then you're a loser, man. A total douchebag."

"Oh yeah, butt wipe? Well take this." I gulped down three shots in quick succession. It felt like molten lava was running down my throat. It took a moment to catch my breath, and I'm pretty sure my heart stopped for several seconds.

"That was stupidly impressive." His head was swaying a bit. "Hey, señor. More tequilas over here!"

"Hold up there, huckleberry; your half is sitting right there…right there in front of you."

"Oh…oh, yeah." He threw the contents of the first shot glass at his face, most of it hit his mouth.

"Two more, sport."

"I know. I know. Just taking a small break…just pulling into the rest stop for a sec."

"Just down 'em all at once. It's easier."

"Listen up, boner, you do it your way, and I'll see to mine. Roger that?"

"Roger that, ghost rider."

He leaned back in his chair, closed his eyes, and put his hands on his head. Just then the waiter dropped off six more shooters. I covered them with my sombrero just as Shane sprung forward, grabbed a shot, and downed it. He made a face like he had just swallowed a grasshopper and then returned to his meditative state. I reached under my hat and slid a full shot across the table. "Come on, man, just two more to go."

"I know. I know." He took a deep breath, opened his eyes, and attacked another. While he was preoccupied with a coughing fit, I snuck over another one.

"Come on, man, just two more to go."

"Hey, don't rush me!" He wiped the sweat from his forehead and choked it down. As he chased it with a beer, I slid another one over.

"You're doing great, dude. Just two more and you got it."

"Screw you, fuck-o, there's only one left."

"Man, you're drunk—look!"

His glassy eyes appeared puzzled as he stared at the two full glasses before him. After a few seconds, he grunted and downed one after the other. "I...I think that's enough for now."

"It's a good thing this stuff's been watered down, or you'd probably be dead."

"Yeah, dead. That's bad."

I laughed, and the next thing I knew a girl was sitting in my lap.

"Hola, chico," she said with a grin. She continued rabbiting on in Spanish. I tilted my head around her appealing body and found a scantily dressed female smothering Shane.

"What the...?"

"You guys look alone. We make company with you." I guess Shane's new friend spoke English—at least as well as we were speaking it at the moment. "You buy us drink?"

"You betcha, babe," Shane declared and was rewarded with a very large kiss.

"Ouch, hey, easy there, señorita." She was climbing all over me, and I couldn't take the rubbing she was giving my sunburn. "Hey now, sister, you're gonna have to get off. Come on, seriously. There you go. Yeah, just have a seat over there."

She stared at me with a pout and settled into the chair. She turned and said something to her friend.

"What'd she say?" I asked.

"She say you *marica*…uh, gay." She smeared some more lipstick on Shane's face and then announced Shane was certainly, "No gay."

"I'm not gay. I'm sunburned. See?"

Both girls squinted in the dim light at my outstretched arms. A few sentences of Spanish flew between them, and they both laughed. Shane's playmate took her top off, straddled him, and began gyrating to the music while pelting him with kisses. My new friend stood in front of me and gently took my hand, placing it on her left breast. At that point, she leaned down and stuck her tongue in my ear. I should have been stunned, but I was too drunk. "Geez, this is kinda nice, dude."

Shane came up for air. "You gotta love Meh-hico."

We were quite drunk. Shane thought we needed to get some water and vitamins into our systems, so we switched to margaritas. The girls were still hanging all over us. I couldn't feel my sunburn anymore. They didn't ask for money, just a few drinks, which they barely seemed to touch. But then again, maybe they were matching us drink for drink—I really wasn't sure; everything was spinning. Somehow my pants had come unzipped. I closed my eyes to shut it all out, and my stomach immediately revolted. I was going to puke. I pushed the girl off my lap and staggered to my feet. Clutching my trousers with one hand, I picked up my sombrero with the other and mumbled to Shane that I had to get outside. He didn't respond. I tried my utmost to bring my vision into focus. He sat there motionless. He was passed out. His girl was sitting next to him.

"Help me get him up," I said.

"We take care of you. We make sure you safe."

We yanked Shane to his feet, and he immediately tried to sit back down, but before he could, I gave him a hard backhand across the face.

"What the fuck?" He was coming around. "Hey, man, let's get some breakfast or somethin'."

I threw a few bills on the table, and with the girls' help, we made it to the sidewalk out front.

"Where you chicos go? We get ride and take you home."

"I don't know," I said with realization. "Shane, where we stayin' at?"

"Biscuits and gravy...and you get the bacon, I think, too...yeah bacon comes with it for sure. And then that syrup and shit...I'm tellin' ya."

I stumbled over to where he was leaning against a brick wall. I had this wild urge to repeatedly punch him. Instead, I threw up on his shoes. He didn't notice. After I caught my breath, and my stomach muscles relaxed, I suddenly felt a whole lot better. The spins had stopped. I turned around and was amazed to see the two girls were still there. Surely that little display would have discouraged them?

"We're staying at the Aztec Hotel. Or something like that," I managed.

In unison the girls asked, "Hotel Tijuana Aztec?"

"Yeah, sure. That sounds about right."

"We get you taxi. Make sure you safe."

Not five seconds later, an unmarked, beat-up blue van pulled to the curb, and the girls herded us into the back.

"Hey wait. Is this a taxi or what?" It sure didn't look like one to me.

"You fine. You fine," Shane's girl reassured. She slammed the sliding door shut, spoke a few words of Spanish to the driver, and we sped away.

I wasn't nearly as drunk as I had been a few minutes earlier. Fear and vomit are pretty good antidotes for inebriation. I had a vague idea how to get back to the hotel, and we sure seemed to be going in the wrong direction. The nightlife had vanished. In fact, life, as far as I could ascertain, had vanished. Only dark, mean-looking buildings passed by now. Several times, I expressed my concern to the English-speaking girl, but apparently she could no longer understand a word I said.

After a few more worrying minutes, the van pulled into a dingy alley and stopped. The girls and the driver got out without uttering a Spanish or English word and briskly walked away.

I shook Shane hard. "Dude, wake the fuck up!"

A forearm materialized around my neck, and I was wrenched from the vehicle and thrown to the ground. I looked up. Three men stood over me. A fourth was dragging Shane from the van. They all wore baseball caps, and bandanas were wrapped around their faces, concealing everything but their eyes.

"Hey, take it easy!" One of them had planted a boot in my chest, stopping me from sitting up. Shane was dumped beside me. He was trying to figure out what was going on. That made two of us. "What do you guys want? Just tell us. Anything you want you can have."

"Your money," one of them said.

"Sure, here, here." I dug out my wallet and tossed it at his feet.

"His too. And the watch."

"Shane give me your wallet. Now."

"What? Why? Man, let me up."

A few words of Spanish were spoken, and two of them lifted Shane to his feet and slammed him into the side of the van. He shouted obscenities and squirmed under their hold while they relieved him of his wealth.

"That's all we have. It's all yours. We ain't gonna call the cops or anything stupid. Just, please, let us go," I pleaded.

"Shut up. We're not done with you. Stand up."

I scrambled to my feet.

"We're taking you somewhere special. Get back in the van."

Thankfully, Shane seemed to be rapidly coming out of his stupor. "Get the fuck off me, man!" Trying to shake loose of his captors, he looked directly into my eyes and clearly said, "I am not getting in there."

"Me either." I nodded.

No sooner had the words left my lips than Shane tore his right arm free and swung his fist squarely into the face of the guy to his left. I kicked the guy nearest me in the crotch and rushed his buddy. I didn't bunch up my fists. I was back on the mat at some long-ago wrestling match. The guy was busy trying to retrieve something from his belt. He never saw me coming. In one swift movement I had his body draped over a shoulder in a fireman's carry. I twisted my hips and threw him to the pavement as hard as I could. Before he could get up, I kicked him in the head with the full force of my leg. I spun around. Shane was complete fury. Both his fists were flying in a blur; his legs were sending out kick after kick as he battled what appeared to be the last two bandits that were still standing. I ran up behind the closest one and pinned his arms behind his back in a double arm bar. Then I front tripped him. His face crunched as it hit the ground. I grabbed a handful of his hair and bashed his head against the pavement until he went limp.

I sucked down air and stood up. Shane was cussing loudly, walking round and round in a tight circle. All four of our abductors were sprawled out, and none were moving.

"Shane!" I caught hold of him. "Shane, come on! We have to get out of here now!" I grabbed his shoulders and shook him. "We got to go, man."

"Yeah, yeah. Okay."

We lurched out of the alley and inspected the dark main street. "Where are we?"

"Don't know," Shane answered. "Wherever it is, it ain't good."

He was right. It wasn't exactly a neighborhood you wanted to take a stroll through at 3:00 a.m. "We sure as shit can't stay here. Let's just pick one—left or right?"

"Screw that, we'll never make it out of here in one piece." He chewed on his bloody lower lip and stared back down the alley. "Come on, we're going back."

"Are you *crazy*?"

He grabbed my arm and pulled me along, jogging back down the alleyway.

When we reached the van, three of the men were still lying where we had left them; the fourth was groaning and attempting to get up. Shane rushed over and kicked him in the face.

"What are you doing? Let's get the hell out of here!"

"That's the plan. Here, take your wallet. Now get in. You drive."

"*What*?"

"Get in the van." He was already halfway into the passenger's seat.

"Jesus, dude, you're fucking nuts! We don't even know if the keys are in it."

Shane was all the way in now. He shut the door. I saw him lean over to the driver's side. A second later, the van roared to life.

He smiled a crazy smile. "Get in!"

"Oh shit." I ran around the front of the van and climbed behind the steering wheel.

We were halfway through our third round of drinks when it was announced over the loudspeaker that the flight to Anchorage, via Seattle, was now boarding. I signaled the waitress for the bill and downed the rest of my beer.

"What if we did kill them?" I asked for the umpteenth time.

"Quit thinking about it! We did what we had to do. Those pricks got what they deserved. You know that."

"I know. I know. It's just that I've never really killed anything before, and the first time I do, it's a man…maybe two."

"Dude, we've been over and over this. First off, you have no idea if you killed anyone. Second, if you did, or if I did, for that matter, it was self-defense. Come on, they abducted us, robbed us, and I don't think they wanted us back in that van so they could take us to Baskin Robbins. And third, we got away scot free."

"Yeah, you're right, I know. I'm just still freaking out a bit I guess."

"You and me both, brother." He slugged down the rest of his bourbon. "Hey, that sounded like the final boarding call. We better get down to the gate, so you can get back to Alaska where it's safe."

Chapter Twenty-Five

Out of the Blue

"Boy, this job is going to take a while," I said.

"Yep, good, steady, outside work for the summer," Tom responded. He tossed a bread crust to Hank. He gobbled it up. He always inhaled anything Tom fed him. I never understood why. Normally, he was quite a selective eater.

"Wow, you think we're going to be here the entire summer?"

"We've been here for two days and only managed to replace four of the lower ones, so you do the math. Don't forget, we have to frame in the new ones and trim them out."

I wadded up my lunch sack and leaned back to get a better view. It was a long, narrow three-story house. It really was unusual looking. It looked like a massive set of stairs that had been chiefly constructed from glass. I took a rough count of all the windows I could see.

"There aren't thirty are there?"

"Actually there are thirty-three on this side, plus we have to replace six on the side walls and two on the front. Now tell me how many skylights there are."

Each level had its own roof. The bottom-story roof ended where the second story began and so forth, which is why it resembled a set of steps. Each roof was peppered with skylights.

"I can't really tell. Some of those on the top two roofs could be two side by side or just one big one. Hmm, I'm going to say fifteen."

"Not even close. There are twenty-four."

"And we have to replace them all? Even the ones at the very top?"

"Yep. And if they are all as difficult to remove as these first four were, we are going to have some fun."

Tom was right. It had turned into a long job, and it wasn't exceedingly fun. It was hard, scary work. Yet, it wasn't all bad. The weather had been excellent, and the view was terrific.

The house sat at the edge of a small tree-ringed lake. Several such lakes dotted the Anchorage landscape, and the shores of a few, like this one, had been developed over time as minisuburbs for the wealthy. I suppose having waterfront property is desirable anywhere, but in Alaska, it meant much more than a bit of fishing and a relaxing view. Without exception, every house on the lake was accompanied by a dock and tied up to nearly every one was a floatplane. The people who lived in this neighborhood could go out their front doors and, within minutes, be perusing the stores of 4th Avenue or go out their back doors and, within minutes, be soaring high above the virgin wilderness.

"All right, this one's loose. You know the drill. Get out there and catch it, then pass it in to me," Tom said, steadying the window. "And remember to be careful."

I jogged down the hallway and climbed out an opened window. My feet blindly searched for the slender plank that was tacked to the roof. When I felt surefooted enough, I heaved my upper body through the hole and carefully headed down the makeshift scaffolding.

"Okay, I'm ready."

"Where's your rope?"

"Quit asking me that. I told you it just gets in the way. I keep tripping over it."

"Well, you should have it on."

I muttered, "I don't think a twenty-foot rope tied around my waist is really going to do much good." I glanced over my shoulder. Below the two-by-twelve I was standing on was a steep roof of metal and glass. It was a twelve-foot drop to the next roof and then a final fifteen-foot drop to the concrete driveway.

"What'd you say?"

"Nothing. I'm all set."

"Okay, it's coming to you."

I supported the base of the window and gently guided it down to the plank. "Shit, that one was heavy."

"Can you lift it in to me by yourself, or do you want me to come out there and help?"

"No, I think I can do it."

"What?" he yelled.

I shook my head and pointed at the lake. Yet another plane was coming in for a landing. It must have been the tenth one to either take off or land that morning. Situated halfway along the lake as we were, our ears were subjected to the full brunt of the thunder created by the plane's engines. We were basically working next to a runway.

As usual, we waited out the noise and became

spectators. The plane's wings were waggling a bit in the breeze, but that wasn't uncommon, as the wind swirled around the lake nearly every day. As the craft dropped toward the choppy water, the seesawing of its wings became much more pronounced. I felt Tom's hand on my shoulder and heard him shout something like, "He's in big trouble."

Yes, yes he was.

The plane struck the water off-balance. The left float was nearly buried in the lake while the right one was two feet in the air. For an instant it looked like it might right itself, but it was too late. The float had sunk too deep; it was pushing the weight of too much water. The left wing suddenly tilted even farther, and a plume of water erupted as it dug into the lake. Presently, the plane turned sideways and cartwheeled down the lake, leaving a trail of debris.

"Holy shit!" Tom's shriek tore through the sudden silence and nearly caused me to lose my footing. "Come on!"

He yanked me through the window hole and we bounded down the stairs. When we reached the shore, we joined a small group of people who had already gathered. A woman was screaming over and over for someone to call 911. The man next to her was stripping off his clothes.

"Jesus, Tom, what do we do?" He was standing next to me with his tongue hanging out of the corner of his mouth and an intense look in his eyes. "Should we go in after them or what?"

Just then, a man raced up and shouted, "Everyone remain calm. The police have been notified. Andy, is that you? Please put your clothes back on. No one is swimming out there. We're not going to make this situation any worse. Doctor Lawrence and some of the other neighbors are already on their way out there in his boat. There they are now."

The boat had just reached the center of the wreckage. I clearly saw three men dive into the water. Two others remained in the boat. Suddenly, everyone on shore was silent. No one was even breathing. At least, I know I wasn't. We watched and waited. I was beginning to fear something awful had happened to the would-be rescuers when five distinct bodies simultaneously broke the surface. Two of them were motionless. The swimmers pushed the inert bodies to the men above who lifted them into the boat. Seconds later, the swimmers were hauled aboard as well, and they angled for shore full throttle.

Without a word, our little group of onlookers rushed in concert down the shoreline, arriving soon after the boat had docked. There was a much larger crowd gathered here, including medical personnel and a cop. We held our distance and watched the scene play out. The end result was that two bodies were loaded onto gurneys, covered head to toe with white sheets, and wheeled into an ambulance. The ambulance left slowly. Its lights and sirens were not on.

"How's it going?" Bryan asked.

"You look a bit spent," Mindi observed. "Tough day at the office?"

I took a seat on Big Green. "Not as tough as some people had."

"Make yourself comfortable, Hank." Bryan laughed. He was nudging his way onto the couch, wedging himself between Bryan and his girlfriend. "So what happened?"

I related the details of the plane crash I had witnessed a few hours earlier.

"That's awful. Are you sure they were dead?" Mindi asked.

"Yep." I made my way to the fridge and liberated a Budweiser. "You guys want a beer?"

"No thanks. Actually, we are just on our way out."

"Oh yeah? Dinner and a movie is it?" I took a large swig. It was amazing how good Budweiser could taste sometimes.

"No, uh, it's a bit more exciting than that," Bryan said.

"Do tell, do tell." I rummaged around the cupboard for something to eat.

"It came as sort of a surprise," Mindi added.

Bryan kept his eyes trained on Hank while he petted him. "I never mentioned anything to you because I really didn't think anything would come of it."

I quit scrounging. I had never known Bryan to beat around the bush about anything. This was not good. I gulped at my beer, waiting for them to deliver the punch, but they just sat there in silence.

"Shall I guess then? Okay, my guess is that Mindi is pregnant."

"No!" She blushed.

"No, it's nothing that extreme. It really is good news. It's just that it's going to affect you, and I don't want you to think we did this behind your back or anything. It's really a bit of a surprise."

"This is sure a strange way to deliver good news. Are you going to tell me or what?"

Bryan gave a sideways look to Mindi, and she picked up the ball. "We started looking at houses last month, you know, just for fun. We didn't really think we had the funds to buy anything, just sort of dreaming I guess. Anyway, last week, we found this really great place.

It's not very far from here. And it was really reasonably priced, and it already had a building report and everything, and, well, we made an offer, and they accepted. We're signing the papers this afternoon." She looked at her watch. "Speaking of that, Bryan we really need to get going."

As they headed out the door, Bryan grabbed my arm and said, "Sorry I didn't give you a bit o' warning about this, but things will work out—you'll see."

"Looks like we'll be finished up by the end of the week," Tom said. "Good thing too. Boy am I sick of windows and skylights."

"Hmhuh," I grunted. My mouth was full.

"I don't think I've ever seen anyone eat that much pizza in one sitting."

I swallowed and took a sip of water. "Free pizza is the best-tasting kind. Thanks for taking me to lunch, by the way." The last time I remember him doing so was in Anchor Point. I assumed he was doing it today because we had reached the end of a long job. I was wrong.

"You're welcome. I just thought it would be a better place to give you the news than the jobsite."

"News?"

"Lisa, the kids, and I are moving to Tucson next month."

"Tucson? What the hell are you talking about? Tucson? Like Tucson, Arizona?"

"Yeah, like Tucson, Arizona."

I was speechless.

"I'm sure I've mentioned Lisa's family lives there, haven't I? I'm sure I have. She went down there last month for a visit—I'm sure I told you that too—and was offered quite a good job by her cousin. We've discussed it at length and decided it was a good time to do it. It would be nice to get established before the kids are old enough to start school. My friend Joe is interested in buying our house, and I've got work waiting for me down there thanks to Lisa's uncle who's also a builder. So the stars have aligned. I didn't want to hit you with this until I was sure, and now, well, I'm sure."

"When?" I managed.

"We don't have an exact date set yet, too many ducks to line up first, but we'll be driving, so we'll have to be on the road before the snow flies."

So that was that. In the span of two weeks, I had been told I no longer had a place to live, and I no longer had a job. Unbelievable.

"Don't worry too much, okay? You have become one hell of a good carpenter, and there's never a shortage of work in this town. It will work out—you'll see."

Chapter Twenty-Six

Gifts from Heaven

"It's been a long time coming, Hank-O, but we are off and running now!"

He wasn't sharing my enthusiasm; he was too busy pleading for his dinner.

"Okay, okay, I guess it's about that time." I fetched some dog food from the back of the truck and filled his bowl. He was eating it before I could set it on the ground.

"So you're hungry then? Me too." I snatched a boiling pot from the fire. I planted myself in the camping chair and surveyed my handiwork while I waited for my meal to cool off.

Ten feet off my driveway (as I had come to call the little track that led to the property) stood the partial shell of a twelve-foot-by-twenty-four-foot cabin. The floor was a couple of feet off the ground, supported by three large beams, which in turn were supported by fifteen posts that were set in concrete. The walls were framed, and that morning, I had started building the roof. It sure was a steep roof, I thought, blowing on my bean mush. "Yeah, but it has to be. That's the only way you're going to get enough headroom up there for a loft," I murmured. "Besides, it will help shed the snow." Hank paid no attention. He was quite used to me talking to myself. Admittedly, this whole thing sure would have been easier if I had drawn up some sort of plan. After all, I had had an entire winter to figure it out. My excuse was I had been too busy to think about it. And it was a pretty decent excuse.

After Tom had told me he was leaving, I panicked. I had no idea how I was going to continue to make a living. So I did what I always did when I was at a loss—I began searching the classified ads. I was dithering between continuing in the construction field and taking a shot at something completely new, when Tom knocked on my door.

"Hey, Tom, come on in."

"So this is the new bachelor pad, huh?"

"Yeah, but we're down to one bachelor—me."

"You can give me the guided tour later; right now I've got to run back to the truck and grab a few things. I'll be back in a tick."

I quickly straightened up the place, which didn't take long. It was a one-bedroom apartment.

He returned with two cardboard boxes, several file folders, a large pizza, and a twelve-pack of beer.

"I thought you were moving to Tucson, not in with me? What happened, did Lisa finally wise up?"

"Ha-ha. That's no way to talk to someone bearing gifts," he said, struggling with his load. "Take the pizza and beer, and let's have a seat. Oh my God, you still have this couch?"

"Big Green lives!"

"Maybe with a whole lot of life support. All right, first things first, hand me a beer."

Four beers and a meat combo later, he placed the boxes on the table.

"Now I know you've been thinking about maybe going into a different line of work, and I just want to say I think that would be a huge mistake. You've learned a lot over the years, and you really have become a good builder, and why shouldn't you be—I taught you! Listen, just because Lisa and I decided to move somewhere a bit more climate friendly doesn't mean you have to end up flipping burgers or mopping floors at the Dimond Center. So here's a few things to help you get started on your own…"

"My God, Tom, I can't accept all this." I examined the tools that covered the table. There were nail punches, saw blades, screw drivers, chisels, router bits, a framing square, a level, and more, much more.

"You can and you will. Look, you know how much gear I have. We can only fit so much in the trailer and car; anything extra has to be shipped down, and that's expensive. So either you take these things, or I'll give them to Goodwill."

"I don't know what to say except, thanks. Thank you very, very much."

"No problem. Like I said, you're actually helping me out. I've got one more thing in here. Call it a farewell present."

"Holy shit, Tom!"

"Nice, huh? It's handmade, just like mine. Go ahead, try it on."

Grinning ear to ear, I leapt to my feet and strapped the custom leather tool belt around my waist.

"Look at that—fits like a glove." He smiled.

"Now I really, really don't know what to say. You didn't need to do all this. I mean…God, thank you."

"You, sir, are welcome. But before you get all teary eyed on me, have a seat and toss me another beer. I've got one last thing to discuss with you."

I reluctantly took off the tool belt and sat back down. He pulled out several sheets of paper from one of the folders. "Now this here is a list of all the clients I have had over the past sixteen years. Underneath each name are contact details—addresses, telephone numbers, and so forth. Beneath that, you'll see some little stars I've hand drawn. The stars are a one-to-ten scale. One star means the people were terrible to work for, and ten means they were great. I don't think there are any ones, or twos for that matter. A lot of the people on this list you'll be familiar with, but there are some that you won't be. Last week, I sent out a form letter to everyone on this list. It basically stated that I was leaving the state and thanked them for their business over the years. I also said I had complete confidence in you and your workmanship and passed along your phone number."

I was absolutely blown away.

"Now in these other folders are copies of the paperwork from, hmm, actually I don't know exactly, the last twenty or thirty jobs at least. I wanted to give you these so you'd have an idea of how I did my bills and estimates. You may want to do yours differently, but this will give you something to go off of. And lastly is a copy of my contractor's license and insurance. You'll need to get both. There's information attached on how much it costs and how to go about getting them. And that's it. I hope I didn't make a mistake doing this. I wouldn't want to crush your dreams of becoming a janitor or anything."

I would never be able to repay Tom for what he had done for me. That winter, I had more work than I could deal with, and I hadn't had to lift a finger to get it. It was a good winter, a lucrative and busy winter. So busy, in fact, I'd completely forgotten about the property. That is, until the snow started melting. Yet, I didn't see how I was going to make the time for a visit, until it suddenly dawned on me that now I, and I alone, controlled my vacation schedule. So I cheerfully penciled in a three-week "holiday" beginning in June.

So there I sat, choking down a mouthful of beans a la Spam. Contemplating the work I had accomplished in just the first ten days, I felt elated. But the feeling was tainted. This wasn't where the cabin was supposed to be. It was supposed to be on the far side of the property, not ten feet off the driveway. It was supposed to be in the spot with the awesome view, the spot I had already cleared. The spot where I nearly got mauled by a bear, I sourly thought, a place far, far from the safety of the truck. I felt like a coward, but at least I was a relatively safe one. Hank's barking tore me away from my musings.

He was staring down the road. I grabbed the shotgun, which was always within arm's reach, and sprang to my feet. It was soon apparent why he'd raised the alarm. A car was bumping down the road. I lowered the gun and stood stupefied. Other people, clear back here? Amazing.

Slowly it maneuvered the rough track, eventually coming to a stop behind the truck. Hank circled it, tail wagging, as three well-dressed and attractive women got out.

"Good evening," the brunette said.

"Oh, what a gorgeous dog." The other two showered Hank with attention.

"Uh, hello."

"We don't mean to intrude, but we've heard faint rumors that someone was back here, and it's such a nice evening that we thought we'd go for a drive and see if we couldn't find this mysterious man. We're from Talkeetna."

"Oh." I had a dream very similar to this just the other night. It was one hell of a good dream.

"My name is Darcy. And this is Sue and Jenny."

I took turns shaking their hands. "Dan," I mumbled.

"Sorry?"

"Uh, my name's Dan."

"Nice to meet you, Dan. And who's this fury friend of yours?"

"That's Hank."

"Such a nice dog." The trio drifted past me and studied my project. "My goodness, but that looks like a lot of work. Are you doing this all by yourself?"

"Uh-huh."

"It sure looks like you're busy, so we won't keep you long, but we were wondering if you would mind giving up just a few minutes to hear us out."

"Uh, yeah, sure. I was just having a bite to eat anyway."

They stood there anticipating something more.

"Oh, um, let me try and find something for you to sit on. I've really only got this one chair, but maybe some of these bigger stumps will work and, oh geez, let me just put a shirt on." I gave an anxious laugh. "I guess I don't need to be carrying this gun around."

A couple of fumbling minutes later, I had the group sitting in a rough semicircle upwind from the fire's smoke.

"This is very comfortable, thank you," Sue said, or maybe it was Jenny?

"Right," Darcy rifled through what looked like a homemade deerskin handbag and removed a stack of papers. "Dan, how well versed are you in the Bible and the teachings of God?"

"Um, pardon?"

"I have some literature here, and I was wondering if I could read a bit of it to you? Perhaps after that, you'd like to comment on how it relates to your own life?"

I cleared my throat. "Sure. I guess that would be okay. But...I don't want to pry or anything...just wondering, you know...are you guys Jehovah's Witnesses?"

"Yes, Dan, we are."

After a long moment of staring into her eyes, an unintended chuckle broke from my throat. "Wow, you guys really leave no stone unturned, huh?"

She smiled. "Where there's opportunity...but believe me, we aren't here to force our beliefs on you. If you'd rather not engage in a friendly discussion with us, that's certainly your right. You just say the word, and we'll leave."

I slowly gazed around the fire at the three pretty women. I reached behind my back and scratched one of a hundred mosquito bites and said, "Please, stay as long as you like, please."

Chapter Twenty-Seven

Drifting On

L ater that evening, after the women had departed, I relaxed in front of the fire, drinking more beer than I ought to.

Most of their lecture had sailed right past me. Except, perhaps, the one idea they kept repeating. The idea that God has a plan for everyone and everything, even me and Hank it seemed. I wasn't too sure about that, and most likely I never would be. Yet, it did start me thinking about plans in general. Had I ever had one? Ever? About anything? I glanced at the half skeleton of the cabin and laughed. I guess the answer was no. I had spent my life inadvertently drifting along in the current, letting it push me wherever it pleased.

So what? I downed the rest of my beer and reached for another. At the end of the day, everything had worked out. I had my own successful business. I had the property. And I had Hank.

What I didn't realize at the time, however, was this wasn't the end of the day—it was the beginning. And this day was going to be just as long, but not nearly so gentle.

And when the sun finally set, I would find myself living in a place very far from Alaska.

Dan currently lives on a warm and sunny, bear-free island. He'll tell you how that came about in his sequel to *Drifting in the Push*, which he is now writing.

Acknowledgments

To Mary, my wife and best friend, it's a great life, thanks to you. You make me a happy man each and every day.

How do I convey sufficient gratitude to the two people that brought me into this extraordinary world? Truly, I can't. I love you both. Thanks for being my parents.

It might seem odd to thank a creature that has no understanding of the written word, yet Hank has earned my everlasting gratitude in every possible way that it can be expressed. I've had a stroke of unbelievable luck a few times in my life and you were certainly one of them. I love you, buddy.

Well, Bryan, it was a long time coming, but you're finally off the hook. No longer will I be asking you to read my latest revision of *the book*. I can hear your sigh of relief from here. Thanks, man.

Shane, next time we get together, you are buying the beers. If you refuse, I'll tell your wife all about our other adventures that I left out of the book.

Thanks, sis, for your input and support; you've always had faith in your little brother.

Thank you, Tom for your friendship and giving me the skills to become a self-employed builder; I'm still putting the tool belt to good use.

To Lindsey Nelson, at Exact Edits, you rock! I couldn't have picked a better editor. Thank you for all your hard work. And who knows, maybe someday I'll figure out how to use those pesky semicolons.

CPSIA information can be obtained
at www.ICGtesting.com
Printed in the USA
LVOW11s1144300517
536290LV00002B/338/P